I0629365

The Artificer of Dupho

THE FIRST THREE EDGEWHEN® NOVELS:

The Dragonslayer of Edgewhen
The Artificer of Dupho
The Klindrel Invasion

EDGEWHEN® NOVELS COMING OUT IN 2015:

The Burglar of Sliceharbor
The Bladesman of Darcliff

Edgewhen®: Fantasy adventure stories of heroism and friendship.
Learn more at edgewhen.com.

The Artificer of Dupho

JASON A. HOLT

This is a work of fiction. All of the characters, organizations, locations, and events are either products of the author's imagination or are used fictitiously.

Edgewhen® is a registered trademark of Jason A. Holt.

Copyright © 2014 by Jason A. Holt.

Cover illustration copyright © 2014 by Kristina Gehrmann – www.mondhase.de.
Map illustration copyright © 2014 by Gillis Björk.
Interior design by the author.

Published by the author.
JasonAHolt.com

print ISBN: 978-0-9860717-3-7
epub ISBN: 978-0-9860717-2-0

Let's be honest: They're all for Sierra.

CHAPTER 1

The Sand Pit

SHIKO REMOVED HER SANDALS and set them in the waist-high grass beside the starting line. She undid the two lowest pins of her chiton and repinned the garment so that its skirt would not bind her legs when she ran. This exposed her brown skin from toe to knee—a style that would have drawn stares on the cobbled streets of Hicho. Technically, it was cheating. She was supposed to be training for situations in which she would not have time to remove her sandals or repin her chiton. But her opponent, being male, could train in a chiton that exposed both knees, and Shiko chose to deny him that advantage.

This time, she would win. Po was quicker, but she was determined to be smarter. She had been practicing a tactic that would catch him by surprise.

Shiko nodded to Elder Badiki to indicate that she was ready. The white-bearded elder stood off to the side so that he could see both ends of the training course concealed in his apple orchard. Shiko and Po, at opposite ends, could not see each other because of the two climbing walls between them.

Elder Badiki acknowledged Shiko's nod with a gentle tilt of his head. His face was obscured by his beard and diminished by distance, but Shiko could tell he was giving her a smile.

The dark-haired man standing beside Elder Badiki did not smile. His dark eyes were cold and impassive. Shiko's heart began to pound—and not just in anticipation of the sprint that lay before her. Higomu was a calculating, exacting man. If he did not like what he saw here today, Shiko would be training for another year before she was considered for a mission.

But Shiko would show him. She had worked hard. She would prove she was good enough to be a striker.

At the opposite end of the training ground, Po must have also given his signal, for Elder Badiki raised his hand, warning them that the contest would begin. Shiko pushed thoughts of the dark-haired man out of her mind and tried to focus on defeating Po. This plan had to work.

With a swiftness uncharacteristic of his seventy-five years, Elder Badiki snapped his hand down, initiating the contest. Shiko's legs pumped as she accelerated through the orchard grass. She knew Po was running toward her from the opposite side with annoyingly effortless speed.

Three pine logs lay across her path, only thigh high. She had learned to hurdle these, leading with her right leg over the first—right, left, right, left, right—left over the second—left, right, left, right, left—and right over the third.

Shiko sprinted along the path and dove into a ceramic pipe. Running along the top would have been more efficient, but it was against the rules. Instead, she scuttled through on her elbows and knees.

As soon as she emerged from the pipe, she accelerated to a sprint that took her into the sand pit. The soft sand drained the energy from Shiko's legs as she slogged toward her climbing wall, but this only encouraged her. Po was quicker, but she was stronger. She imagined herself gaining ground with every step toward the daub-and-wattle wall.

The climbing wall simulated a shuttered-windowed, two-story house typical in most districts of the city of Hicho. Shiko leapt from the sand to grab the ground-floor shutter. Using her momentum, she pulled herself up to grasp an edge with one foot. Her other foot found purchase on a hinge, and she raised her body until she was standing on top of the shutter. After two years of training, her toes were as strong as her fingers.

A hole was gouged in the plaster just above the wooden crossbeam that separated the two stories. She wedged a toe into the hole and pushed herself toward the upper window. One hand on the shutter hinge, the next hand on top, now catch the hinge with the toes, and up! Before she could think about it, she stood on the upper story's shutter, from which her fingertips could reach the edge of the red-tiled roof.

Shiko wrestled one elbow onto the roof. She swung her bare leg up to grasp the edge with her toes. Her toes pulled, her elbow shoved, and she was lying with her belly pressed against the tiles. She only paused for a quick breath before scrambling on all fours up the slope of the roof.

Cresting the top, she saw that Po had surmounted his climbing wall first. As always.

The two climbing walls were like two pieces of a house that had been sawed in half. They were separated by a gap of forty paces which was spanned by a redwood beam. The length of the beam guaranteed that the two contestants, no matter how disparate their speeds, would meet in combat two stories above the sand pit. In theory, it was possible to win by crossing the shoulder-width beam and running the opponent's half of the course in reverse. Shiko had once tricked Po into attempting this by lying in wait for him on her rooftop. That had been her only victory against Po.

Until today, she thought, placing a bare foot on the redwood beam.

She was still panting, but it was considered poor form to pause for breath. With dark-eyed Higomu watching, she did not want to show poor form.

By reaching the beam first, Po had the right to choose the place of combat. He had chosen a point that would force Shiko to cross two-thirds of the beam while he waited and rested. Three months on Elder Badiki's estate had taught the recruit that demonstrating tactical sense was wiser than flaunting his speed and agility.

Shiko moved toward Po with a steady walk that she hoped would appear confident to the two men watching from below. Po assumed a low stance. Shiko revealed nothing as she approached, but she smiled to herself. In their recent contests, she had been using low attacks that Po could best counter by crouching lower.

As Shiko quickened her steps, Po sank deeper into his backstance, offering his front leg as bait for another failed leg sweep. Shiko closed the distance. Po's eyes narrowed, and she could tell he wondered why she was moving so fast. Left, right, left, right, left! Shiko leapt into the air and soared over her surprised opponent's head.

She had fooled him! Her plan had worked!

Po's hand pushed aside her trailing ankle, inducing a slight rotation just before her lead foot landed on the beam. Her trailing leg reached forward to grab the wood, but her center of balance was already off line. Shiko tipped off the side.

It was a two-story drop to the sand pit. Shiko had made that drop often enough to know how to recover in time for a safe landing. She tucked to increase her spin, reached out to catch the ground with the side of her hand, rolled along the curve of wrist, elbow, and shoulder, and landed flat on her back, striking the sand hard with her other arm and both feet. Po had defeated her again.

Now what?

Another year of training, probably. Unless Elder Badiki chose to ignore Higomu's advice and promote her anyway.

Two pairs of sandals stepped into the sand pit. Shiko wanted to lie on the soft sand, stare at the feathery clouds in the blue sky, and contemplate what she could have done better, but it was unwise to appear to be playing for sympathy. She sat up and shook the sand from her brown curls.

Elder Badiki's eyes twinkled in his leathery face. She realized he had expected this outcome—she lost to Po every time, didn't she?—but the manner in which she had chosen to lose pleased him.

Pale-skinned, dark-eyed Higomu showed no expression. During their few brief encounters, Shiko had never seen any emotion in that man's face. Higomu was a striker. Perhaps the work was too dangerous to allow one to indulge in emotions.

Well, Shiko might have failed the physical test, but she could demonstrate emotional discipline. She asked the

Goddess of Knowledge to give her a calm mind and clear thoughts. She would accept Higomu's judgment. She would keep training. She would not give up. Shiko took a deep breath and exhaled some of her disappointment and frustration.

Po dropped from the beam and landed with a pleased grin. He extended a hand to help Shiko up.

She accepted his help. There was no need for her to be rude. He had won fairly. He had earned the right to feel triumphant. But she wouldn't have minded if he had worn the same impassive mask as Higomu.

"That was, in truth, quite well done," Po told her. "You took me completely by surprise."

"Thank you," she said, because she knew that Po was trying to be nice and that he did not realize how humiliating it was to receive compliments on her effort from a recruit who had been on Elder Badiki's estate for only three months.

Elder Badiki turned to his companion. "Higomu, have you met Po?"

"No, I haven't."

The two men exchanged nods.

"Seminary graduate?" Higomu asked.

Po's face grew even more radiant. "Yes, Higomu. I graduated at the end of last year."

Higomu nodded. "It shows," he said.

The Seminary was the second oldest educational institution in Hicho. It had been founded by a group of theologians who believed that their people had become too focused on the Goddess of Knowledge.

Shiko had attended the Hicho Academy—the oldest educational institution in the world—where nobody worried about becoming too focused on Knowledge. Knowledge was the deity who had created their people. In a sense, Knowledge had even founded the Academy. It seemed only natural that people whose name for themselves was "Children of Knowledge" would focus on service to their creator, regardless of the merits of the other deities.

But Seminary theologians advocated balance. Students were expected to learn what each deity had to offer before choosing a focus. Po had chosen to serve the God of the Lith—the god of conflict, combat, and war—and so Po had already studied martial arts for nine years when he had arrived at Elder Badiki's estate. Po and Elder Badiki were quite willing to explain this to Shiko every time Po defeated her. Shiko had trained especially hard since Po's arrival, struggling for respect instead of condescension. The result of her labors was sand in her chiton.

"Higomu is a Seminary graduate himself," Elder Badiki explained. To Po, not to Shiko. No recruit ever met Higomu without learning where he had studied.

"In truth?" said Po. "Which school?"

"The School of Knowledge," said Higomu.

"Ah," said Po. "I graduated from the School of Lith."

"I spent much of my free time in such studies," said Higomu. "You will need a handkerchief."

"I will?"

"Are you aware that we are standing in the sand pit?"

Confused, Po looked at his feet. Higomu punched him in the nose.

The stunned recruit sat down. Blood trickled from his nose. Higomu opened his fist, dropping a linen handkerchief into Po's lap.

Shiko felt sorry for Po. Higomu did that to every recruit. In Higomu's time, any form of trickery had been allowed in the sand pit, so that recruits would learn to outthink their opponents. In recent years, the tradition had largely died out—except when Higomu visited the training grounds.

Elder Badiki shook his head. "I did warn you, Po." Shiko noted that the bearded elder was standing well out of Higomu's reach.

Something white flashed at Shiko's head, and then she was sitting in the sand beside Po, holding her stomach.

"How can you become cunning and vigilant if you don't

practice in the sand pit?" Higomu asked, turning away. "Really, Elder Badiki, why aren't you teaching them? The boy offered her a hand up and she actually took it. In the sand pit."

Pinching his nose with his new handkerchief, Po said, "That was well done, Shiko. You blocked his feint."

Shiko realized that her left hand had caught the handkerchief Higomu had thrown at her face to create an opening for the stomach punch. Perhaps she would have found this more consoling if the wind had not been knocked out of her. She nodded to acknowledge Po's compliment and tried to breathe.

Elder Badiki called, "When you are ready, Shiko, I would like to speak with you in the quiet room."

Shiko pushed herself to her feet. Looking down at her training partner, she gasped in enough breath to say, "Excuse me for not helping you up." Holding her stomach, she staggered out of the sand pit.

CHAPTER 2
The Quiet Room

THE DISTANCE through Elder Badiki's blossoming apple orchard to his grand house was enough that Shiko was able to breathe normally again by the time she entered the "quiet room". According to lore passed from recruit to recruit, the quiet room's walls were filled with sound-absorbing reeds and strung with iron chains that would confound anyone attempting to spy with elemental senses. Although most chambers in Elder Badiki's rambling home had curtained doorways like those in normal houses, the quiet room had a heavy wooden door that sealed the room shut. Closing it made Shiko feel as though she were leaving the world. Certainly she had left behind the pleasant Purplemonth day, for she was now in a windowless cubical chamber that was lit only by light released from a light box—an artifact that used mirrors to trap light and store it for later use.

Higomu and Elder Badiki were already seated on cushions on either side of the room's knee-high central table. Shiko picked up a cushion near the door and approached the two men.

Higomu looked up. His hard, black eyes shone like obsidian in the glow of the light box.

Elder Badiki indicated that she should sit next to Higomu. Higomu's body language indicated otherwise. Shiko chose to sit at a corner of the table, keeping herself just out of Higomu's reach.

Elder Badiki smiled and gave Shiko a congratulatory nod. "Before I describe your mission, let me be the first to welcome you as a full member of the Order of the Lock."

Shiko shot a glance at Higomu. His face held no expression.

"I passed?" she asked.

"You have learned all I can teach you here," Elder Badiki said. "Higomu agrees with my decision to send you on a mission."

So she hadn't exactly passed, but she was getting a mission anyway?

"Am I to be a striker?" she asked.

Higomu rolled his eyes.

Elder Badiki's eyes twinkled. "I would like you to be one of my strikers, yes. Assuming that is still what you want?"

"Ah … yes," Shiko said. "Forgive me, I'm just— Yes. That is what I want."

Finally, she would be able to use her knowledge! At the Academy, Elder Badiki had taught her all about elemental resonances and how they could be bent by properly constructed artifacts. Shiko had never developed the talent to construct artifacts herself, but this had not troubled Elder Badiki.

It had troubled Shiko. One afternoon, she had confronted him with the fact that she would never be an artificer. He had replied that artificers were not the only ones who needed to know about artifacts. And then he had suggested that, after graduation, she should consider joining the Order of the Lock.

The Order was the society responsible for guarding the secrets of forbidden artifacts. Most of the artifacts Shiko had studied were benign—like the knife that could slice through granite, or the box that trapped light—but some artifacts were more sinister. Elder Badiki had told her about devices that could give a person elemental power equivalent to that wielded by dragons, about devices that opened paths to the negative Elemental Realms, about devices that allowed direct contact with a demon. The secrets of creating such objects must never become common knowledge. The Goddess of Knowledge wanted her people to learn, but she also warned them that some knowledge must remain hidden. In the study of artifacts, the Order of the Lock guarded the secrets.

The Order's founders had been actual locksmiths and metalsmiths—and "smith" was still the title used for someone like Elder Badiki who collected information and decided what to do about it. Elder Badiki's informants were called "jewelers". The Order's first spies had been actual jewelers—people who might be called upon to decorate the devices an artificer made—but now anyone could be an informant for the Order, and only Elder Badiki knew his jewelers' true identities.

Strikers were named in analogy to hammer-wielding blacksmith's assistants. Higomu's job was to do whatever pounding was necessary to keep forbidden artifacts hidden from potential demon worshippers. And that was now Shiko's job, too.

"Higomu will be your partner on your first mission," Elder Badiki said.

"Ah!" she exclaimed. Why was he treating her so coldly, then? "Thank you," she added.

Elder Badiki said, "Higomu, you could move over and give her some room to sit beside you."

"She has plenty of room," Higomu grumbled as he shifted over. "I don't know what you're afraid of," he said to Shiko. "I never punch my fellow strikers outside the sand pit."

Shiko shifted closer to Higomu and laid her hands neutrally in her lap, keeping one arm relaxed so that, if necessary, she would be able to snap it upward to block a punch.

"Well," said Higomu, "what's our mission?"

"Shiko will be going with you to Dupho," Elder Badiki said.

"What? I never said anything about taking her with me to Dupho."

"You agreed to guide her through her first mission."

"But I thought you had something for us here," Higomu said. "Her first mission should be something simple—like searching someone's library for forbidden texts—and she shouldn't be leaving Hicho."

Elder Badiki shook his head. "I don't have a mission for you here. I have a mission in Dupho, and it needs to be done now."

"Then send me alone," Higomu said. "I'll work more quickly without her."

"I thought we agreed that it is time for Shiko to learn by experience. Was that not the point you were making when you punched her in the stomach?"

"I just didn't want the boy to sit in the sand by himself."

Shiko glanced at Higomu. She couldn't tell if he thought he was making a joke or not.

"Higomu, do you intend to make this difficult?" asked Elder Badiki.

"Missions to Dupho are always difficult," Higomu said.

"Why?" Shiko asked. Dupho was the capital of the Theocratic Empire of Beauty. The Children of Beauty had an army and a navy, but the civilians were best known for artwork, jewelry, glassware, and absurdly romantic stories. What made the missions difficult?

"For one thing," Higomu said, "it is difficult to blend in when everyone else is twice your height."

"Ah," said Shiko. Yes, that would be a problem. Children of Beauty were giants—tall enough to see over an ox's back. Of course, looked at another way, Children of Knowledge were half-sized. Either way, Shiko and Higomu would be conspicuously small.

Elder Badiki said, "But the main difficulty is that Higomu has taken some risks in the past that have drawn the attention of the local authorities."

"I just did what was necessary to complete the mission," Higomu said.

"Yes, well," said Elder Badiki. "Regardless, it is my hope that concern for the safety of your partner will inspire a little more caution."

"Now, wait," said Higomu. "What's the priority here? Watching your new striker or completing the mission?"

"As always," said Elder Badiki, "you must do whatever is necessary to secure any dangerous artifacts and prevent anyone else from learning how to make them."

"And that's our top priority?" Higomu asked.

"It is," said Elder Badiki.

"Good," said Higomu, and his shoulders seemed to relax a little.

"But assuming you can accomplish that," Elder Badiki said, "then I would like both my strikers to return alive."

"Of course," Higomu agreed.

"So our mission is to confiscate a dangerous artifact?" Shiko asked.

"I don't think it's complete yet," Elder Badiki said, "and I'm not certain it's dangerous. That is the main reason I am sending you, Shiko: You understand artifacts well enough to figure out what this one does. One of my jewelers has sent me information concerning an Emotion artificer—"

"They have those?" Higomu asked.

"They have one in Dupho," said Elder Badiki, "and the Order needs you to decide whether to take him into custody."

"What has he done?" Shiko asked.

"As far as I know, he has done nothing wrong yet," said Elder Badiki. "My jeweler says he applies optical principles to elemental Emotion. He has invented a mirror that reflects Emotion the way a mundane mirror reflects Light."

Shiko was intrigued.

Higomu frowned. "What application does that have?"

"None, as far as we know," said Elder Badiki. "Nor has my source reported an application for his emotional lens."

"But you think he might be working on something that has the potential to aid demon worshippers," Higomu said.

"My jeweler thinks that is a possibility. I need you to help Shiko find out all she can about this artificer's techniques and creations. You will have to decide for yourself whether he is dangerous, based on what Shiko can tell you."

Shiko realized that this wasn't just a training mission. Elder

Badiki thought Higomu would actually need her expertise. Maybe that was why he had decided her performance above the sand pit was good enough.

"Very well," said Higomu. "When do we leave?"

"I will make arrangements for you to travel with the next shipment from the Green Chalice Glass Company," said Elder Badiki. "It leaves Hicho Harbor at high tide in three days."

"I shall be there," said Higomu.

The two men looked at Shiko expectantly.

"As will I," she said.

Elder Badiki nodded his approval. "If you have no more questions at this time, you may go."

Higomu nodded to indicate that he had none.

Shiko had many questions, but none that seemed important enough to ask in the quiet room. She stood up with the men and tried to sort out her thoughts as she followed Higomu to the door.

Elder Badiki placed a gentle hand on her shoulder before she could leave the room. His eyes watched Higomu until the dark-haired man was out of sight. Then he gave Shiko a comforting smile.

"Do not let Higomu fool you," he said. "He has respect for you and your abilities."

"What makes you think that?" Shiko asked.

"He punched Po in the face," Elder Badiki said. "But he deemed you worthy of a feint."

CHAPTER 3
A Long Voyage

THE PENDANT OF SACRED STONE caressed Shiko's skin as she lifted its cord from her neck. Losing contact with the water-smoothed lava rock was like seeing her soul's sunshine go behind a cloud, but she gave up the cord-and-stone to the ritesmaster's ink-stained fingers. Her pendant bounced off Higomu's with a click.

The ritesmaster carried their pendants to his library's central table and suspended them above the candleflame. Shiko watched her sacred stone, anxious to get it back.

She had picked up the rounded chunk of porous rock during her pilgrimage to the peak of the Sacred Mountain, twelve years before. Seeing it in the ritesmaster's hands made her feel vulnerable. Which was absurd. The purpose of the ritual was to request extra protection. The chunk of lava rock had no power. Protection and guidance came from the Goddess of Knowledge. Shiko suspected that her irrational attachment to the rock was somehow impious, but she could not help sighing with relief when the ritesmaster handed it back.

She rolled the stone between her palms to be certain it was not too hot. In theory, a hotter stone would be more likely to draw the Goddess's attention, but in practice, anyone foolish enough to get burned during a ritual would probably be deemed unworthy of notice.

The warm stone embodied two of Knowledge's dominant elements—Earth and Heat. Shiko added the third element, Thought, by pressing the stone to her forehead and praying, *Knowledge, please grant me the wisdom I need to complete this mission.*

A gentle warmth flowed into her bones, like sunlight in autumn or a smile from a friend. Shiko felt no wiser, but she knew she had been heard. She knew she was watched. As the poet said, "The pious find comfort in the Goddess's gaze."

Shiko put on the cord and tucked the sacred stone back into its place below the neckline of her chiton. She smiled at Higomu and nodded to indicate that she was ready to go.

Higomu's eyes acknowledged her nod, but his solemn face did not return her smile. He thanked the ritesmaster and led the way out onto the cobbled street.

Did the man feel nothing? And after a dozen years of service, would that be Shiko's fate as well?

She didn't want to believe it. They were undertaking a mission to discover new knowledge and determine the dangers it posed. Technically, the Order of the Lock was a secret society, not a religious organization, but Shiko felt as though she had been given this assignment by the Goddess herself. Surely Higomu felt something similar. The Goddess of Knowledge expected her people to control their emotions, but she did not require them to have no emotions at all.

As they stepped onto the broad boardwalk connecting the piers of Hicho Harbor, Higomu said, "If I had known you grinned so much, I would have asked the company to assign me someone else."

"I am sorry my happiness displeases you," Shiko replied.

"You can be happy or not," said Higomu. "I do not care. But if you insist on beaming like it's the first day of school, the buyers will not believe you are a serious cloth merchant."

"I see," said Shiko. "I will be more careful."

Shiko was grateful that her dark skin never revealed a blush, for she felt embarrassed at having forgotten to act her part. She and Higomu were not strikers on a secret mission for the Order of the Lock. They were cloth merchants working for the Long Creek Linen Company. They had booked passage on a Green Chalice Glass ship bound for Dupho, where they would look for merchants interested in importing linen. Higomu had traveled to Dupho as a cloth merchant several times in his career, and this time Shiko was to travel with him in the role of a young woman learning the trade—a lie that matched the facts nicely.

So: how would a cloth merchant act on her first voyage to a foreign port? Shiko did not find cloth to be exciting, but a cloth merchant might—especially if, after two years of working for her company, she was finally being sent out to deal cloth. Wouldn't she feel exactly the way Shiko did? Wouldn't Shiko seem more out of place by acting as solemn as Higomu? She was only two years out of the Academy. High spirits were normal for people her age.

Of course she could not bring up any of these points while she and Higomu were pretending to be cloth merchants. And because of the intimacy of sea travel, they would need to maintain the pretense until they reached Dupho, three or four weeks away. Shiko scowled at Higomu. He glanced at her, and for the briefest instant, his eyes twinkled.

They said no more as they walked along the boardwalk between the piers and the warehouses. Most of the ships that would leave harbor with this tide were already loaded, so the boardwalk was empty except for cheese vendors offering one last bite of fresh food, off-duty captains discussing business with other off-duty captains, and small clusters of people bidding family members farewell. Even the gulls seemed to be sparse on this spring morning. Shiko realized that she was more used to the crowded Fish Wharf.

A man wearing a light-blue chiton shaded his eyes from the late morning sun as he watched them approach. Shiko could tell he was a captain not only by the color of his clothing, but also by the way he stood on the pier, as though he were both a guardian and a gate.

"Long Creek Linen Company?" he asked, when they were within speaking distance.

"Captain Muzer?" Higomu asked.

The captain nodded, and his dark face broke into a white-toothed grin. Higomu did likewise, as though facial expression came easily to him. He was good at pretending.

"Come aboard, come aboard," Captain Muzer said, spreading an arm to indicate the gangplank.

Higomu led. The captain followed behind Shiko.

"I see that someone has spent some time aboard ships," the captain observed.

Shiko realized that her strides up the gangplank had not been timid enough. "I was in the fishing program at the Academy," she said.

"Ah, fishing," said the captain. "An admirable profession."

He was being polite—either that, or he was the only merchant captain on the Moonaway Coast who did not look down on those who stayed within a halfday of port.

Shiko had focused most of her studies on metaphysics and locksmithing, but every student at the Academy also had to learn a skill that produced food. The tradition originated from the time when Hicho was a village and the Academy was the only school in the world. At that time, every Child of Knowledge between the ages of eighteen and twenty-seven had been enrolled, and food production had been the most important skill they could learn. The tradition had persisted partly for completeness of education and partly because it provided a way for students to pay their tuition.

Shiko had learned to hate fishing at sea. It was nothing like helping her parents trap fish in the eddies of the Redwood River. Sea fish were smellier. The sea was too deep. The ship was always tilting under the crew's feet as they hauled in the nets. And they often had to work in the rain.

Shiko realized she was in for several weeks of shipboard life, with few ports until they reached Dupho. She hoped the weather would stay nice.

Two rowers pulled in the gangplank and stowed it as a walkway resting on the thwarts—the ship-spanning planks on which the rowers would sit. The craft had eighteen rowers on each side, all Children of Labor.

They were people, but built like oxen—huge, strong, with a thick leather hide. Their legs were bigger than Shiko's entire body. They were expensive to hire. Only merchants could afford them. But they must have been worth it, because nearly all merchant vessels—whether shipping for Children of Knowledge or for Children of Beauty—were propelled by rowing crews composed of Children of Labor.

Shiko had never been so close to one before. On the streets of Hicho or down at the Fish Wharf, she had occasionally seen an injured Child of Labor, cast out by his or her rowing crew, begging for work. But now she would be living among them.

The males wore vests that left their navels exposed. Their skirts covered their laps, but not their knees. The females—few in number—dressed similarly, except that the lacing of their vests seemed designed to draw attention to their giant bosoms. It was not the sort of clothing that Shiko would wear, but then, the climate was much hotter sunward, where the rowers came from.

She tried not to be intimidated by biceps the size of her head and thighs of greater circumference than her hips. This would be good practice. By the time she reached Dupho, Children of Beauty would seem short and slender.

Captain Muzer led Shiko and Higomu to the foredeck, which was a small platform just big enough for someone to stand on and watch for hazards. He showed them an oilskin stowed under the deck in which they could wrap their satchels. "It looks like there will be enough room for one of you to sleep here, too," the captain said. "I admit I was expecting you to have more luggage."

"We find it easier to travel with only small samples," said Higomu. "Please accept this handkerchief."

Shiko flinched. But of course, Higomu the cloth merchant did not punch anyone in the nose.

"Thank you," said the captain, holding up the handkerchief to examine the embroidery in the sunlight. He nodded with approval. "A sea otter. Neatly stitched."

Higomu nodded to acknowledge the compliment.

Shiko wondered why the captain had chosen to stow their expected luggage below the foredeck. The point where wood met wave was the roughest part of the ship. Then she remembered that Captain Muzer was shipping for the Green Chalice Glass Company, and deduced that the best locations for cargo already held crates of glass.

Captain Muzer stuffed his new handkerchief inside his chiton. "Now then, I know you both are experienced sea travelers, but it is customary for me to review some of the points of shipboard etiquette."

Shiko was at once surprised and grateful. During her time on Academy fishing boats, she had not seen much etiquette. As it turned out, however, "etiquette" was Captain Muzer's term for practical common sense, including such topics as which corners of the ship provided the best shelter during a storm (it depended on the direction of the wind) and which way the contents of the waste bucket should be dumped after it had been used (also dependent on the wind). The lesson was concluded in the time it took them to pass between the thirty-six rowers to the aftdeck, where they were introduced to Vadu, who held the title of first mate, being the only other Child of Knowledge aboard.

Vadu nearly looked like his own species of person. His skin was wrinkled by weather and tanned by the sun to a color almost as dark as Shiko's. His shaved head reminded her of a rotten apple.

Vadu gave the passengers an indifferent glance before reporting, "Ready to depart, Captain."

Captain Muzer nodded. "Then do so, please."

Vadu waved a wrinkled brown arm. A rower at the opposite end of the ship began shouting commands in their language. Great hands began hauling on the rope that dangled over the starboard bow, pulling the ship away from the dock while lifting the anchor up.

The shouting man sat at the bow, but because the rowers

faced the stern, he was behind his subordinates. That way, his shouts would be heard by all even when he was rowing. In theory, Shiko should know their language: The God of Labor had decided his people would speak the language invented by the Goddess of Luck, and at the Academy, Shiko had learned a variant of that language. In practice, however, Shiko recognized none of the foreman's words.

Perhaps it was only a difference in pronunciation. Children of Beauty, for example, spoke the same language as Shiko's people, except that they were notorious for inserting *m* and *n* sounds into certain words. For a moment, Shiko worried that she would be unable to understand anyone in Dupho. But if the Dupho dialect were really so different from her own, wouldn't Elder Badiki have mentioned it?

Once the anchor was stowed, the rowers signaled they were ready to begin by leaning forward and dipping their oars into the waves.

The foreman barked. Thirty-six rowers pulled. Thirty-six oars pushed the ship through the water, and they were underway.

The green-vested foreman gave the rowers a cadence, but once he was satisfied with the vessel's speed, he fell silent, trusting them to maintain the rhythm. Which they did.

Shiko looked over the aftdeck's railing to see the red-tiled roofs of Hicho drifting away. She shivered, partly because of the morning breeze, but partly because it reminded her of how she had felt eleven years ago, when she had left her riverside village to study metaphysics, locksmithing, and artifacts with Elder Badiki. She had never realized that the Redwood River could carry her so far.

Hicho Bay had a few navigational hazards, but they were easily avoided. Only occasionally did Vadu need the steering oar at the stern. Satisfied that his first mate had everything in hand, Captain Muzer turned to Higomu and asked, "Do you play pegboard?"

Higomu did.

The captain produced a cedar board with brass pegs, and the two men faced off. By the time Vadu reported that the ship was making for the coastal current, Captain Muzer had played enough to inform his first mate, "He plays better than you do, Vadu."

"Is he a good match for you, Captain?"

"I'll say he is. He won!" To Higomu he said, "Let's play again."

Shiko soon grew tired of watching Higomu defeat Captain Muzer. She watched the ocean for whales or dolphins—or anything, really—as the sparkling lith made its circle around the lithward sky. Eventually, that heavenly body sank beneath the waves. The lavender moon settled toward the coastal mountains. Still the men played.

When the lith rose again, it marked noon, and Shiko realized that Higomu and Captain Muzer had been playing for an entire lithic—one-ninth of the day.

Vadu broke out the food for the midday meal, but he only offered enough for the four Children of Knowledge. Shiko felt that the eyes of all thirty-six rowers must be on her as she accepted a chunk of bread from Vadu.

"When do the rowers eat?" she asked.

"Children of Labor eat only twice a day," Vadu told her.

"But they eat a lot," said Captain Muzer.

"How long will they keep rowing?" Shiko asked. They had already rowed an entire lithic without breaking cadence.

"They could row forever," Vadu replied. "Nothing seems to tire them. But at dusk, they get food and sleep. Very adamant about that."

"They sometimes rest when we put up the sail," Captain Muzer observed.

"Oh, yes," said Vadu. "They appreciate a break. But they hate being idle for long. And because they see anything other than hard physical labor as idleness—" he nodded his bald, brown head at the pegboard, "—they have nothing they want to do except row."

The rowers had a point. Shiko had disliked standing in the pouring rain hauling up stinking nets of fish on Academy fishing boats, but sitting idle made her back itch. She had trouble enjoying the meal and the warm spring afternoon.

After lunch, she walked between the laboring rowers to the tiny foredeck. The sea was smooth enough that the deck was dry, for now. She opened her satchel and took out the oilskin pouch that held *A Recent History of Dupho*, the authoritative guide that had been written by Tazhubo fifty-three years before Shiko was born.

Moments later, she was joined by Higomu.

"You brought a book to sea?"

"Elder Badiki loaned it to me," Shiko said. "He has two copies."

In fact, Shiko had transcribed this second copy for him as part of her tuition, but Higomu did not need to be reminded that she was not long out of school.

Higomu grunted.

Shiko opened Tazhubo's *Recent History of Dupho* to the page she had been reading last. Higomu stood on the tiny deck, staring ahead.

Shiko found it difficult to read with Higomu looming above her. "What are you looking for?" she asked.

"I'm not looking," said Higomu. "I'm standing."

He turned so that the line of his shoulders matched the line of the ship.

"Why are you standing?" Shiko asked.

The foreman looked back at them. Curious brown eyes met hers.

"The sea reminds me of cloth," Higomu said.

"Cloth?" Shiko asked.

"Yes. Cloth."

Shiko saw no reason to be reprimanded. He was the one behaving oddly. She was just asking questions. It was exactly what she would have done if she were a cloth merchant.

The foreman had apparently lost interest, but Higomu

spoke loudly enough for him to overhear: "The patterns of the weaver are like the waves of the ocean. When I am done, I recommend that you stand here a while and see if you, too, cannot learn more of our craft. Perhaps it will inspire you to discover new patterns."

With that, he turned to face the stern, staring enigmatically over Shiko's head.

What was he saying? Was he trying to teach her something, or was he just being rude?

Well, perhaps he had the right to be rude. She hadn't demonstrated any skills worthy of his respect. At least, not yet. But she would. She would prove to Higomu that she could be a striker.

THE CITY OF
DUPHO
& SURROUNDINGS

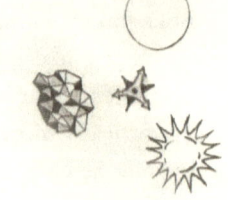

EMPEROR'S PALACE

TEMPLE OF BEAUTY

RED PALACE

AGAVE PLAZA

WHALE PLAZA

GRAND MARKET

DUPHO HARBOR

FISH PLAZA

TEMPLE OF THREE SISTERS

CHAPTER 4
Unexpected Visitors

ZEFI WALKED ON THE SUNNY SIDE of the avenue, even though the paving stones were so hot that she could feel the warmth through the leather soles of her feet. The sunny side was uncomfortable, which meant that it had fewer people in her way. The citizens of Dupho hated discomfort.

They stared at her as she passed, their auras turning blue to reveal their curiosity. Zefi was a Worker Person—a head taller than everyone else, and nearly twice as wide. She hunched her shoulders to make her body seem smaller, but no matter how small she made herself, her blond hair and brown skin would stand out in a city where everyone else's hair and skin were black or white.

They didn't need to stare. They should be used to seeing Worker People in Dupho.

To Zefi, citizens of Dupho were Decorator People, but in their language, they called themselves "Children of Beauty". They called Worker People "Children of Labor" … when they were being polite. Sometimes they called Zefi a "filthy leatherskin", but rarely to her face.

Another word for people like Zefi—Worker People who had suffered injuries at sea—was "orphans", because an injured rower would find himself out of a job at the ship's next port. In most ports, such unfortunates were simply "beggars" hoping to find work until they were strong enough to join a rowing crew again. Zefi thanked the gods that she had been abandoned in Dupho. Her foreman had dropped her off at the "orphanage" run by the Church of Three Sisters.

How ungrateful Zefi had been! It shamed her to recall how

sorry she had felt for herself. She had not known that the miraculous techniques of the Church of Three Sisters would completely heal her injured knee. She had not known that they would find work for her so she could repay her debt. She had not known that they would assign her to a man like Kittiwake.

Zefi had been ungrateful, but she had been an ignorant child of sixteen. Now she was seventeen, and so much wiser. She had learned their language. She had lived in their culture. She could understand the emotions they expressed with the colors of their halos. She had fallen in love.

Today was the fourteenth day of spring's Redmonth. Her year-and-a-day of service was at an end. Zefi did not want to leave.

Did that make her ungrateful? Or just disobedient? And which was the greater sin?

Zefi followed the broad avenue to the Agave Plaza, named for the bushy succulent growing in a pot built into the central fountain. Some people nicknamed it "the Rooftop Plaza" because it held numerous rock gardens featuring the ornamental plants that also decorated the flat rooftops of the city. One cactus in the plaza was as tall as a tree, with branches reaching like fingers into the sky. One garden held pots of short cactus—spiny balls arranged on tiers to form a mound with a gnarled juniper emerging from the summit. In another garden, succulent-leaved stonecrops sprouted from holes carved in a porous lava-rock monolith.

As on the rooftops, neighbors liked to gather in the Agave Plaza to exchange gossip. Zefi never felt welcome among the neighbors, and today she intentionally avoided them. She feared that if she made eye contact they might remember how long she had been living in the House of the Four Wrens.

Would the Orphanage send someone after her, or was it Kittiwake's responsibility to bring her back? Zefi hoped it was up to Kittiwake. She was sure the man was so focused on completing his artifact that he did not know her term of service was done.

No white-robed healer-priests waited for her outside the single-story house whose mural depicted four wrens as big as Zefi. She entered without knocking and shut the door behind herself with relief. Kittiwake's blue-haloed head did not even look up.

Passing into the cool workshop from the bright streets of Dupho was almost like walking into a cave. Blazing white sunlight poured in through the house's window, but this only made the rest of the one-room house seem darker. Even Kittiwake's halo seemed dim until Zefi's eyes adjusted.

The shop's two workbenches sat side by side against the wall with the window, an arrangement that Kittiwake said he had learned when he was studying optics. Sun now lit the afternoon workbench, where Kittiwake worked on the angular pieces of the artifact.

"I'm glad you're back," he said. "I need you to hold this face of the octahedron. Did Diamondback have any more silver foil?"

Zefi laid Kittiwake's notebook on the morning workbench, dark and bare at this time of day. "He did," she said. "Two sheets." As instructed, she had placed them between the pages of his book, to protect them while she carried them home.

Kittiwake looked up at her with a smile in his eyes. His irises were red, a color Zefi had once found shocking. Now she found it beautiful, especially when his halo turned red, as it did now, revealing true affection.

"Wonderful, Zefi!" he said. "You are a treasure! Come hold this, please."

Zefi floated over to stand behind him. A treasure! She was his treasure!

She leaned toward him so that her yellow vest touched the back of his red linen gown. Reaching over his shoulder, she wrapped her hand around his and pressed her fingers gently against the handle of his pliers. "I have it," she assured him.

With a trust that came from months of working together, Kittiwake released the pliers and slipped his hand, white as a cloud, out from underneath hers. His shoulder gently brushed against her body as he stepped aside to get the angle clamp.

He was unaware of the contact. His aura had returned to blue—which it always did when he focused on his work. This did not disturb Zefi. His passion was for artifacts, not for her.

Kittiwake stepped back into Zefi's embrace. As he applied the angle clamps that would hold the two pieces together, Zefi breathed in the scent of his long, straight, black hair. "Unrequited love." That was the phrase a Decorator Person would use to describe her feelings. Zefi was not certain she understood the word "requited", but she understood the phrase. It meant she was in love with him and he was not in love with her. To Decorator People, unrequited love was beautifully tragic. To Zefi, it was simply beautiful.

True, when she had first realized she loved him, it had been agony. But time had taught her to be grateful. A romance between them would have been doomed. The gods had not made it possible for different peoples to intermingle. So Zefi thanked the gods for giving her the chance to love Kittiwake without distracting him. She knew how much he loved his work.

Perhaps that was why she loved him. No. She loved him for his kindness, first of all. But his dedication was why she was attracted to him. He was beautiful not because he was a perfect-skinned Decorator Man, but because he understood the value of work. Kittiwake made things. He could barely sleep while a creation remained unfinished.

What would happen when he finished this one? Did he know that she was supposed to return to the Orphanage today? When he leafed through his notebook seeking inspiration for his next project, would something in there remind him that Zefi had arrived at his home exactly one year ago on the fourteenth day of Redmonth? Zefi could not remember the last time either of them had mentioned that she would not remain in Dupho forever. The fact had gone unspoken for months.

Someone knocked at the door. Zefi dropped the pliers as though they were red hot.

"I'm so sorry," she told him.

Kittiwake, too, had been startled. His aura showed the green of fear. The color darkened, then slid toward yellow anger, but he was not angry with her.

"You have done no harm," he said. "It is clamped now."

Kittiwake pushed himself up on his tiptoes and leaned across the bench, almost sticking his head out the window so he could see who was at the door. Zefi wished she had barred it.

"Guardians," Kittiwake said, his halo flickering turquoise with confusion.

Zefi breathed a sigh of relief, for she had feared it would be priests from the Orphanage. But then she wondered if they might not send soldiers instead. Perhaps not showing up on time was considered a crime.

The knock came again, this time followed by a voice: "Artificer? We are guardians-of-the-peace with a message for you."

Kittiwake forced the fear from his aura as he crossed to the door. Many Decorator People could control their auras, just as some Worker People disguised their true feelings by masking their facial expressions, but in Kittiwake's case, this talent was magical. The gods had granted him command of elemental Emotion.

Zefi wished she had more control over her fear as Kittiwake opened the door to reveal four soldiers. They were called "guardians-of-the-peace"—a name that was supposed to distinguish them from the branch of the Theocratic Army that drilled for battles—but their iron helmets, iron breastplates, and iron-headed spears gleaming in the afternoon sunlight made clear exactly what would happen to people who disturbed the peace they were guarding. One of the four was marked as a sergeant by the triangular pennant painted on his right cheek. The pale green paint stood out boldly on his charcoal-black skin.

It was too late to hide from them. Zefi moved to stand beside Kittiwake. These soldiers would need to be careful about the way they chose to deliver their "message".

The green tinge of fear crept into the auras of the sergeant's three subordinates, and Zefi felt rewarded.

The sergeant glanced up at Zefi, then returned his gaze to Kittiwake. His dull, silver halo wavered only an instant.

"Citizen, are you Kittiwake the Artificer?" the sergeant asked.

"I am," said Kittiwake, holding his chin high. "Is there something I can do for you?"

The sergeant handed Kittiwake a rolled-up piece of paper tied with green yarn. "I have been ordered to deliver this request from Commander Fox. I will return on the twentieth to receive your answer."

Kittiwake glanced at the paper in his hand, but he did not untie the yarn.

"I bid you good day, citizen."

"I bid you good day," Kittiwake replied.

As soon as the soldiers were gone, Zefi closed the door and barred it.

Kittiwake cast the message onto the shadowed workbench, where it rolled until it bumped against his notebook. He went back to work in the sunlight. He removed a small, silver magnifying lens from its covered box and held it so that he could examine the pieces he had just clamped. His hand shook.

Zefi stood to one side, biting her lip.

"Thorns," he murmured. "My heart pounds so hard I cannot even hold the lens."

He slipped the lens back into its box and selected a snipping tool instead. Hastily, as though by working faster he could still his shaking hands, he cut the green yarn and unrolled the paper onto the space beside his vise.

Zefi tried to wait quietly, but when Kittiwake's aura turned dark and troubled, she asked, "What says it?"

He released the paper and the ends curled toward each

other. Kittiwake looked up, frowning. "It says that Commander Fox requests me to move into a room at the Red Palace to make artifacts for the guardians-of-the-peace."

Zefi knew the Red Palace was the headquarters of the soldiers who policed the streets of Dupho. "Commander Fox is the head guardian?" she asked.

"He is," Kittiwake said. "And he is also among the wealthiest people in the city."

"Wealthier than your patron?" Zefi asked.

"I don't know."

"What offers Commander Fox?" Zefi asked. "A better shop? More rooms?"

"The message doesn't say."

"Then why thinks he you will go? He should offer more than Legislator Whitedove."

"Zefi, he thinks I will go because he can send soldiers to fetch me if I refuse."

"Oh."

He put a hand on her arm. "Ah, Zefi. Do not let it trouble you. I will not be bullied."

The dear man still thought of her as a child, but she was not. She covered his hand with hers. "It troubles you," she said. "Tell me."

Kittiwake exhaled and sat down on the three-legged stool.

"Commander Fox can make this difficult," Kittiwake explained. "He might convince other crafters to stop selling us materials. Or he could find a reason to confiscate my tools. He could send guardians to our door every day to keep me from getting my work done. If Commander Fox wants me for his own, I have no doubt that he will do whatever he can to make our current situation seem worse than imprisonment in the Red Palace."

"But you will not go?"

"Never!" Kittiwake slapped his knee. "I'll not have my creations twisted to suit the whims of the Army."

"Your patron—could he help you, you think?"

"Perhaps. I hope so."

"He makes the laws," Zefi said. "Commander Fox must obey laws. Yes?"

Kittiwake shook his head. "Legislator Whitedove makes the laws for the city and the province. Commander Fox obeys orders from the generals and the Imperial Council. He and Whitedove do not get along."

"But your patron can do something perhaps," Zefi said. "You should ask him. And I will pray for you."

Kittiwake nodded thoughtfully. "You are right, Zefi. I don't know what Legislator Whitedove can do, but if he wants to keep me, he will find a way to protect us."

Legislator Whitedove provided Kittiwake with the workshop, materials, and money for food and clothing. He was wealthy, with a lavish villa on the Heights. Kittiwake was sometimes invited to parties where Whitedove would ask him to demonstrate his artifacts. Although Zefi did not like working with the kitchen servants at the villa, she enjoyed walking home with Kittiwake after these parties. He was so happy when his work was applauded.

"I think he will keep you," Zefi said. "He likes you."

Kittiwake chuckled as he rose from the stool. "Yes, Zefi. Or at least he values my work, which is what truly matters."

She had said something that amused him. His aura glowed an affectionate red. Zefi was glad her clumsiness with the language had lifted his spirits. If she had been a Decorator Person, her aura would have flashed red, too, … and she had heard enough of their stories to know where that would have led. For the briefest instant, Zefi wished that she were not herself. But she was herself. And Kittiwake was an artificer.

Kittiwake bent down and picked up the pliers that Zefi had dropped. "We will go talk to him tomorrow," he said. "Today, let us seal the edges of this octahedron."

CHAPTER 5
Hazards of Sea Travel

THE GREAT CHANNEL reminded Shiko of a river. The distant ship off the starboard bow could have been a pinecone fallen into the water. The mainland's coastal mountain range and the long shoreline of Movozo Island could have been river banks. In truth, the Green Chalice Glass ship was at least half a day from either shore, being rowed lithaway with the channel current.

Higomu and Captain Muzer were playing pegboard. Again. Still. On the aftdeck, pegboard was not a game to be won and put away; it was a constant occupation, as though Captain Muzer were determined to prove that Children of Knowledge could play pegboard for as long as Children of Labor could row.

Shiko did not play, and she had lost interest in these games days ago. The outcome was always the same: Higomu won. But at breakfast this morning, Captain Muzer had announced that he planned to try a new strategy based on a historical battle of the Theocratic Empire. Shiko had decided to watch this game. After twenty days of sea travel, she was eager to see something new.

Vadu was also watching, his wrinkled brown forehead further wrinkled in concentration. Unlike Captain Muzer, who delighted in pursuing victory against a superior foe, Vadu had become frustrated by the game. He said he used to defeat Captain Muzer roughly one game in three, but the captain had improved so much that Vadu had not won in days—not since leaving Kozhimu, the tiny colony port where they had resupplied.

Vadu frowned as Captain Muzer pushed another peg into the board. Shiko, too, wondered why he had played there. She expected a strategy based on military history to be too sophisticated for her to understand. But Muzer's play did not seem sophisticated; it seemed random.

Higomu placed a peg to threaten two of Muzer's and said, "I must confess, Captain, that your opening has me completely baffled."

Vadu nodded in agreement.

"At least that part of my plan is working," Muzer said, pushing another peg into the board.

Normally a deliberate player—one who could spend a dozen oar-strokes considering his move—Captain Muzer now played without contemplation, as though his choices did not matter. Higomu matched the captain's steady pace, but his moves had the precision of a martial arts form. Every one of Muzer's careless blunders was swiftly punished.

By the end of the game, the captain was shaking his head sorrowfully. "Ah, you win again," he said. "So much for the wisdom of General Victorious."

Higomu said, "I have always found Victorious's theories to be quite sound."

"But in analyzing the Battle of Peachgrove, did he not say that the Winelanders won because chaos evens the odds?"

"He did."

"And have I not disproven that theory?"

Higomu shook his head. "You have not."

"But I played to create chaos," Captain Muzer said. "And the outcome was much worse than usual."

"You played randomly," Higomu said. "That created chaos for you, but not for me."

"How else can one create chaos on a pegboard?" Muzer asked. "Or are you saying that the theory has no application here?"

"Oh, it does," said Higomu.

"Then show me," said Captain Muzer. "I will play as well as

I am able, and you defeat me with chaos."

Higomu shook his head. "General Victorious was giving advice for dealing with a superior foe. He said chaos *evens* the odds. Against you, forgive me for saying so, that is not my best strategy."

Captain Muzer nodded thoughtfully. "Yes, I see your point."

"The Winelanders had little chance in a conventional battle," Higomu said. "To win, they had to defy convention. I could teach the strategy to Vadu, but you would not like it."

"What? Nonsense! I would be glad if my first mate could play a more challenging game."

Higomu shook his head. "I fear you do not understand," he said. He glanced at the first mate. "But perhaps Vadu does."

Muzer looked at Vadu.

Vadu looked away. "I should raise the sail," he said. "This is a good breeze."

Higomu's dark eyes twinkled as they followed the first mate's passage to the mast.

"Emperor Zealous claimed that all battles are winnable," Captain Muzer said. "But I suspect he would have felt differently if he had ever played pegboard against you."

"Emperor Zealous always had the bigger army," Higomu observed.

Captain Muzer frowned and scratched his chin where his beard was beginning to grow. "And the Theocratic Emperor *still* has the bigger army," he said. "The only army."

Higomu nodded and leaned back against the railing, as though getting comfortable for the ensuing conversation. Two days spent in the company of Captain Muzer were sufficient for one to learn his politics. Higomu and Shiko had been on his ship for twenty. Any moment now, he would say—

"Every one of our schools should teach military history. It should be required knowledge for enrollment at the Academy."

Higomu nodded in agreement.

"Why do our people insist on remaining defenseless?" Muzer asked. "How long can the Children of Beauty maintain an army before they point their spears at us?"

Over two hundred years and counting, Shiko thought. But she wasn't interested in arguing. Muzer's fears were so far-fetched. The Children of Beauty had gold, silver, cotton, and citrus fruit. They could trade for any goods they needed. The vast stretch of coastline between Hicho and Dupho provided them plenty of room to expand. War was illogical.

"You mark my words," Muzer said. "We'll see an invasion within the next two decades. The Children of Beauty are a warlike people."

Higomu shook his head—much to Shiko's surprise, for he rarely contradicted their host. "Children of Beauty want violence no more than our people do," Higomu said. "It is only the Theocratic Army that is violent."

"Yes, yes, of course," said Captain Muzer. "But all it takes is one ambitious emperor."

"Which is why the Church has not appointed an ambitious emperor in a hundred years," said Higomu.

"But wouldn't we be safer if we had our own army?" Muzer asked.

"We would," Higomu said. "And we should certainly encourage young people to learn military tactics. But I do not expect we will need to use that knowledge against the Children of Beauty."

Against the demons, Shiko thought.

"Against the Children of Lith, then?" Captain Muzer asked.

"That seems more likely," said Higomu. "Their kingdoms have historically been aggressive and unstable."

Captain Muzer nodded. "I have always thought that Emperor Zealous's fortress strategy in the Wineland River Valley might also apply to the defense of mountain passes …"

Shiko arose and left them to their discussion. The nine peoples had been created to fight the demons, not each other. What made people forget that?

She nodded as she passed Vadu, who was discussing the weather with two of the rowers. The Children of Labor were allowing themselves a break after helping Vadu put up the sail, which displayed the outline of a chalice painted in green.

Shiko stepped lightly onto crates of glassware or onto the rowers' thwarts. While the rowers rested, she did not have to worry about timing her steps to the strokes of moving oars. She exchanged a smile with Timon, the green-vested foreman, before stepping from his thwart onto the foredeck.

Perhaps the armies get tired of constantly training, Shiko thought as she assumed a relaxed stance on the foredeck with her feet shoulder width apart. *If they believed they would someday have a chance to use their skills against the demons, perhaps they would not start wars with each other.*

Shiko was glad that Elder Badiki was giving her a chance to use her skills. She had continued to study artifacts even after she had realized that she did not have enough magical talent to make them herself. On this mission, she could finally put that knowledge to use. And although she certainly did not plan to fight anyone, her combat training gave her the confidence to face giants without fear.

Shiko bent her knees and leaned forward as the foredeck bobbed over a wave. Maintaining one's balance on the most dynamic part of the ship could be quite challenging. Cloth buyers could not spar or practice forms, but they could "seek inspiration for new patterns of cloth." When she had figured this out, Higomu had actually smiled at her. Briefly.

Shiko adjusted her stance so that she faced more toward starboard. The distant ship had drawn closer during the peg-board game. Perhaps it was heading to Hicho.

She caught sight of Higomu stepping from crate to thwart, as surefooted as a mountain goat. She turned to face him, pleased that she could do so without reaching for the railing.

"Have you found any new patterns?" Higomu asked as he approached.

"I enjoy the traditional ones," she said.

Higomu sat down on the edge of the deck. It was an amusing reversal of roles: When he came to practice his balance, Shiko was usually sitting there reading.

"Do you need the deck?" she asked.

"No, don't let me interrupt," he said.

He continued sitting. Higomu never simply sat. He was always practicing his balance, discussing military history with Captain Muzer, or playing pegboard. Even when pretending to be a linen merchant, he was constantly in training. Shiko suddenly realized that even the pegboard was training.

"Does military history really apply to pegboard?" she asked.

Higomu looked up at her, weighing her merits with his dark eyes. He reached a decision and rose to stand beside her.

"Yes," he said quietly.

Shiko could find no reason for his tone.

"Could Captain Muzer use the chaos strategy to defeat you?" she asked.

"No," said Higomu, as though confiding a secret. "He doesn't understand it. But Vadu does. He's playing against the captain now."

Shiko followed his gaze aft. Unsure of how to react to this revelation, she contented herself with saying, "Oh."

Higomu held up a hand to forestall her next question. He watched the aftdeck intently, as though he could see the game from here.

Shiko waited politely for Higomu to explain what they were watching for. A few moments later, her patience was rewarded by the sight of a small cedar board spraying brass pegs as it whirled off the aftdeck. It landed in the sea with a tiny white splash.

Captain Muzer emitted an incoherent cry of anguish.

"Chaos evens the odds!" shouted Vadu.

Higomu heaved a sigh of relief. "Twenty days of pegboard," he murmured, "but I've finally won."

Shiko stared at him. "You *don't* like pegboard?"

He looked into her eyes, "Shiko, I—"

His gaze shifted out to sea. "That looks like trouble," he said.

The ship off the starboard bow was raising its sail. The sail was unmarked, like those on the fishing boats that operated out of Hicho Harbor. This confused Shiko, because she believed they were more than a day from any fishing port. Sails on merchant vessels usually bore identification symbols, like Captain Muzer's green chalice.

Higomu was already moving aft.

The unmarked vessel was crewed by Children of Beauty, black- or white-skinned giants with auras illuminating their heads. They were famous for decorating everything. Why did they have a plain white sail? And how could it billow into the wind?

Shiko followed Higomu. As soon as Higomu reached the aftdeck, he pointed out the approaching ship to Captain Muzer.

"Pirates!" the captain yelled. "Lower the sail and take us cross wind!"

Timon the foreman repeated the order in the rowers' language. The giants amidships began lowering the sail. By the time they had it secured, however, the other ship had closed the distance, sailing under the power of an opposing wind.

"A windmaster?" Shiko asked, as she stepped onto the aftdeck.

Higomu nodded.

Although rowers had been the primary means of ship propulsion along the Moonaway Coast for more than two centuries, magical techniques for moving ships had not been forgotten. Anyone with enough power over Air and Motion could become a windmaster, but such power was rare. Shiko guessed the windmaster was the man in the purple gown who stood on the other vessel's aftdeck, facing the sail. Beside him, a white-skinned man with long black braids shouted orders. The words sounded foreign until Shiko's mind adjusted to his accent.

"Man the oars!" he was shouting. "Man the oars, or they shall escape us!"

Escape was exactly Captain Muzer's intention. The Children of Labor were now rowing the ship toward Movozo Island. The island was too distant to provide safe harbor, but the course would force the pirate ship into an awkward heading.

That was the intent, but the crosswind caused no trouble for the enemy ship. It altered course, but its unmarked sail did not slacken. The pirates took oars in hand, and their ship drew even closer.

Shiko hoped the Children of Labor would prove to be stronger rowers than the Children of Beauty. Perhaps they were, but they could not match the other ship's supernatural wind. The pirates were now so near that Shiko could see that they hid their faces behind domino masks. Their hair was done in the "jellyfish style" of many short braids. Only their proud leader stood out, for his black braids were so long that they fell over his shoulders.

Higomu frowned. "Captain," he said, "I recommend negotiation."

"Where's the bloody Theocratic Navy when we need them?" Captain Muzer asked.

"Ship oars!" called the enemy captain as the pirates drew alongside. "Ready javelins!"

Two dozen spear points gleamed in the sunlight.

"We yield!" Captain Muzer shouted. "Full stop," he ordered his crew. "We yield!" he repeated. "What are your terms?"

"Tie our line," ordered the masked captain with the long black braids. A skinny, knobby-kneed pirate tossed a line weighted with a fist-knot. One of Muzer's rowers stood up and caught it.

The pirate captain threw his javelin through the rower's throat. Her eyes screamed as she fell onto her thwart, but her voice was only a sickening gurgle.

"Tell your leatherskins to remain seated," the pirate captain said. "We have more javelins."

Timon the foreman began shouting at his horrified crew.

"Vadu, tie that line," Captain Muzer murmured.

The wrinkled brown man scurried over the crates to the fallen Child of Labor. He did not attempt to take the line from her flailing hand. Instead, he cut it and hastily secured the new end to the railing. On orders from their captain, the pirates hauled on the line, dragging the two ships close enough for them to lash the vessels together.

The pirate captain's thin lips twisted in disgust at the gurgles of the dying woman. "Quiet her, Brutal."

The person indicated by this name was a broad-shouldered, long-armed man with a scar on his jaw. His aura glowed yellow-orange as he leapt aboard to stand above the fallen Child of Labor. He swung his iron-headed hatchet into the woman's skull, and her noises ceased.

One of the rowers near Shiko murmured a prayer.

Shiko broke out in a sweat. She wanted to kill them. She wanted to kill them all. But the pirates held the advantage, and any counterattack would likely result in the deaths of more rowers.

"Be certain your leatherskins remain still," the masked captain said. "We do not wish to use our hatchets against your crew."

Timon translated.

The masked pirates crossed onto Captain Muzer's vessel, each with a hatchet in hand. At first, Shiko thought they intended to scuttle the ship, in which case resistance, no matter the odds, would be the logical course of action. But the Children of Beauty dealt only incidental blows to the hull. They were intent on destroying the crates of glass.

With so many men, they worked quickly, smashing crates while the rowers watched in fright or in stoic anger. Shiko was baffled. She wanted to ask Higomu what it meant, but she had lost track of her partner.

A moment later, Higomu announced his location to all: The

pirate ship's mast fell and toppled overboard.

"My mast!" yelled the giant captain. His black braids swung away from his shoulders as he turned on Captain Muzer. "What treachery is this?"

Higomu, aboard the pirate ship, had cut the lines that lashed the two vessels together. He picked up a javelin and pressed it against Captain Muzer's ship. One of the rowers, seeing Higomu's intent, assisted him by pushing off with her oar.

"Back to the ship!" cried the pirate captain. "Back to the ship!"

The skinny, knobby-kneed pirate raised his hatchet to strike the woman who was helping Higomu push the ships apart, but Timon stood up, grabbed the pirate from behind, and threw him onto the enemy ship. At the sound of the foreman's battle cry, the Children of Labor rose to grapple with the hatchet-wielding pirates, whose auras flared into a wildfire of yellows, oranges, and greens.

The long-braided pirate seized Captain Muzer's throat in his bone-white hand. "How dare you defy me!" he snarled, thrusting Muzer up onto the railing above the stern. For an instant, Captain Muzer tottered there, and Shiko did not know which way he would fall. Then the giant slammed his left forearm up into Muzer's jaw, knocking him overboard.

"Back to the ship!" cried the masked captain. Placing one hand on top of his head, he leapt across the widening gap.

Vadu was yelling, "Push off! Push off!"

Shiko pulled the pins off the shoulders of her chiton and tore off her linen belt. Her garment fell to the deck as she clambered onto the railing.

Captain Muzer was lying face down in the sea, his blue chiton billowing around him. Shiko dove.

The rowers separating the ships were unknowingly pushing their vessel away from Captain Muzer. Shiko's dive came up short, and she had to swim a dozen strokes before her hand brushed his blue chiton. She grabbed it at the nape of the neck.

Kicking with her legs and pulling with her free arm, she was able to maneuver the captain's limp body so that his head was out of the sea. While the unconscious captain coughed up water, Shiko heaved in great breaths and wondered how to catch up with the retreating ship.

"Grab this!" Higomu called.

Shiko looked up to see a javelin flying toward her. It missed by only an arm's length.

It was the foe's javelin, but apparently it had been thrown by Higomu, for a line was attached to it and the other end was secured to the ship.

Shiko grabbed the line with her free hand. One of the rowers began pulling her in.

"Go!" Vadu yelled, and thirty-four oars dug into the water. Shiko and Captain Muzer were dragged behind. As the vessel picked up speed, the pull of Captain Muzer's body grew heavier. The rower on the aftdeck was hauling them in, but was Shiko strong enough to hang on against this extra force? She had to be.

As they neared the stern, Shiko's body began rising out of the sea. The rower was hauling them up as though raising an anchor. As the captain's bulk rose from the waves, Shiko's burning arms told her that the weak link in this chain was about to give.

"Stop!" she called.

The giant stopped pulling.

Shiko allowed herself to slide back down the rope so that the sea would bear more of the captain's weight.

"What is it?" Higomu asked.

Shiko looked up into his worried face. "He's too heavy," she said. "I won't be able to hold him if you try to pull me out of the water."

Higomu nodded and disappeared.

A moment later, Vadu's bald head appeared over the railing. He lowered a line with a double loop on the end. Shiko recognized the knot as a "deadman's bowline".

"Can you get this around him?" Vadu asked.

I will have to, Shiko thought.

To free a hand, she held the captain's body with her legs. She grasped his chiton with her toes for extra security. The speed of the ship and her grip on the line kept their heads mostly above water.

With her teeth and her free hand, she managed to get one loop under Muzer's arms. Then she used her feet to slip the other loop around his legs.

She looked up to Vadu and nodded.

Immediately, the rowers began lifting the unconscious man from the ocean. Water from his chiton rained down on Shiko's head. She clung to her line with both hands and waited until the rain stopped.

Finally the bowline was lowered for Shiko. She slipped into its loops. The rowers hoisted her up. Giant hands grabbed her and deposited her on the aftdeck. As soon as her bottom hit the planks, Higomu was dropping her chiton over her.

"I wouldn't mind drying out first," she said.

"Your lockpicks," he murmured.

Oh. She had not taken the time to remove her tools, which were on a waist belt that had been concealed by her chiton. She would have to wipe them dry when no one was looking. Seawater was probably bad for lockpicks.

Shiko wriggled free of the bowline. She lifted the folds of her chiton to cover her chest, brushing her fingers against her sacred stone pendant to assure herself it was still there. When Higomu had finished pinning the chiton back on her shoulders, she reached up and touched his wrist.

"Thank you," she said.

His dark eyes studied her face, as though the droplets sliding down her cheeks told him something of her worth.

"That was well done," he said.

CHAPTER 6
Whitedove's Villa

OVERLOOKING the crowded housing blocks of Dupho, the villas on the Heights stood apart from each other. With their numerous living chambers, their courtyard gardens, and their open-air atriums, Dupho's villas could have been called "palaces", but that term was reserved for government buildings and imperial residences in the city below. Wealthy locals on the Heights called their homes "villas".

Kittiwake sat in the atrium of Legislator Whitedove's villa on a familiar bench. The sculptor had carved the bench from a single block of wood, rounding the corners for comfort and decorating the edges with a flying-dove motif. Kittiwake traced the line of doves with his finger and wondered how much longer he would be waiting.

His other hand held the message from Commander Fox. If Legislator Whitedove had known that his artificer was threatened with conscription, perhaps he would have abbreviated his conference with the Inspector of Aqueducts. Surely he would have. Kittiwake was losing time that he needed for his work.

Kittiwake found it difficult to sit quietly, yet Whitedove's spacious atrium was designed to be soothing. The four walls were painted with a blue gradient that seemed to merge them into the sky above. Around the gurgling central fountain stood serene-faced statues depicting Legislator Whitedove, his older brother, his younger sister, and his older sister, whose statue faced away from the other three, to indicate that she no longer lived.

Kittiwake knew nothing of Whitedove's brother, except that he ran a vineyard elsewhere and that the legislator did not mind having his brother far away. His living sister, however, had rooms in this villa, as did her middle-aged son.

A servant girl poked her head out from a window on the sunlit side of the upper story. No doubt she had hoped to enjoy a moment of the quiet morning, but on catching Kittiwake's eye, she ducked back into the room. Servants didn't like to be caught enjoying the day.

Zefi never had that problem. She was enjoying the day most when she was helping Kittiwake work. The girl was fond of him. Children of Labor had no halos, but Zefi's feelings were strong enough that Kittiwake sometimes felt her elemental resonance even when he was focused on something else.

Zefi was across the atrium in the kitchen now. She was always taken away to the kitchen when Kittiwake arrived at the villa. He would have preferred to have her by his side. She hated sitting idle, but so did he, and it would have been nice to have her company.

Perhaps he enjoyed her company too much. Her term of service had ended yesterday, but he had not sent her back to the Orphanage. He needed her help to finish the emotion box. Zefi hadn't said anything. Perhaps she was unaware that her year-and-a-day had passed. Or perhaps she felt as he did: that it wouldn't hurt for her to stay a few more days to help finish Kittiwake's latest creation.

His greatest creation. A box that could trap elemental Emotion and hold it indefinitely. It was beautiful because it proved his theory that Emotion could be contained. As soon as he could align the indicator garnet and attach the directional resonance spigots, it would be complete. He was so close! He could be finishing it now if Commander Fox's soldiers had not interrupted him yesterday.

A man in a green gown walked out of Legislator White-dove's study. He passed Kittiwake's bench without a glance and strode across the atrium. The fountain embroidered on the back of his gown reminded people he was Dupho's Chief Inspector of Aqueducts. His bearing indicated that he thought he was too important to notice Kittiwake. Why did bureaucrats think themselves more important than artisans? What had the inspector ever made?

The inspector departed, echoes from the entry chamber announcing that the door had closed on his haughty back. A moment later, Whitedove's manservant emerged from the chamber and approached Kittiwake. Badger was husky like the animal he had been named for, yet his walk was always delicate, as though he were barefoot on a rocky beach.

Kittiwake stood to receive Badger's acknowledgment that it was finally his turn for an audience, but the sound of a female voice in Whitedove's study indicated that his turn had not yet come. Whitedove's sister, Opuntia, must have entered from the courtyard garden on the other side. Kittiwake sat back down on the atrium bench. Badger gave Kittiwake a polite nod and assumed a post near the door to the study.

What was the sister prattling about? Kittiwake's problem was urgent. And he needed to get back to work. Ah, well. He couldn't fault the most powerful legislator in the province for taking time to talk to his sister.

Kittiwake contemplated his troubles and watched a cloud drift above the atrium. Finally, the siblings' conversation ceased. Kittiwake rose and looked to Badger. The manservant inclined his head and entered the study. After brief words with the legislator, Badger re-emerged and indicated that Kittiwake could enter.

In the darkness of the study, Kittiwake was greeted by his patron. Although Whitedove had represented Kittiwake's district for years, he still had the face of a man in his thirties. His white skin was unwrinkled, and no trace of silver could be seen in his black hair.

The blue of Whitedove's aura revealed his curiosity. As they seated themselves on opposite sides of the marble-topped desk, Whitedove said, "I assume you have come to tell me of your progress on our artifact. Is all going well?"

"I fear it is not," Kittiwake said.

Legislator Whitedove's aura darkened with disappointment. Tinges of green revealed his apprehension as he asked, "You will have it ready in time for the party, won't you?"

"I will," said Kittiwake. "That is, I plan to, but—"

"Are you short on materials?" Whitedove asked, leaning forward. "Tell me what you need and I can have it brought to you while you work."

"No," said Kittiwake. "We have found what we need. No, I requested to speak with you because I have a different sort of problem. A political problem."

Legislator Whitedove sighed with relief. "Ah, then I am glad you came. Yes, let me handle your problem so you can concentrate on our artifact. Tell me all about it."

"The guardians-of-the-peace came to the shop yesterday to deliver this message." He handed it to his patron.

Whitedove unrolled the piece of paper. Kittiwake held his emotions under control, projecting an aura of patience while his patron read the message. Twice.

Whitedove did not offer the message back. Instead, he stood up and paced to the corner of his office where he kept his pair of caged doves, as though the birds had the answers he sought.

"Commander Fox must hold you in high esteem," he said.

"I'm not accepting his offer," Kittiwake said. He wanted to be certain that was clear.

"No, of course you're not," said Whitedove. "It isn't really an offer, is it? This message reads more like a threat."

"Yes," said Kittiwake.

"But you are wondering what you can do, is that it?"

"Yes," said Kittiwake. "I am but a simple craftsman, whereas you are one of the most powerful legislators in the Assembly. The guardians-of-the-peace must answer to you."

"Yes," agreed Legislator Whitedove. "That is so."

In fact, Kittiwake did not know if it were so. The policing of Dupho was handled by the Theocratic Army, which took orders from the Imperial Council, from the Church of Beauty, sometimes even from the emperor, but not from Whitedove's Provincial Assembly. Nonetheless, Kittiwake hoped his patron's power would be good for something.

Whitedove said, "It is a pity that Fox should choose to come after you now." He spoke to Kittiwake, but he seemed to be addressing the doves. He cooed softly to them. Kittiwake remained silent to let the man think.

Whitedove nodded to himself.

"It is a threat," he decided. He took a wooden box down from a shelf. "But it is not a threat against you, my dear artificer," he said as he placed the box on his marble desk. "Commander Fox simply wishes to anger me."

The box was decorated with an image of the sun rendered in an angular style traditional for three-tone wood inlay. Legislator Whitedove lifted the lid to reveal a magnifying lens with a silver handle tessellated with point-work doves. He took the lens and a bronze lamp out of the room to the sunny garden courtyard and returned a moment later with the lamp lit.

"Anger does not suit great people," Whitedove said as he returned the magnifying lens to its box. "Anger is for thumb-fingered soldiers—for generals and commanders—not for visionaries like you and me."

Whitedove lifted the scrolled message and ignited it in the lamp's flame. He set the paper down to burn on the marble desktop.

"Kittiwake, it grieves me that you have been disturbed by this. It is an unfortunate consequence of my influence that my enemies, seeking to harm me, sometimes threaten those who are near to me—people like you, whom I hold in esteem, whose skill and loyalty I value. But I beg you to see—" Whitedove gestured at the burning paper, "—that Commander Fox has no power over you. Your work is the highest art. It is no crime. And so the guardians-of-the-peace cannot touch you. Is that clear?"

"Yes," said Kittiwake, although he did not find this answer satisfactory.

Whitedove put a friendly hand on Kittiwake's shoulder.

"My brother's birthday party is just four days away. He turns seventy-two. I dearly want to give him the most appropriate gift I can. Please, Kittiwake. That artifact must be complete. For him. In a way, my brother has been waiting to see your creation for six dozen years. I know you don't want to disappoint."

"No," said Kittiwake.

"Good, good." Whitedove smiled and gave Kittiwake a pat. "So don't let this unfortunate incident distract you. My influence will keep you safe."

Kittiwake swallowed. "And what should I tell the guardians if they come back?"

"Simply tell them you won't go," Whitedove said. "Tell them you are mine."

CHAPTER 7

Arrival

SHIKO LEANED ON THE RAILING of the foredeck, contemplating the glow where the sun had set. She felt too tired and empty to sleep.

"You should sleep," Higomu told her, appearing with his customary stealth. "We arrive in Dupho the day after to-morrow, and you will need to be rested."

That was logical. But Shiko didn't feel like being logical. Which implied that she was tired. Which meant she should go to sleep.

Instead she said, "I should have done something."

"You did do something. You saved Captain Muzer's life."

"But I should have saved *her*, too."

"How?" Higomu asked. "She was dead the moment she stood up."

Higomu was right, of course. Shiko could not have saved the rower. Shiko could have joined in the melee that started when the pirate captain ordered the panicked retreat, but it would not have made a difference for the woman whose body they had just buried at sea.

Higomu had done something, moving so stealthily between ships that not even Shiko had noticed him, disabling the enemy windmaster, slicing the lines, chopping down the mast. Higomu had known how to secure a tactical advantage. Higomu was a striker for the Order of the Lock. Shiko had just watched, wasting two years of training.

"When did you cross onto the pirate ship?" she asked.

"As soon as the first hatchet smashed glass," Higomu said.

"They were all looking down, and no one could hear a thing. Once I was on their ship, I could stay low enough that no one could see me."

"And how did you get back?"

"I jumped as they were jumping the other way."

"Didn't they try to stop you?"

Higomu shook his head. "They had other things to worry about."

Shiko finally found the courage to ask, "What should I have done?"

"You should have snapped the long-braided man's knee joint when he picked up Captain Muzer. He wasn't looking at you. A side thrust-kick would have done it. Alternatively, you could have hamstrung him."

That sounded grisly, but it had logic to it. "I didn't bring my knife," Shiko said. "Elder Badiki said they are illegal on the streets of Dupho."

Higomu frowned. "Don't you know the location of every weapon on this ship by now? You could have taken the carving knife from the toolbox. Or you could have used the lemon knife."

Shiko nodded. "I was thinking of them as tools. I should have realized they could also be weapons."

"A weapon is just a tool for causing injury," Higomu said. "And any tool can be used to cause injury."

Shiko's stomach tightened as she recalled the use the scar-faced pirate had found for his hatchet. "I wish I had done something," she said.

"I wish you had snapped their captain's knee joint," Higomu said. "I would have liked to keep him aboard for questioning. But you showed good instincts in saving Captain Muzer. We make decisions in an instant and live with the consequences forever. That's the way it works in this business."

"You mean the cloth business?" Shiko asked.

"Of course," Higomu said. Neither his voice nor his pale

face expressed any irony.

"But I'm glad you are asking questions," Higomu said. "Success depends on good judgment, and judgment improves by thinking about the decisions you have made. The Goddess knows we don't have time to think *before* we make them."

"Thank you, Higomu." His words had made her feel better—which she had not expected.

"Training you is my job," he said.

"Of course," she replied.

"So now you will get some sleep?" he asked.

"I will try," she said. "Only …"

"Yes?"

"Higomu, why did they destroy the cargo instead of stealing it?"

"Because someone paid them," Higomu said.

"Really? Who?"

Higomu turned to face her. "His name is Fox," he said. "He commands the unit of the Theocratic Army that enforces the laws in Dupho."

"And you know him?"

"We have crossed paths," Higomu said. "I do not know Fox as well as I would like, but I know that he controls the Chuckwalla school of glassblowers and that glass from the Green Chalice Glass Company has been selling well in Dupho. Commander Fox is most intolerant of those who challenge his territory."

"You know this from personal experience," Shiko guessed.

"I do," said Higomu.

"So what will we do when we get to Dupho?" Shiko asked.

"About Fox? Nothing. Our mission is to investigate the artificer. We can accomplish that best by staying out of Commander Fox's way."

"Very well," said Shiko. She wanted justice, but that was not her job. Her job was to protect the world from dangerous artifacts. She could not let this incident distract her from the mission.

"Of course, Fox might not stay out of *our* way," said Higomu. "It depends on whether his thugs recognized me."

"What did you do the last time you were in Dupho?" Shiko asked.

"Roughly the same thing we are planning to do this time," Higomu said. "Now get some sleep."

They arrived at the Bay of Dupho two days later at midday, with the red moon high in the sky. Captain Muzer asked the rowers to stroke at double time, so that the ship could reach the harbor before the tidal currents turned against them. Despite injuries suffered while driving off the pirates, the rowers complied.

As the docks of Dupho drew nearer, Shiko realized she had arrived at a different place. The flat-topped buildings made it seem as though the city had been built from a child's blocks. Brightly painted warehouses lined the docks, but most of the city was built on the plain above, presenting a wall of multihued facades to the harbor. The hill above Dupho was terraced by vineyards and orchards that climbed from the plain of the city up to the line of lavish houses known as "the Heights".

Knowing what to look for, Shiko spotted the aqueduct winding its way along the contour of the hill. It descended in a series of stair-step cisterns into the background of the city. The Theocratic Empire had invented plumbing, and Shiko's people were still trying to catch up.

"Commercial docks there; fishing docks there," said Higomu, pointing them out.

"So far apart?"

"It seems only half as far to them," said Higomu.

Shiko nodded.

Higomu pointed: "There's the Temple of Three Sisters up on the Heights."

A white marble structure on the hill gleamed in the hot noon sun.

"I imagine it is quite impressive up close," Shiko said.

"Yet not nearly as imposing as the Temple of Beauty," Higomu said. "The Theocratic Empire likes to make an impression."

"In truth," said Shiko, "I am most impressed by their aqueduct."

"Do you see the sewer?" Higomu asked.

"I thought it was a covered river running under the city," Shiko said.

"It is," agreed Higomu. "But it comes out right there. See that jetty on the right?"

"I do."

"That marks the sewer outflow. It's easier to see at low tide."

"Wouldn't high tide make the sewer flow backward?" asked Shiko.

"Are you doubting the competence of imperial engineering?" Higomu asked.

"No, no. But does it back up?"

"Rarely," said Higomu.

Shiko sighed. "I wonder if they'll ever finish the plumbing of Hicho."

"In Hicho the problem is more complex," said Higomu. "The engineers have to bring water through a thousand-year-old city. Dupho is better designed not because the Theocratic Empire is smarter, but because Emperor Zealous decided to build a new capital after his army had destroyed Old Dupho." He waved at the location of Old Dupho in a distant part of the bay. The tiny cluster of buildings looked no bigger than the village Shiko had grown up in.

"I wonder if any of them still remember," Shiko said. Dupho had been conquered two hundred years ago.

"Some do," Higomu said, with a certainty that surprised her. "The empire is governed from Dupho Province, but the government is controlled by the Theocratic Province. Some citizens of Dupho resent that."

"You know much about Dupho," Shiko observed.

"I've done some business here."

While they talked, the ship rapidly approached the docks until First Mate Vadu gave the order to come about. Under oar, the ship pivoted gracefully so that it could approach its dock stern-first. Shiko could see that this made rowing awkward, but at least the rowers finally got to face the direction the ship was moving. On Vadu's signal, two of the rowers dropped the stone anchor overboard. Some of the portside rowers used their oars to keep a safe distance between ship and dock, while others, each holding a short line, sprang onto the dock to tow the ship into the position indicated by a dockside official—a broad-shouldered Child of Beauty with a silver-streaked black braid so long that it wrapped across his shoulder to lie against the front of his richly embroidered yellow gown. First Mate Vadu announced to Captain Muzer that they had arrived at Dupho.

Shiko was almost eager enough to leap the gap between railing and dock, but she waited politely for the gangplank. Once the plank was in place, the privilege of using it first was taken by the Child of Beauty in the yellow gown. He wore no mask, and his single braid was nothing like the short "jellyfish-style" braids the pirates had worn, but Shiko felt uncomfortable at seeing him board their ship.

Irrational. He was no killer. He was a jovial man who greeted them with, "Welcome to Dupho. I am the harbor-master."

A scribe followed him onto the ship and poised his pen to write in the record book.

"Welcome aboard," said Captain Muzer. "I am Captain Muzer, from the port of Hicho, representing the Green Chalice Glass Company."

"Good day, Captain Muzer. What will you be declaring?"

"Five crates of glassware, two damaged." That was all that had remained after the destroyed crates had been jettisoned.

The harbormaster's smile faded. "Rough seas?" he asked.

"Pirates," the captain spat.

The harbormaster put his hand over his heart and grasped the end of his braid. "Did they steal much cargo?" he asked.

"No, they didn't steal it," said Captain Muzer. "They just smashed it."

The harbormaster frowned and twiddled the end of his braid between his fingertips.

"This does not surprise you," Higomu observed.

The giant shook his head. "No. Piracy is on the rise this spring."

"Especially against glass shipments," Higomu said.

The harbormaster nodded. "It grieves me to say that it is so."

"Then I shall not worry," said Higomu. "For I was but a passenger. I am in Dupho to deal in cloth. Perhaps my company's ships shall have better luck."

The harbormaster smiled. "I certainly hope so." He turned to his scribe and asked, "Do you have it written down?"

"Five small crates, two damaged," the youth repeated.

The harbormaster sighed. "Captain Muzer, you have my sympathies. But no matter how unpleasant your journey, I hope that you enjoy your stay."

Once the port officials had left, Shiko and Higomu thanked Captain Muzer and said good-bye to him and Vadu. Shiko hoped he could get a price for his remaining glass that would at least cover his costs for the trip. Profit margins were substantial on crafted goods, but she suspected the glass company would be taking a loss.

The wharf and piers of Dupho were stone surfaced, not wooden as in Hicho. After two weeks aboard a ship, the stone felt hard and unforgiving. Shiko's head still rocked with the waves, making her feel as though she were bouncing through the crowd of colorful gowns. She hoped she would soon be able to move gracefully, as Higomu was doing, but at least she was walking the way a sea-traveling cloth merchant would.

A guard stood near a flight of stone steps leading up from the docks to the rest of the city. Shiko reminded herself that a cloth merchant would not be afraid of this soldier, who held a spear even longer than the javelin that had killed her ship's rower. Or perhaps a cloth merchant *would* be afraid of all armed giants, if she had recently been attacked by pirates. Higomu ignored the guard and climbed the stairs. Shiko followed his lead.

From Tazhubo's *Recent History of Dupho*, Shiko knew the place above the commercial docks was called "the Whale Plaza". Vendors announced dried apricots, ripe citrus fruits, and fresh-baked bread—foods that made a seafarer's mouth water. Shiko wanted to purchase a small sample of—of anything, really; it all sounded good—but Higomu led her instead to the fountain in the center of the plaza.

A marble whale spouted water out of the top of its head. The water cascaded down its back where it collected in a chest-high basin. Unobtrusive holes perforating the base of the statue drained the water so that the basin would not overflow.

"We may drink some?" Shiko asked.

"We may."

Shiko reached into the basin with cupped hands. Because of the awkward angle, she was able to get only a scant amount of water, but it tasted good. She ran a cool, wet hand through her curly hair. Dupho was four weeks sunward of Hicho, and Redmonth seemed much hotter here.

From the Whale Plaza, Higomu led her along a stone-paved avenue that was more like a canyon. It was wide enough for multiple donkey carts to pass, which several did, traveling in either direction. The buildings, although only two or three stories high, were twice as tall as buildings in Hicho. They were decorated with fanciful murals depicting what artists thought life looked like under the sea, ignoring the fact that most sea creatures lived at depths where the water was monochromatic.

"The districts are identified by the murals," Higomu explained, as though she had not spent the last two weeks rereading Tazhubo's *Recent History of Dupho*. "These buildings are in the Aquatic Wonders district."

"And we are traveling due moonaway toward the Fish Plaza," she concluded.

"Yes," said Higomu.

Dupho was laid out geometrically, with grand avenues running straight through the entire city in the three cardinal directions. These sliced the city into triangular districts, each of which was painted according to its own theme. Tazhubo said that this geometric order was only superficial and that within each district, the twists and turns of the streets could be as complex as in Hicho.

"What do they call this avenue?" Shiko asked. That was something she had not been able to find in Tazhubo's *History*.

"They don't name avenues," Higomu said.

"Why not?" she asked.

"Buildings are named for their murals. Districts are named for their themes. Avenues have no art, so they deserve no names."

Was he mocking her? His face remained as solemn as always.

As they walked along, the feeling gradually grew inside Shiko that the buildings were missing something—that they were somehow naked, despite their fanciful murals.

"Where are the shutters?" she asked.

"There is no burglary in Dupho," Higomu said. "And so they need no shutters."

"And no locks on their doors," said Shiko.

"Precisely."

"But I thought I saw ..."

"What?"

"On the shop back there with the open doorway: I thought I saw a bracket inside so they could bar the door."

"Oh yes," said Higomu. "They don't lock their doors when they leave, but they do bar their doors when they are home."

"Why?" Shiko asked.

"To keep out murderers," Higomu said.

"They have murderers, but not burglars?"

"Murder is a crime," said Higomu. "But burglary is a sin."

"I'm afraid I don't follow the logic," Shiko said.

"For servants of Beauty, every act of creation is sacred," Higomu said. "Therefore, every object becomes sacred, by virtue of being created. Burglary of any home is the same as stealing from a holy shrine. Furthermore, no one in Dupho buys anything without knowing who made it, for whom it was made, and how the seller acquired it. Providing such information could be problematic for a burglar."

"I see your point."

Higomu nodded.

"But Dupho has murderers?" she asked.

"Children of Beauty have difficulty controlling their tempers," Higomu said.

"Very well. That explains why they have doors that can be barred only while they are home. But why don't they have shutters?"

"No murderer would come in through the window. It would be inelegant and undignified."

Was he mocking her, or them? Or perhaps himself? The man was unreadable.

"Ah there it is," Higomu said. "The House of the Flashing Tuna."

"Who lives there?" Shiko asked.

"We shall. It is an inn."

The House of the Flashing Tuna was near enough to the Fish Plaza that Shiko could smell the day's catch. A man in a midnight blue gown stood in the doorway to greet arriving guests.

"Good evening, Topaz," said Higomu. "Have you a room for two?"

The giant blinked in surprise. Then his face broke into a grin. "Higomu! How glad I am that you remembered me. And how pleased I am to meet your wife!" Topaz reached out a silver-painted arm toward Shiko.

His hand offered nothing to her, so Shiko wondered if he

expected her to put something in it. One of Higomu's hand-kerchiefs, perhaps?

"Not my wife," Higomu said. "My business partner. Shiko, meet Topaz. He wants to hold your hand."

"Oh," said Shiko. "Hello." She held out her hand.

The innkeeper's fingers pressed against hers warmly and tenderly. "I am glad to meet you," he said.

Turning his glowing blue head to Higomu, he asked, "But you did say one room for two, did you not?"

"I did."

"I have two rooms available in your size."

"We shall only require one," said Higomu. "With two cots."

"Ah," said the innkeeper. "Yes. Of course."

"Don't business partners usually share the same room among your people?" Shiko asked.

"Yes," said Topaz. "Ah, business partners usually do, although they are usually two men, do you see? Or sometimes two women."

"But not a man and a woman?" Shiko asked.

"Ah ... not unless they are husband and wife," said Topaz.

"Our custom is different," Higomu said.

"Yes, I see," said Topaz, looking at Shiko appraisingly. "But if I may say so, Higomu, your custom is not without merit."

Shiko was not sure what he meant by that.

CHAPTER 8
Commander Fox

BY THE TIME COMMANDER FOX returned to Dupho, the sun and moon had both set. A soft sea breeze followed him up from the docks and along the broad avenue. The paving stones, having soaked up a full day of sunshine, were now relinquishing their heat to the evening. Couples strolled hand-in-hand, halos glowing pink with affection. Neighbors conversed on the flat rooftops above. From the open doors of the taverns, music and laughter drifted out onto the streets. On a night like this, with temperatures too cool to flare tempers, it would not be until the eighth lithic—when all the sensible people were in bed—that trouble would begin.

The citizens of the Theocratic Empire were passionate people. When it came time for a pleasant evening to end, some were grateful for a rest from their passions, but always a few would overextend themselves. Sometimes, a quiet word was sufficient to calm them down. Sometimes, they needed to spend a night in the Red Palace. The guardians-of-the-peace sorted out the troublemakers, and Commander Fox watched over the guardians.

Two soldiers on duty at the edge of the Imperial Plaza saluted hand-to-heart as he passed. Fox returned the salute with a quiet smile. The male soldier had allowed fear to seep into his aura, but Fox did not rebuke him. Fear should not be shown to civilians, but a brief trepidation was acceptable when encountering one's commander unexpectedly.

Pink-haloed couples roamed even here. It took a special sort of person to see the romance of imposing palaces, bloody battle murals, and grandiose statues of the Empire's greatest military leaders, but the Imperial Plaza had its admirers, especially on moonless nights. The artwork of the plaza's architecture was illuminated by hundreds of lamps, making it the brightest plaza in the city.

Fox crossed the paving stones to the Red Palace. It, too, had lamps and torch sconces to illuminate its many fine features, but these were unused. Commander Fox kept the palace exterior dark, to remind people that it was a military headquarters. Only the front of the palace was lit. The two bronze basin lamps flanking the pillared entrance were beacons guiding home soldiers returning from patrol.

Fox himself had not been on night patrol in a long while, but sometimes he thought he would prefer an evening spent sorting out the city's troublemakers to a day spent listening to General Tern at Camp Shenkerwo. Not for the first time, Fox wished he had been smart enough to remain a captain. The captain's job was tactical. A commander had to be political.

Although Fox spared the olive oil on the exterior of his headquarters, the interior was kept well lit. Soldiers should walk confidently, not bumble about in the dim light of their own auras. Commander Fox set an example with his bearing as he walked through the foyer, past the saluting guardians, up the red marble staircase, and down the hall to his office.

He lit a taper off of the hall lamp and used its light to check his message box by the doorway. The box was empty. Good. That meant the near future held no meetings with imperial officials; he could spend tomorrow evening with his wife.

Fox made a circuit of his office to light the four corner lamps. He had ordered the room repainted fifteen years before, when he had moved in. Underneath the paint, the outlines of the battle scenes that had once adorned the walls could still be discerned by a scrutinizing eye. The scenes had been painted by someone with an artist's understanding of light but no understanding of how to hold a shield while thrusting a spear into an enemy's neck. Fox hoped evidence of the artist's genius lived on elsewhere in the city. In his office, the walls now depicted a mountainscape.

Fox completed his task by lighting the brass desk lamp shaped like the animal for which he was named. He extinguished the taper and returned it to its holder by the doorway. With his office now brightly lit, he would not have long to wait for the captain's report.

Captain Faith did not disappoint. Fox had just sat down at his desk when she appeared at his door. Although she wore her black hair in feminine ringlets, she carried herself like a warrior worthy of the line-dot-line forehead-symbol that marked her as a captain in the Theocratic Army. As was customary in Dupho, she also painted the two triangles on her cheek to mark her as a captain of the guardians-of-the-peace. She had chosen blue paint tonight, in a shade light enough to contrast prettily with her black skin.

The marble of Fox's desk took on a pinkish hue, reflecting the affection he felt for the woman. Had she not been his subordinate, she would have been his friend, for she understood the problems he faced, and she knew how to deal with many of them.

"Enter, Captain."

"Thank you, Commander. We are glad to have you back." Her red aura demonstrated that her words were genuine. "How was your visit to Shenkerwo?" she asked.

"The new recruits are looking good enough," he replied. "But General Tern is a ponderous bore who never stops talking. If you have my chevron someday—" he gestured at the mark of rank painted on his forehead, "—I do hope you get it after General Tern has retired."

"Perhaps once *you* are the general," Captain Faith suggested.

Commander Fox chuckled. "You know I would not take that job, even if they offered it. I love my work in this city."

"Perhaps you could move the provincial headquarters back to Dupho, Commander. Once you are general."

"An interesting thought, Captain. Yes, I have often said that it would be better to train our guardians here, in the city, to be guardians, instead of training soldiers and then trying to choose guardians from among them."

"It would make our jobs easier, Commander. Our recruits soak up so much at Shenkerwo. To make them worth anything, my sergeants must squeeze it all out of them."

"Well said." Fox chuckled. "And now, Captain, what news do you have for me?"

"Tonight has been quiet, Commander, although I suspect the street patrols will be bringing in guests later. Currently we have two murderers in the cells: one awaiting transport to the Greenmount quarry and one awaiting trial."

"We had another murder?"

"Last night."

"I wish people would stop to think more. What were the circumstances?"

"Two men disputed which of them had the prettier wife, with the result that one fell off the roof."

"Witnesses?"

"I have their names recorded, Commander. You needn't worry about this one."

"Very well."

Fox hoped the man would be found guilty of a lesser crime. The murder count for the year was above average so far.

"Anything else to report?" he asked, knowing that there was, and hoping the report would be favorable.

"I sent a patrol to deliver your message to Kittiwake the Artificer, Commander."

"And?"

"They delivered it."

"Was there a reply? Or a reaction?"

"Sergeant Obsidian reported that the artificer seemed subdued," said Captain Faith.

"Did you remind him that the artificer can project a false aura?"

"I warned him before the mission."

"Very well. Did the sergeant report anything else?"

"He said that Kittiwake's servant, a Child of Labor, was displeased by the squad's visit."

"But the leatherskin took no action?"

"None. The message was delivered without incident."

"Good. I commend you for choosing a sergeant who would not let himself be provoked."

"Thank you, Commander."

The question, of course, was whether the message would provoke Whitedove. Fox believed it would. The legislator thought his political power was unassailable, or else he would not have stolen Chuckwalla the Glassmaker.

Under the law, Chuckwalla was a free man who could work under whichever patron he chose. When Chuckwalla decided to abandon Fox and put his glassblowing school in the hands of Whitedove, Fox had no legal recourse. True, Fox had several illegal recourses, but he knew that was Whitedove's game: If Whitedove could goad Fox into abusing power, then his agents could control Fox with blackmail. Fox had let the glassmaker go.

But he could not let Whitedove believe that he would retreat in the face of every attack. The counterattack on the artificer was designed to keep Whitedove on the defensive, until Fox had found opportunities to do favors for the new members of the Imperial Council.

Captain Faith was still standing before him, so he asked her, "Can you spare any bareheads for day duty?"

Captain Faith smiled, and her aura grew brighter. She was training an elite group of guardians to fight smuggling and foreign espionage. They worked clandestinely, without spears, breastplates, or helmets—hence the name "bareheads". Fox knew that Captain Faith enjoyed any excuse to put her innovative methods to the test.

"I should be able to spare a few," she said. "What did you have in mind, Commander?"

"You were telling me last month about their surveillance training. Let us give them a test with this artificer. I want him watched all day, every day, and I want reports on where he goes when he leaves his house."

"Gladly," she said.

"And …" He thought a moment. How hard did he want to play for the artificer? "See if they can find evidence of something we can arrest him for. Anything, really, but it must be legitimate."

"Understood."

"Thank you, Captain. You may go."

"I would, Commander, but I have more to report."

"Oh. Do so, then."

"Darkheart has returned. He is staying at the House of the Flashing Tuna."

"Darkheart! You should have told me at once. How did you learn this? Did your bareheads track him?"

The bareheads were to report Darkheart on sight, but they were forbidden to follow the spy, so as not to reveal themselves.

"No, Commander. Darkheart was discovered by a citizen observer."

"How did a civilian recognize Darkheart?"

"I gave out his description to a few selected innkeepers."

Ah, but Faith was clever!

"Very well," Fox said. "But what if your innkeeper gave the game away?"

"Whether he did or not, I cannot say. It was a risk worth taking."

"It was," Fox agreed.

"Topaz said that Darkheart is using the name 'Higomu'."

"That was the name he gave last time," Fox said. "Why would he be so incautious?"

"Perhaps he trusts Topaz. The innkeeper's cooperation came at a high price."

"Do I want to know how high?"

"I am sure the details of how he came to be in our service will not concern you."

So she had either blackmailed him or threatened him. It was always risky to use underhanded tactics, but Fox chose to trust his captain's judgment. He was certain Faith had weighed the risks and determined that if any wrongdoing were revealed it would not incriminate her commander.

"Very well, Captain. Good work."

"Thank you, Commander. I have additional information as well."

"Do tell."

"He has a woman with him—another Child of Knowledge. Topaz describes her as brown and curly-headed. He also describes her as 'short', but I doubt that is helpful."

Fox agreed. Bookers were usually about waist-high. If the innkeeper had thought she seemed tall, that would have meant something.

"His wife?" Fox asked.

"Topaz denies it. Or, rather, he said Darkheart denied it and referred to her as his business associate. But they did take the same room."

"Interesting."

Captain Faith nodded. "She may be a weakness for him."

"Ah, but does Darkheart have weaknesses? First, he would need to have feelings, and we have no evidence of that."

"That is true, Commander."

"If he is here on 'business' then it would be strange for him to bring along weaknesses."

"Also true," Captain Faith agreed.

What was Darkheart playing at? On his previous visit to Dupho, he had abducted the city's most prominent artificer and stolen the Lamp of Darkness—not the most charming of artifacts, but certainly one of the most famous. Fox found it difficult to believe that Darkheart would return with his wife for a sight-seeing tour.

"Captain Faith, be certain to have your best bareheads watching Kittiwake. If Darkheart visits the artificer, they are to report this immediately."

"Yes, Commander."

"But the order against engagement stands. They should make no attempt to follow or contact Darkheart."

"Understood. What about the woman?"

"Ah, I see what you mean."

Commander Fox pondered that mysterious woman. Darkheart would not have brought her along unless she were essential to his plan. But that did not mean she was as cunning and vicious as Darkheart. In all the world, there could be only one person like him.

"If they can identify her, if they are certain who she is, and if they are certain she is alone, then they are to arrest her."

"Not follow her?"

"That would give us more information, Captain, you are correct. But if they were to follow her too far, they would find Darkheart following them."

"Understood. Arrest her then. On what charge?"

"Espionage, of course. All foreigners are guilty of espionage."

CHAPTER 9
Legislator Whitedove

THE YOUNG WOMAN reminded Whitedove of his dead sister. The curled ends of her bone-white hair caressed her shoulders, where the cut of her gown revealed her sweet black skin. As she spoke to him, a tear glided along the curve of her cheek and despair trembled in her vulnerable throat.

Exquisite. Certainly worthy of his attention, even this late at night.

"And since then, we have been looking for another apartment," she concluded, "but there is nothing we can afford."

Her husband squeezed her hand. Whitedove wondered how such a skinny, gawky potter could ever have attracted this beauty. Doubtless the potter often wondered the same.

"Do not despair," Whitedove consoled them. "You have come to the right person. Tell me: When is the scheduled demolition?"

"In two days," her husband replied.

"Then be certain both of you are home all day tomorrow, for someone will be arriving to move you into a new apartment."

"Can't you stop the demolition?" the husband asked.

Whitedove shook his head sadly. "I fear that not even the Emperor could stop the demolition now. If only you had come to me sooner."

"But we were told only three days ago," the husband wailed.

Whitedove nodded. "Yes. That is a great misfortune." He smiled at the woman, "But be brave. All will be well."

The woman made the effort to return his smile. Ah, the

poor thing was dispirited now, but she would be grateful to him once she had settled down in her new home.

Whitedove licked his lips. Yes. Very grateful.

He called for his manservant: "Badger!"

The husky man stepped softly into Whitedove's study and bowed.

"Please escort this young couple to the door, and then return, for we have matters to discuss."

"Very good, Legislator. If I may inform you, your nephew has returned from his voyage and waits outside."

"Ah, I see." Whitedove had not expected his nephew to return until later in the month, but perhaps this was for the best. "Very well. Tell him he may come in. He shall fetch you when he and I have finished talking."

"Very good, Legislator." Badger bowed to the couple. "Follow me, please."

They left. Snowgull stalked in, glowing yellow with anger. It was not a pretty color for a man with white hair and white skin.

He sneered, "Badger made me wait for those slum-dwellers?"

Dupho had no slum-dwellers, for the fair city had no slums, but Whitedove chose to not take offense. The way Snowgull wrinkled his nose reminded Whitedove of Opuntia, Snowgull's mother, Whitedove's living sister.

"Would you have preferred that they wait in the atrium, overhearing the news you bring?" he asked.

"You could have sent them home."

"And I have done so."

Snowgull opened his thin lips to say more stupid things, but Whitedove was quicker: "Snowgull, do you know how mosaics are made?"

Whitedove walked over to the shelf near the bird cage and lifted the lid off a cedarwood box. A naval captain had given him the box out of gratitude for helping the captain's niece get a wine stall on the Grand Market. It held birdseed and a slender silver spoon set into copper brackets in the lid.

"The pieces in a mosaic are unimportant. You could replace any one with another—in fact, you could even lose a piece—and the mosaic would seem unchanged."

Whitedove removed the spoon from its brackets and dipped it into the birdseed. He brought the spoon to the bird cage, poked it in between the bars, and dumped the seed into the male dove's feed bowl.

"The mosaicist knows this, and yet he cares for every piece." Whitedove fed the female, with a hand so young and steady that he lost not a single seed. "Do you know why?"

Snowgull sighed. "Why."

Whitedove ignored his nephew's insolence. "Because only through attention to detail can the mosaicist build the whole picture."

Whitedove replaced the spoon and closed the lid.

"That potter is no more than a piece in the background—you are correct—but the woman, Snowgull, is the daughter of a friend of the wife of the admiral. Tomorrow, she will be moving into a new home. I have rescued her. She will be grateful. She will tell her mother, and her mother will be grateful. Her mother will thank the admiral's wife, who will take pride in having the influence to put her friend's daughter in front of a man as influential as I am, even so late at night, after I have returned from a party.

"But her connections give her influence only if they remain influential, so the admiral's wife will continue to support our arrangement with the admiral, and I believe, Snowgull, that you find this arrangement to be in your best interests?"

Snowgull nodded.

"So you see, it was not truly the potter's interests I was serving, but yours."

Whitedove smiled at the caged birds pecking at their food. With clipped wings, they were totally dependent on him. So many things were.

"But you have not come to me this late at night to argue over whether nephews should be allowed to interrupt meetings with potters. You want something that only Uncle Whitedove can get for you. Tell me what it is."

"I want to kill a man."

"Oh." Whitedove did not try to hide his surprise. Snowgull knew he had said something shocking.

"I prefer that you do your killing on the seas," Whitedove said. "Murder in Dupho draws too much attention."

Unless one is highly skilled, he added to himself.

"But you said that if a man does me harm, I should make him pay doubly."

"Snowgull, there are other forms of revenge more effective than murder. Life is sacred. It should only be sacrificed when it brings you an advantage."

"It would bring me pleasure."

"Pleasure is pleasant," said Whitedove. "But it is not an advantage. Greatness is not about using power to pursue one's every whim. Greatness is about using power for others and receiving, in return, the admiration and loyalty that expands one's fame. To be great, your personal pleasure must be as nothing to you when compared with the esteem of others."

"Then use your power to bring me pleasure," pleaded Snowgull. "Help me find this man so I can kill him. Please."

"When you beg, you look like your mother."

"Then you will help me?"

"Tell me first who he is," Whitedove said.

"He is a booker."

Whitedove showed his surprise. "What did he do?"

"He attacked my ship."

"By himself?" Children of Knowledge were half the size of people.

"It wasn't my fault. My men should have seen him sneaking aboard."

"Perhaps you should begin at the beginning," Whitedove suggested.

"Yes, of course," said Snowgull. "We were at sea, in the current between the coasts, where the Hicho ships prefer to travel. We spotted a vessel bearing the Green Chalice on its sail."

"Ah, now I begin to understand."

Hicho's Green Chalice Glass Company was creating prismatic stemware. Prismatic stemware was also one of the signature products of the Chuckwalla school of glassblowers, which Whitedove had recently acquired. Whitedove had used his social standing to make prismatic stemware the most fashionable way to drink Whitedove wine. The fashion had spread, as fashions did, from the houses on the Heights down to the masses, including those who could not afford to order from Chuckwalla.

One of the young upstart legislators on the Assembly had gotten the idea that he could import prismatic stemware from Hicho and sell it at prices more people could afford. Of course, it was not as prestigious as Chuckwalla stemware, but Chuckwalla's rivals were spitefully proclaiming that it was superior in quality. Whitedove did not want to move against the young legislator directly—he often needed the boy's vote—so he had offered to pay Snowgull to attack the glass shipments.

This solution solved several problems at once. It made it difficult for the importer to turn a profit. It satisfied his sister's desire to see her son get paid for something. It pleased his nephew to be able to employ skills learned in the Theocratic Navy. And it removed his nephew from the villa for weeks at a time.

"Tell me what went wrong," Whitedove said.

"Nothing, at first. I didn't show the sail until they were too close to escape. We caught them easily, and they surrendered. To show that things would go poorly for them if they tried to fight us, I killed one of their leatherskins. Took her right through the throat!"

"Well done!" said Whitedove.

Actually, he thought it was ghastly, but he knew his nephew was proud of his skill with a spear. The boy could be such an embarrassment in so many ways that it was necessary to encourage him to take pride in the few skills he possessed.

"Once we had them intimidated, we boarded their ship and smashed their cargo."

"Did you remember to act as though you were searching for hidden caches of coins?" The pretense was important. Otherwise, people would soon deduce that piracy was not the true object of the attacks.

Snowgull's aura flashed green. "Yes," he lied.

Whitedove gave him a look.

"No," he admitted. "But we didn't have time. While we were working, this little booker chopped down our mast."

"Ah."

"I ordered everyone back to the ship, but he had also cut the lines and pushed the ships apart."

"Ah."

"Uncle Whitedove, it was humiliating. The leatherskins turned on us as we retreated. Several of my men were injured, and one drowned."

"Why didn't you keep someone behind to guard your ship?"

"I did! It was the windmaster's job."

"I see. So what happened?"

"The booker assaulted him."

"Really?"

"Incapacitated him. We found the windmaster lying underneath the aftdeck, tied up, with linen handkerchiefs stuffed in his mouth."

"A Child of Knowledge did this?"

"That is what the windmaster said. He also gave notice that he was leaving the crew as soon as we reached Dupho."

"But you dissuaded him, of course."

"I threatened to withhold his wages, but he would not change his mind."

Whitedove shook his head sadly. "Snowgull, that is no way to inspire loyalty. You should have offered him a hazard bonus."

"I wasn't certain you would give me the money."

"I would not have. You would have paid him from your own salary."

Snowgull nodded dolefully. "And that is the way the wind blows. We tied him to the spare anchor and threw him overboard."

"Such a waste," said Whitedove.

"He didn't have the heart for piracy," complained Snowgull. "He would never kill anyone. Next time, find me a windmaster with some military training."

"Windmasters are rare, Snowgull. If you need to go against the wind, I fear your men will be required to row from now on."

"They won't like that."

"Then you will have to find a way to make them like it."

"If I had your powers, I could keep them in line."

"I have earned my powers by long and devout service to the Goddess. If you wish to have powers of your own, you must do the same."

Snowgull scowled. "I serve faithfully, yet she denies me even the meanest of boons."

"Your service is not as faithful as you pretend. She sees into your heart. Never hold her in contempt, but let your thoughts and feelings be those of love and devotion. Great is her power."

Snowgull opened his mouth to say something contrary, but he thought better of it and said, "Yes, Uncle."

"There. That is a good start."

Whitedove knew the Goddess would never grant Snowgull great powers. Snowgull was unimportant. He could hold together a gang of bestial thugs, but he would never command the loyalty of hundreds and the admiration of thousands. Whitedove could give Snowgull a ship, a job, and a crew. He could share his home, his food, and his money. But he could not grant the powers he had from his Goddess. They were hers to give, and she found Snowgull unworthy.

This saddened Whitedove. And truth be told, it humbled him. But it was no shame to be humbled by the Goddess—She Before Whom All Will Be Humbled.

"Snowgull," he said, "you need to learn ways to inspire loyalty. I have an idea for you."

"Yes, Uncle?"

"When you tell your men they will have to row, remind them that this is not your fault. Tell them they must row because this Child of Knowledge humiliated them."

Snowgull chewed on this a moment. "True, but—"

"But you can console them with the promise of a new pair of gloves, made from this man's skin."

Snowgull's face lit up with joy. "You will help us find him?"

Whitedove nodded. "I will."

Why not? No one in Dupho was likely to care about a Child of Knowledge, least of all the guardians-of-the-peace, who regarded them as spies against the Empire.

"Oh, thank you, Uncle!"

They embraced and, in gratitude, Snowgull kissed him on each cheek.

"I am glad I have made you happy," said Whitedove. "Now, tell me: Are you planning to spend some time here with your mother tomorrow?"

"Of course."

"Good. She and I are making plans for your uncle's birthday party, and it seems right that we should share them with you."

"Oh. How old is Uncle Feldspar?"

"He will turn seventy-two the day after tomorrow."

"I am glad I will be here, then."

Whitedove smiled and patted his nephew on the shoulder. "As am I. Before you go to bed, Snowgull, would you find Badger and ask him to come here?"

"Certainly, Uncle. Good night."

Snowgull departed then. Whitedove smiled at his nephew's pink halo bobbing across the atrium. Whitedove enjoyed helping people.

He had a carter at the docks whom he paid to deliver goods that had avoided the imperial tariff. If the Child of Knowledge were indeed in Dupho, this carter's inquiries would find him. That would help Snowgull.

For the woman who wept so sweetly, Whitedove would go through the list of tenants and find someone to evict. She was sad now, but after a few days in her new home, she would be grateful. Badger would discover when the gawky husband hawked his pots so that Whitedove could schedule an appropriate time for a building inspection, during which he would allow the woman to show her gratitude.

Whitedove piously thanked his goddess for bringing him the woman to remind him of his long-dead sister. And his goddess rewarded his piety by promising that, this time, he would not be required to wrap his fingers around the woman's vulnerable throat.

CHAPTER 10

A Visit From Thugs

ZEFI'S TERM OF SERVICE had ended. Now, each day was a gift—a gift from her to Kittiwake as gratitude for his kindness and a gift to Zefi from the gods, who generously allowed her another day in the company of such a remarkable man. Even if he made her leave now, she would always be grateful.

And perhaps he *would* make her leave now. He had needed her help to finish his latest artifact, but now it was done. Or was it? She and Kittiwake had glued the wooden casing together last night, but the artifact had not yet been tested.

Kittiwake peered through a magnifying lens at the artifact's glued seams. His eye paused at the dark red garnet set into the top of the box. The garnet had to line up with the topmost point of the artifact's metal heart. Kittiwake lingered over it some time before raising his red-irised eyes to smile at Zefi.

"The glue has set," he told her. "Now we must perform the test that will tell us whether our work is done."

Zefi nodded and smiled back. She hoped it worked. Even though she knew that Kittiwake might dismiss her if the artifact was completed, she wanted him to succeed. Creation was so important to him.

It was an emotion box, designed to hold Emotion the way a jug holds water. The actual magical box, Kittiwake had told her, was the metallic heart inside the wooden case. The heart was shaped like two pyramids, with their square bases stuck together. Kittiwake said that this shape trapped Emotion inside. It could get in, but not out.

Kittiwake picked up the artifact and turned the spigot that would allow Emotion to flow in. "What should we put in here,

Zefi? What should we put in here?"

The box could hold any emotion, so Zefi suggested the first one that came to mind: "Hope?"

Kittiwake smiled. "Oh, Zefi. Yes, hope is what we feel, isn't it? But it is such a slippery emotion, sometimes so passive that it does nothing but sit and wait. We should think of something more powerful."

Zefi thought that hope was very powerful indeed, for hope could conquer despair.

"We need an emotion that drives someone into action," Kittiwake said thoughtfully.

I love you so much I could kiss you, Zefi thought. *But I don't want my love shut up in a box.*

"Zefi, would you strike a blow with my hammer?"

That was the confusing thing. Emotion didn't just mean how people felt. Kittiwake said Emotion was the thing that made people do what they did. "Emotion" was one of those words whose meaning twisted in translation.

Kittiwake set a piece of scrap wood on the other work-bench and handed Zefi his heaviest shaping hammer.

Zefi tapped the wood.

"Yes, Zefi, just like that," Kittiwake encouraged her. "Except that I want you to make a strong swing and truly smash that piece of wood. Smash it as though it were a hornet that has made you angry, or ... well, just think of a good reason and smash it."

Zefi did not need to search for a reason. She knew that if she smashed it hard enough, that would make Kittiwake happy. She lifted the hammer, focused on the scrap, and brought the hammer down.

For an instant, it seemed as though swinging the hammer to please Kittiwake were her only purpose in the world. She drove the blunt hammer into the wood with a bang that produced the deepest satisfaction. As the echoes rang in her ears, Zefi became aware of the pounding of her heart in her chest.

Kittiwake had struck the blow with her. He had some

magical way of making emotions bigger than they were, and he had enhanced Zefi's desire to swing the hammer so that it would be easier to capture in his box. She was glad he never tried to enhance her other desires. They were difficult enough to control.

Kittiwake's face glowed with wonder. "We did it," he said. "It's in there."

The red garnet in the lid of the box was now as bright as Kittiwake's eyes. It reminded Zefi of the difference between dried blood and fresh blood, as though the box had been brought to life.

She asked, "What you will do with it?"

Kittiwake looked puzzled for a moment. Then he chuckled. "Zefi, I don't know." He burst into joyful laughter. "I don't know!"

Zefi was baffled. The box was so important to him that she had just assumed he had a reason for making it. But Kittiwake was a Decorator Person. The things his people made did not need to have a function.

Zefi began to laugh with him. He had spent months on his greatest creation, and he did not even know what it was good for. Zefi would never have done that, but Kittiwake was Kittiwake. She loved him for it.

They were too joyful to be startled by the knock at the door. In fact, for a moment, they shared a silly grin at the thought of being caught in the middle of their laughter by whoever was on the other side. But then Zefi remembered that she was living with a man after her term of service had expired. As green tinges of doubt crept into Kittiwake's aura, she also remembered that, just three days before, it had been soldiers knocking.

Kittiwake set the box back on the workbench and leaned forward to look out the window for their caller.

"Should I open?" Zefi asked.

And as she said the words, she realized they had options. It was morning. They had not yet unbarred the door. They could go up the ladder onto the roof and keep on going, from one rooftop garden to the next, until they dropped down into someone's courtyard where they could take a passage to a hidden side street along which they could slip away, perhaps to a quiet village upriver or perhaps to the docks, where they could board a ship and travel back to Zefi's people. They did not have to live under the rule of the imperial soldiers. They did not have to fear the arrival of healer-priests from the Orphanage.

But this moment of freedom was all in Zefi's mind.

"I don't see anyone there," Kittiwake said, as the knocking came again.

Glowing blue with curiosity, Kittiwake crossed to the door and unbarred it. When he pulled the door open, Zefi saw no one. Then she looked down.

At first, she thought they were children wearing bedsheets. One was brown, darker than Zefi. She was the size of a little Worker Person girl, but her build was slight, her hair was in curls, and her face seemed mature. The other was almost white, with black hair, giving the impression of a miniature, short-haired Kittiwake—until Zefi saw his dark eyes and realized he was a well-seasoned man whom life could no longer surprise.

"Good morning," he said, his face making it clear that he was completely indifferent to their enjoyment of the morning and that the phrase was meant strictly as a formal greeting. "My name is Higomu, and this is my associate, Shiko. We are looking for Kittiwake the Artificer."

They were not children, but Thinker People, and they spoke Kittiwake's language. The little man's pronunciation was odd, but Zefi could understand his words.

Kittiwake identified himself proudly, saying, "I am Kittiwake."

The little dark-eyed man nodded. "Our employer is very interested in your work," he said. "We would like to learn more about it."

Kittiwake was puzzled, but he beckoned them inside. The

little woman smiled and nodded at Kittiwake and Zefi. Zefi stared back, realizing too late that it would have been more polite to return either the smile or the nod.

Among Worker People, Thinker People had the reputation of being small, intelligent, and polite, and the pair in Kittiwake's shop seemed, at first glance, to fit what Zefi expected. Kittiwake introduced Zefi, and they greeted her politely. Kittiwake offered them the room's only stool, and they said they were happy to stand. The curly-haired woman regarded Kittiwake with a smile.

"You have a spacious workspace," observed the man as his dark eyes flicked about the room.

"Yes," said Kittiwake. "I am quite pleased with it."

"I should think you would be," said the little man. "Not many houses in Dupho have a window facing due sunward."

"Yes," said Kittiwake. "I enjoy working in the sunlight."

Zefi glanced at the morning workbench where the emotion box sat in the sunbeam, red garnet gleaming.

"Do you work with Light, then?" the man asked. "I had heard you have an affinity for Emotion."

"You have heard correctly," Kittiwake said. "But I apprenticed with an optician for a time, and I learned to value windows."

The little man nodded. "I hope we aren't interrupting your work," he said.

"Not at all," said Kittiwake. "In fact, Zefi and I were planning to take the day off."

"Oh?"

"Yes, we were just celebrating the completion of my latest artifact." Kittiwake gestured at the emotion box.

"Oh really?" said the man. He and the little woman stood on tiptoes to get a better view. "And what is that?"

"The emotion box," said Kittiwake.

"And what does it do?"

"Ah. Are you familiar with the light box?"

"Yes."

"Well, just as a light box traps and stores light—" Kittiwake frowned. "Who is your employer?"

"Ah, yes," said the little man. "I represent Long Creek Linen. Would you like a sample?" From somewhere inside his bedsheet garment he produced two tiny handkerchiefs. He handed one to Kittiwake and offered the second to Zefi.

Zefi inspected the dainty thing, wondering what she could possibly use it for. "Thank you," she said.

"But why would a linen manufacturer be interested in artifacts?" Kittiwake asked.

The little man threw up his hands. "Why is *anyone* interested in artifacts? Your patron, for example, doesn't he have a business?"

"Yes," said Kittiwake. "Several, in fact."

"What is the most famous one?" the man asked.

"Well, I suppose he is best known for the Whitedove vineyards."

"Oh. Is Legislator Whitedove your patron?"

"He is."

"I thought that …"

"Thought what?"

"I thought perhaps you were under the protection of Commander Fox," the little man said.

Fear crept into Kittiwake's halo and he shook his head. "No," he said. "I have no association with Commander Fox."

"Really?" asked the little man. "Have you never seen any guardians-of-the-peace near your home?"

"How did you know about that?"

"I guessed," said the little man. But his tone of voice had lost its pretense of innocence.

Kittiwake frowned.

The little man asked, "Have they been just watching, or have they come inside?"

"Why are you here?" Kittiwake asked.

"I told you: Our employer is *very interested* in your work."

Zefi had the feeling that they were supposed to understand

something from that, something more than what was said.

"I am quite happy working for Legislator Whitedove," said Kittiwake.

"Has Fox made you an offer?" the little man asked.

He was threatening now. He wasn't even tall enough to see above the workbench, but somehow, he managed to look dangerous. The curly-haired woman had stopped smiling, and now her face was worried.

"I'm not taking Fox's offer," said Kittiwake.

"Do you really think he will accept your refusal?" the little man asked.

The curly-haired woman finally spoke up: "Please understand, we are not here to scare you. We simply wish to know about the artifacts you make."

"I don't think I should tell you anything," Kittiwake said.

"You've already told me enough," said the dark-eyed man. "You've told me that the guardians have visited you—very recently, if I am to judge. You've told me that Fox has scared you badly. And you've told me that your patron has left you here, vulnerable to Fox's soldiers, while he sits in his home on the Heights drinking Whitedove wine."

"I thought you said you weren't here to scare me."

"She said that. I made no promises."

"What do you really want?"

"We want you to come with us. For your own protection." The dark-eyed man looked at Zefi. "And you may come with us or stay, as you prefer."

"We aren't going anywhere," Kittiwake said.

"We aren't leaving Dupho without you," said the little man.

"Then you shall be staying in Dupho a long time!" Kittiwake shouted.

The woman crouched low, then, but not in submission. She looked poised to spring. The man, impassive, did not even flinch. Zefi prepared to help Kittiwake with whatever he was planning to do, but Kittiwake did no more than clench and unclench his fists as the light faded from his yellow-green aura.

"We shall give you some time to think about it," the man said. "But not much time. We'll come for you tomorrow. Fox will not allow you to defy him long."

The woman relaxed and assumed a normal posture again. "Please consider our offer," she said. "If you are in danger here—" she looked at Zefi, "—either or both of you—then returning with us to Hicho may be your best option." She nodded her head.

The man turned his back on them, opened the door to let the woman out, and pulled the door closed behind himself.

"Who were they?" Zefi asked.

"I don't know," said Kittiwake. "But I don't think they were linen merchants."

"How know they so much?" Zefi asked.

"They are Children of Knowledge," said Kittiwake. "They have spies everywhere."

Zefi frowned. "What if they come back?" She felt sure the little man would not have threatened them unless he truly had some means to force Kittiwake to leave.

"What if the guardians come back?" Kittiwake asked, his aura shading green with trepidation.

Zefi looked at the hole in the wall that served as a window. Shutters didn't even exist in Dupho. She could bar the door with the stout oaken beam, but she had no way to prevent entry through the window.

"We should take the emotion box to Legislator Whitedove right now," Kittiwake decided. "It will be safe in his villa."

But what about all of Kittiwake's tools? "Think you that I should stay here?" she asked. "To watch the shop?"

"No!" He grabbed her by both arms and looked up into her eyes. "No, Zefi, come with me. I'll make Legislator Whitedove keep us both safe."

Zefi feared that only the gods would be able to keep them safe.

CHAPTER 11

Surveillance

AS SHIKO FOLLOWED HIGOMU past an artistic arrangement of succulent-leaved cliff plants, she wondered why he had thought it necessary to threaten the artificer. She decided to ask him as soon as they got back to the inn. As strikers for the Order of the Lock, it was their duty to acquire and guard knowledge of dangerous artifacts, but Shiko had yet to see proof that Kittiwake's work could aid demon worshippers.

Shiko tried to look like a cloth dealer as she and Higomu passed within sight of children playing in the Agave Plaza's central fountain. The children stopped splashing and stared.

It was difficult to become accustomed to the stares in Dupho. People stared simply because they did not see many Children of Knowledge—at least, not this far from the docks—but Shiko could not suppress the feeling that they suspected something. She reminded herself that her anxiety was illogical. The only way they could guess that Shiko was on a secret mission would be if Shiko herself betrayed that secret. If she acted normally, they would react normally. And of course, their normal reaction was to stare.

Higomu led her past a short-haired yawning man and out of the plaza. The murals on the left side of the avenue depicted an agricultural theme: fields being planted and harvested; grapes growing on vines; baskets of colorful pumpkins, squashes, and gourds. Shiko realized she had not seen this district yet.

"This isn't the way back to the House of the Flashing Tuna," she said.

"No," said Higomu. "It is the way to the Temple of Beauty."

"Oh! Are we going to visit the temple?"

"No," said Higomu, turning onto a side street.

The side streets of Dupho had only a fraction of the width of the avenues, and they didn't run straight. They reminded Shiko of the streets of Hicho, except that they were paved with polygonal slabs of stone, not with cobbles.

"What is down here?" Shiko asked.

"We are," said Higomu, quickening his pace.

He tugged her hand, drawing her into an unlit passage. The quick-step scrape of their sandals against the paving stones echoed off the cool walls and arched ceiling. Such passages offered a way to pass between courtyard and street without going through the buildings in the block surrounding the courtyard. What business did Higomu have down here? Shiko looked at him quizzically, but it was a wasted gesture. It was too dark in the tunnel for them to see each other's facial expressions.

When they were halfway to the gate at the other end of the passage, Higomu stopped. "Be small," he murmured, and he tugged at her chiton to indicate that she should crouch low, as he was doing.

Shiko already felt small in this city, but she followed his example, crouching beside him and facing the street from which they had come. They waited. And as they waited, Shiko realized what they were waiting for.

When staring is normal, then the person who doesn't stare is the one to be suspicious of. The yawning man they had passed as they left the plaza had hardly seemed to notice them. What color had his aura been? Shiko realized she should have paid more attention. She could not even remember his face.

She crouched in the passage, listening to the blood pulse in her ears. Beside her, Higomu was silent. She could not even hear him breathe. They waited, but no one came.

Higomu straightened up. "We'll go into the courtyard," he said.

"Why didn't he try to follow us?"

" 'He'? There are three of them."

"I saw only the man who yawned as we walked by," Shiko said, following Higomu to the gated end of the passage.

"Did you?" Higomu asked. "You didn't show it."

"I didn't realize he was pretending not to watch us. Not until we got here."

"Good," said Higomu. "I counted on that."

"You counted on me not being intelligent enough to recognize we were being watched?"

"And I was right."

Shiko felt chastened. "Yes. You were."

"Elder Badiki said you are good with locks. How would you get past this gate?"

Shiko looked up. The wooden gate was so high that not even a Child of Beauty could have seen over it. The face of the gate was made of split poles, with the flat sides against cross-boards and the round sides facing the passage. The gaps between poles were three fingers wide, allowing Shiko to see the trees and potted plants in the courtyard beyond.

"It has no lock," she said. "The gate is latched from the other side."

"And?"

Shiko reached up and slipped her fingers through the gap. She found the latch at what would be chest height for the giants who would use the gate. She tried to lift it, but her fingers slipped and the latch fell back into place.

It was just a simple latch. No lockpicking skill was required—provided one could reach it. Shiko slipped her hand inside her chiton and found her lockpicking tools. She selected the pry lever, a stout blade-like tool for pushing aside catch mechanisms on the crudest locks. Using the pry lever's extra length, Shiko lifted the latch. She pushed the gate open triumphantly.

As they entered the courtyard, Higomu asked, "Wouldn't it have been simpler just to climb over?"

Shiko had not thought of that.

Higomu shut the gate, jumped up, and flipped the latch back into place.

"Stay low," he murmured. "People visit courtyards at all times of the day."

The courtyard provided plenty of cover. Wooden planters, stone statues, shrubs, and trees subdivided the courtyard into intimate garden nooks—an arrangement which could have allowed Shiko and Higomu to move unseen even if the courtyard had held a dozen people. Higomu led Shiko along the maze-like paths until they came to a building that jutted into the corner of the courtyard. Higomu avoided the doorway and chose instead to approach the side of the building that had a ladder built into its wall.

Shiko looked up to the top of the wall. It was only a one-story building, half as high as the rest of the buildings in the block. Of course, a one-story building in Dupho had walls as high as the two-story climbing walls at Elder Badiki's estate, and the ladder had wide gaps between rungs, but the climb would present little challenge.

Higomu removed his sandals and gripped them in his teeth. Shiko did likewise and followed him up the ladder to a flat roof intermediate between the courtyard and the rooftops of the enclosing buildings. Higomu led her up another ladder, and Shiko was on top of Dupho.

The rooftop gardens were said to be a second city, waking up as the sun set and the avenues emptied. This time of day, with the sun rising, the hot, flat roof was deserted, but it was not bare. Flowerpots with green yuccas lined the edge of the building. Carved wooden benches flanked by potted agaves provided seating. A trapdoor, unobtrusively off-center, indicated how the denizens below Shiko's feet would access their garden-in-the-sky come nightfall.

Higomu—who was still carrying his sandals, but in his hands now—did not pause to admire the garden. He led Shiko to the edge of the building and up three steps to the roof of the building adjacent. Despite the careful planning evidenced by Dupho's wide, straight avenues and hexagonal plazas, the buildings of Dupho were of nonuniform geometry. In this two-story block, each house had its own idea of how high those stories should be, with the result that crossing from one rooftop to the next often required stairsteps.

They moved softly from one building to another, staying in the middle of the rooftops so that they would be hidden from anyone on the streets below or in the courtyard in the center of the block.

Higomu wanted to move more swiftly than Shiko could in her ankle-length chiton. She stopped, undid the bottom two pins, and repinned them to bring the chiton up to knee-level.

"I wondered when you would realize you needed to do that," Higomu said.

"I didn't want to look out of place," Shiko said.

"You're half their height and wearing something they think is a bedsheet. You're already out of place. Just pretend it is Hicho's latest fashion. The people here won't know the difference."

That was logical.

Shiko's adjustment had the desired effect. She was able to match Higomu's pace.

"Higomu," she asked as they descended two steps to another building, "if you knew that the yawning man was watching us, why did you walk straight toward him?"

"I wanted him to think I didn't know," said Higomu.

"If he had followed us, what would you have done?"

"He would not have followed us far," Higomu said. "The passage was dark enough that he would not have seen us, even if he had thought to look."

That made sense.

"Do you know why he was watching us?" Shiko asked.

"He wasn't," said Higomu. "He was watching our friend the artificer. We drew his attention by visiting the building he watched."

"Oh," said Shiko. "Was he there when we went in?"

"Yes."

"Then why did we go in?"

"Because the woman at the fountain recognized me before I realized she was a guardian-of-the-peace. If we'd gone anywhere except where she expected us to go, she would have known I had seen her."

Shiko dimly remembered a woman at the fountain. She had thought the woman was supervising the children.

"How did you know she was a guardian-of-the-peace?"

"Because I've never seen her before, but she recognized me."

"How could you tell she recognized you?"

"I've been a striker a long time. I've learned to read people's faces."

"Is that why you keep your face so unreadable?"

Higomu stopped and looked Shiko in the eye. "No. I'm really like this."

Crossing the next rooftop, Shiko saw two wet gowns drying in the sun. "Is anyone likely to come up here in the daytime?" she asked.

"We're expecting no one will," said Higomu. "But remember, if someone does come up on the roof, they won't be expecting us. Hide if you can. If you can't, just hold still. People have difficulty seeing things they aren't expecting. Here we are. What luck: Your curly head matches this juniper."

Higomu knelt by the potted shrub and Shiko did likewise. She gave him a sidelong glance, but his solemn face did not indicate that he thought he had made a joke.

From their position, they could see down into the Agave Plaza. Kittiwake's single-story shop, named "The House of the Four Wrens", jutted out from the two-story block across the avenue. The shop's roof was decorated with cactus and two colorful rugs. A ladder led up to the neighboring rooftop.

"I see," said Shiko.

"What do you see?"

"You were just bluffing when you threatened the artificer.

Now you want to see how he responds."

"No and yes."

Shiko considered. "You weren't bluffing?"

"We can't leave him unsupervised in Dupho," Higomu said. "We'll have to take him back—one way or another."

"But he has done nothing wrong."

"Hasn't he? How do you know? He told us he has found a way to trap elemental Emotion in a box."

In truth, the artificer had stopped short of telling them that, but by then he had already revealed too much to keep them from guessing what he had not wanted to tell them. According to Elder Badiki's source, Kittiwake was applying optical principles to elemental Emotion. For a man raised in Dupho, among the best Light artificers in the world, an Emotion artifact that worked like a light box would be a logical step.

"What harm can he do?" Shiko asked. Light boxes were not forbidden artifacts. They were becoming common among the professors at the Academy.

"It has been a while since I took a metaphysics class," said Higomu, "but isn't the soul made of elemental Emotion?"

"Not pure Emotion," Shiko argued. Higomu knew full well that the soul was also composed of Thought. "Are you saying you think this artifact can trap souls?"

"I think it is our job to find out."

"But wouldn't it also have to trap Thought?" Shiko asked. "I don't think trapping Emotion would be sufficient."

"Did you learn any funeral theory at the Academy?"

"Funerals have a theory?"

"We covered it in depth at the Seminary," said Higomu. "When a body dies, its soul can go directly to Heaven, but often the soul gets stuck with the body. It stays attached. People who can see Emotion or Thought have verified this empirically."

"Yes. I did know that," said Shiko.

"Did you know that souls are sticky?" he asked. "If they come unstuck from their bodies, they often attach to the place of death, or to a meaningful object. Ghosts and spirits rarely roam free, and if a bodiless soul appears to be doing so, it is usually just moving within the confines of a larger place."

"Very well," said Shiko. "Souls are sticky."

"Yes," said Higomu. "Now if I want to trap your entire body, all I need to do is hold your wrist. So why wouldn't Kittiwake be able to trap your entire soul if he can trap the Emotional half of it?"

"I would like some time to examine your argument before conceding your point," said Shiko. "I would not want us to be misled by false analogy."

"Take all the time you need," said Higomu drily.

The door to the House of the Four Wrens opened.

"Aha," said Higomu.

The artificer emerged in his scarlet gown. He glanced around the plaza in a manner which marked him as a hunted man, even to an observer high above. A moment later, the Child of Labor emerged from the building carrying a bundle of cloth about the size of the emotion box.

The artificer pulled the door shut, and the two of them set off across the Agave Plaza.

"They have no way to bar their door when they leave," Shiko observed.

"They don't," Higomu agreed.

"Because there is no burglary in Dupho?" Shiko asked.

"Precisely," said Higomu. "Except when I am in town."

As Kittiwake and his servant left the plaza, a woman who had been sitting on a bench by the fountain stood up, stretched, and began following them. A man left the plaza at the same time, but in a different direction. Shiko could not recognize him from above, but he left from the location where she had seen the yawning man. Kittiwake's head darted nervously as he and his servant walked away up the avenue, but he did not look behind him.

Remembering what Higomu had said, Shiko whispered, "Where's the third?"

"Ahead of them. At the citrus stand now."

Shiko spotted the figure indicated. As the artificer and the servant advanced, the supposed citrus buyer strolled ahead, pausing to admire a mural or to inspect a vendor's wares. His stops would enable him to glance back without seeming to be watching over his shoulder.

"That's a good technique," Higomu said. "Fox has learned a few tricks since I visited last. Look: Our yawning man is heading toward the Imperial Plaza instead of following our artificer."

"What does that mean?" Shiko asked.

"It means that we don't have much time, so we had best move now."

CHAPTER 12
Burglary

WEARING THEIR SANDALS AGAIN, Shiko and Higomu crossed the Agave Plaza. Shiko's chiton was still pinned high. Higomu wanted her to be ready to run, and Shiko agreed that it was logical to assume that no one would know she was wearing her chiton improperly. But she knew. The knowledge made her irrationally self-conscious.

"We belong here," Higomu reminded her. "Kittiwake has invited us to come into his shop and wait until he gets back."

Shiko nodded and put on her confident face. It didn't sit well.

The wooden door was painted as part of the mural on the House of the Four Wrens, its brass door handle camouflaged among the yellow desert grass in the mural's foreground. Without knocking, Higomu pushed the door open. As soon as they were inside, he closed the door and dropped the oaken beam into place.

Shiko could feel the shop's emptiness … and also her own foreignness. The furniture was designed for giant bodies, the tools for giant hands. No, she could not make herself pretend that she belonged here. She was trespassing.

Higomu crossed to a square wooden hatch set into the stone floor. He opened it and disappeared into the pit below. A moment later he began handing up bottles.

Not trespassing. *Investigating.* This was her job. Shiko uncorked a bottle and sniffed it.

"Wine," she said. "Do we need to investigate the artificer's wine?"

Higomu handed up a half loaf of bread and a box that

smelled strongly of cheese.

"I want to see what is in this crate underneath," he said.

Shiko corked the bottle and peered down at Higomu. He heaved a wooden crate until it was resting on top of his head.

"Can you lift this out?" he asked.

Shiko did so. It was heavy, but her fingers were strong. She set the wooden crate beside the cheese, the bread, and the wine bottles.

Higomu grabbed the edge of the pit and pulled himself out.

"Open it," he said.

Dupho has no burglars except us, Shiko thought, borrowing one of Kittiwake's chisels. The nails in the lid were loose, and the crate opened easily.

"Raisins," she announced.

Higomu grunted and went to look through the artificer's bedding.

This wasn't right. Kittiwake had not given them permission to wait here for him. In fact, Kittiwake had fled his home in terror of them.

"Why did you decide to do it this way?" she asked. "Couldn't we have just requested to see his artifacts?"

"We could have," said Higomu. "But we don't want to see his artifacts. We want to confiscate them."

"But what if they prove to be harmless?"

"I thought we settled this: He is working on a box that can trap souls."

"That might not be his aim," said Shiko. "Perhaps he wants to trap joy or ... control his anger."

"His aim does not concern us," Higomu said. "If his box can trap souls, it is forbidden."

"But who are we to decide?"

Higomu stopped poking at the artificer's mattress and looked at Shiko. "We are not to decide. Elder Badiki will decide when we present him with Kittiwake and his artifacts."

"So we must bring Kittiwake in for trial, even though he has committed no crime?"

"A striker does what must be done," said Higomu. "Now help me search for— Aha!"

He sprang off Kittiwake's bed to pluck a book off a high shelf. His sandals landed gently on the stone floor.

"A notebook?" Shiko asked, coming to see.

Higomu handed it to her. "Check the most recent pages," he suggested.

Shiko did so. None of the illustrations resembled the cubical box she had seen on the workbench, but when she glanced at the written descriptions, she learned that the wooden box was simply a case. The octahedral object in the drawings could be embedded inside, with corner points fitting into divots at the center of each face of the box. One drawing, in particular, showed how a corner point could be matched to a resonance bracket that would change the color of an inlaid indicator garnet when the octahedron held elemental Emotion.

"This is a clever design," she told Higomu, who was climbing up on the artificer's stool so he could see the work-benches better.

"Do you know much about light boxes?" she asked.

But Higomu had seen something out the window. He jumped from the stool and said, "To the roof!"

Higomu dashed to the back of the workshop and leapt onto the first rung of the ladder. He seemed to sprint up the wall to the ceiling, where he unlatched the trapdoor.

A fist pounded against the front door. "Open for the guardians-of-the-peace!" Higomu had been clever to bar that door upon entering.

A blue-haloed, helmeted soldier peered in through the window. He saw Shiko and demanded, "Open the door, foreigner."

"Toss me the notebook!" Higomu ordered as the soldier began clambering through the window. Apparently the soldier wasn't worried about looking inelegant or undignified.

It didn't seem right to take Kittiwake's only book, but how else would they learn whether he had discovered forbidden knowledge? Shiko ran to the base of the ladder, tossed the book up to Higomu, and followed it upward, grateful that her partner had talked her into keeping her chiton pinned high.

By the time she reached the top rung, Higomu had already secured the book somewhere inside his clothing. He reached down and helped her up onto the roof.

They had seen Kittiwake's rooftop from the building across the plaza. It was sparser than others in the block. It had no benches. The only seating was provided by two rugs spread out in the sun. The only plants were a row of potted cactuses along the edge overlooking the plaza. Kittiwake was not much of a gardener.

The one-story workshop abutted a two-story building. Higomu stood next to a ladder set into the wall, but he made no move to climb it.

A spear flew over their heads and bounced off the wall. Into Shiko's mind flashed the memory of the rower with the javelin through her throat.

"And that is why we will not climb the next ladder yet," Higomu explained.

"Darkheart is on the roof!" called a voice from the plaza.

"What *will* we do?" Shiko asked.

"Wait."

They waited.

The dark hole in the roof took on a yellow glow. A helmeted head popped out. Higomu kicked it. It bounced off a roof support beam and dropped out of sight.

Higomu dropped the trapdoor back into place. "Now we climb." He nodded at the ladder.

Shiko accepted his invitation to climb first. No spears slammed into the wall—or her neck—so she deduced that the soldiers were now inside the workshop. Higomu was right behind her—even giving her a push on the rump when she was near the top.

He sprinted across the rooftops, dodging around garden benches and jumping up steps between buildings. Shiko followed, thankful for the time she'd spent on Elder Badiki's training grounds. She was competent, but still slow. Higomu had to wait for her at the other edge of the block.

A bridge spanned the gap separating them from the next block of buildings. Higomu knelt there and motioned Shiko to go ahead. She ran across the bridge, her sandals pounding on the wood high above the back alley.

She waited for Higomu on the other side. When he passed her, he found enough breath to say, "Don't wait." They were sprinting again.

From behind, a voice cried, "Careful, Sergeant: Trip cord here!"

A voice answered, "Then cut it, Soldier!"

"Still five of them," Higomu said. "Ah, junipers! This way."

The scrubby trees lined the edge of the next building. It was five stairsteps lower, so Shiko could see only the junipers' tops. Instead of using the steps, Higomu jumped into one of the trees.

Shiko did likewise and found that the juniper's pot was not as heavy as she had expected. As her weight bent the tree, the pot tipped. Shiko let go and landed on the roof with a roll.

"Hide," said Higomu, gesturing to the junipers against the wall. Shiko ducked into the hedge and waited, grateful for a chance to catch her breath, yet afraid she might not keep her breath for much longer.

Higomu disappeared from view.

The hedge of potted junipers obstructed Shiko's view of the garden, but the corridor that it formed with the wall of the adjacent building gave her an unobstructed view of the steps. A moment later, the soldiers' leather-hemmed skirts and sandaled feet descended. Higomu had thought there were five soldiers left, but Shiko saw only three of them. Perhaps the trip cord had worked after all.

"Where did they go?" one asked.

Shiko hoped the soldiers would think she and Higomu had climbed down through the building's trapdoor, but if everyone kept their trapdoors latched, as Kittiwake's had been—

"I don't think they went anywhere," another voice answered. "Search this garden."

Sandals scuffed urgently on the roof's clay surface. Shiko held still and hoped her head truly did look like a juniper.

Near the steps, a spear thrust into the hedge. It disappeared, then flashed into the hedge again, nearer this time.

How thorough would the soldier be? It looked like he was striking every gap. If so, Shiko realized, he might miss her. All she had to do was line up with a juniper—strike!—and hope that he did not—strike!—break the pattern.

Her adversary was deliberate. The flashing iron point drew steadily nearer. Shiko could not help but count down to herself as the spear struck five gaps in front of her. Four. Three. Two. Strike! It just missed her nose.

Shiko tensed, hoping the next strike would not be through her neck, but the soldier had stopped.

Without moving her head, Shiko looked sideways at the bare, white leg standing beyond the branches of her juniper. Had the soldier seen her?

His spear reached into her juniper—tentatively this time— and pushed branches aside. Shiko looked up into the green eyes of a helmeted man.

He turned his silver-haloed head and called to the others, "I found Curls!"

Shiko leapt through the gap he had opened, seized his spear at the midpoint, planted her feet in front of his, and pulled downward. This would have pulled a Child of Knowledge off balance, but Shiko had not allowed for the giant's weight. She wasn't heavy enough keep her feet anchored.

The soldier stepped back and yanked his spear from her grasp. Shiko crouched into a defensive stance, and her mind reflexively broadened her focus. She was aware of the soldier before her, the position of his feet, the angle of his spear. She was aware of the other two behind him, approaching in response to his call.

A pale sandaled foot flashed out from behind a potted agave, snapping the rearmost soldier's knee with a gristly pop. The man crumpled with a cry of pain.

Shiko's adversary turned his head, and this time Shiko ran away. She dove over a waist-high stone bench, but no spear had been thrown at her. The soldiers had other cares, Shiko surmised when she saw Higomu use a spear to vault into the air so he could kick one in the face.

Shiko squeezed between two agave pots—leaping over the agave's saw-like leaves seemed unwise—and bolted for the next set of steps. They were three, and they led up. Shiko climbed them without breaking stride.

Sandals slapped behind her, but she recognized the sound as Higomu's tread. If he was running, then running was a good idea. This rooftop garden was mostly open, trimmed only with wooden planters holding ornamental grass. Shiko hurdled the two benches in the middle and was almost onto the next rooftop when she was presented with a new obstacle: a trap-door opening directly in her path.

A helmeted head popped out of the hole and flashed bright blue as she leapt over it. Her landing foot skidded on the clay of the rooftop, but she regained her balance. The clang of sandal against helmet told her that Higomu was close behind.

The block of buildings they were running on was trapezoidal, enclosing a courtyard. The ladder down into the courtyard was just around the corner, and three soldiers were climbing up it. Reinforcements. Shiko did not need to look back to know that they still had soldiers behind them. They would be trapped at the corner.

Higomu caught up with her, and their strides hit the roof of the corner building at the same time. "We must jump it," he told her. "Keep running."

Shiko hurdled a planter of aloes and wondered if that were the "it" Higomu wanted her to jump. Soldiers were spreading out to keep them from going around the corner. Higomu kept running straight ahead.

Shiko realized that "it" was the edge of the block. Only a narrow alley separated them from the next block of buildings, but there was no bridge here.

Higomu leapt. His legs wheeled underneath his chiton as he crossed the gap. He passed cleanly over the edge of the building opposite and landed in a sagebrush hedge.

Shiko had no time to hesitate. A leaping stride carried her from the rooftop clay to the lip of a flower planter on the edge. She pushed off the planter and soared through the air.

For a moment, as she floated above the dark alley, Shiko thought she would make it, but the edge of the opposite building rose up rapidly before her eyes and she realized she would strike the wall instead.

She touched the wall with her lead sandal and twisted to absorb the impact with her forearm, upper arm, hip, and thigh. As she fell, her toes brushed a windowsill. She flung an arm out into the empty space and caught herself with an impact that bruised her arm and jarred her shoulder.

The room outside which she was hanging seemed dim in contrast to the bright morning rooftop gardens, but it was lit by the blue glow of a girl who stared at Shiko in astonishment. The girl held a brush. She had been practicing calligraphy.

"Can you—? Do you think you could help me in?" Shiko asked.

A spear hit the wall beside the window and stuck there.

"Never mind," Shiko said. She let go.

The windowsill was not much higher than the plank above Elder Badiki's sand pit. The major difference was that the ground was covered with paving stones, not sand. Shiko tucked and rolled, turning a bone-crushing impact into a body-bruising tumble. She would have liked to lie there in the alley until she had taken stock of her injuries, but it seemed unlikely that the soldiers would give her the time. She could hear their voices high above her, yelling for the residents of the corner building to open the trapdoor.

As Shiko got to her feet, Higomu dropped over the side of

the building opposite the soldiers and plummeted after her. Halfway down, he caught the spear that was still stuck in the wall. It bent under his weight—a much gentler impact than slamming into the windowsill. The spear came loose, but Higomu seemed to have expected that, for he held on to it and scraped it along the wall as he descended, only releasing it just before he hit the paving stones. He tucked and rolled away from Shiko in a flurry of legs and linen, using the last energy of the roll to pop himself onto his feet. It looked elegant and painless.

But it could not have been painless. His knees started to bleed.

"Can you walk?" Higomu asked.

Shiko nodded.

"Let's go," he said.

They left the alley and ran across a broad avenue at a pace that Shiko felt she could maintain for a quarter-lithic—or until her mind realized how much she had hurt herself in her fall, whichever came first. Glancing back at the building she had jumped from, she saw there would be no more pursuit. The soldiers had not yet found a way down. Just before she and Higomu passed into a side street, an orange-haloed soldier raised his fist and shouted down, "The demons take you, Darkheart!"

CHAPTER 13

Conversion

KITTIWAKE, with the emotion box under his arm, was not the only citizen at the villa waiting to speak with Legislator Whitedove. As the morning approached afternoon, a table was set up in the atrium and spread with bread, cheese, olives, dried apricots, and citrus fruit, because Legislator Whitedove was not the kind of patron who would let his people go hungry. Kittiwake did not feel like eating—his stomach was twisting too much—but he went to the table because Zefi was there, helping the villa's kitchen servants.

A worried frown creased her forehead. "You should try the olives," she told him. "They are fresh still."

Kittiwake could not help smiling. He patted her arm and said, "I will do so, Zefi."

He was glad she had eaten something. He hoped it was more than a nibble. Children of Labor needed to eat, and Zefi was young enough that she might still be growing.

Her term of service had ended four days ago. Thus far, she had said nothing of it. Kittiwake believed she knew, and he was certainly not going to mention it. She could stay as long as she wished. She could stay forever.

But how could he protect her? They were vulnerable in the workshop. The guardians-of-the-peace could have them locked up in the Red Palace long before word reached this villa on the Heights.

And who knew what those Children of Knowledge would do? They were a magical people. Perhaps it was from extra study, perhaps it was from extra talent, but elemental affinities were more common among them.

As an artificer, Kittiwake knew that elemental resonance was not inherently threatening. He never thought of Emotion as a weapon. But a man—even a half-sized man—who could resonate with Heat or Motion could be more dangerous than a soldier with a spear.

A few years ago, Otter the Artificer and his bride had disappeared. It was rumored that her brothers had killed them or that the couple had run away to one of the independent colonies, but now the rumor at the forefront of Kittiwake's mind was the one that said Children of Knowledge had abducted Otter because he knew more about Darkness than anyone living.

And Kittiwake? The artifact he now carried in the crook of his arm took Emotion beyond what others had thought possible. If the Theocratic Army wanted to use him as a weapon, would not the magicians of Hicho seek a way to steal him for themselves?

Whitedove, Fox, and Higomu. An artisan with a choice of patrons was worse off than an artisan with no patron. That was the price of his brilliance. Once his emotion box was revealed, how many other powerful people would be competing to seize control of him?

Kittiwake had to make Legislator Whitedove understand the gravity of the situation. Whitedove protected what was his. He would protect Kittiwake, too, if he understood that Kittiwake was at risk.

Whitedove's tall, husky manservant approached the food table. To Kittiwake, he said, "Legislator Whitedove will see you now."

This was out of turn. Temerity the Glassmaker, a woman from Chuckwalla's school, murmured in surprise. The Feathered Flowers Mural Inspector, who had been waiting nearly two lithics, glowed yellow with anger. As Kittiwake followed the manservant across the atrium, he congratulated himself on having chosen the right patron. Legislator Whitedove understood the value of genius.

The legislator's still-young face smiled at him in greeting as he entered the study. To the manservant, Whitedove said, "Thank you, Badger. Please make certain we are not … disturbed."

"Ah. Of course." The manservant drew a black curtain across the doorway to the atrium, leaving the room lit only by light filtering in from the garden doorway. Scraping sounds, muffled by the curtain's thickness, suggested that the manservant was removing the bench outside to make it clear that loitering near the study was unwelcome.

Kittiwake felt flattered. In all his visits to the villa, he had seen the black curtain drawn only twice. This was the first time it had been drawn for him.

Legislator Whitedove placed his hands on his marble desk and leaned forward eagerly. "I see you have it."

Ah, that explained the special treatment. Kittiwake knew that his news was urgent, but the legislator did not. He had assumed Kittiwake's visit was solely to demonstrate the emotion box. Kittiwake unwrapped the box from its linen sheet and laid it on the writing desk.

Legislator Whitedove ran a finger along the wood, tracing the geometric chain pattern carved into the top.

"Did you carve this?" he asked.

"No," said Kittiwake. "The box was made in Bluemonth by Acorn the Woodcarver."

"She did a fine job," said Whitedove. "The theme was well chosen."

"Thank you," said Kittiwake. Actually, Acorn had introduced two irregularities into the chain pattern to make it come out right, but Kittiwake had not complained. The purpose of the wood was to protect his own artwork, which lay within.

"And these are?"

"They are spigots," Kittiwake said. "Opening this one allows Emotion to flow in for storage. Opening this one allows stored Emotion to flow out."

"I see. Perhaps I should let you demonstrate?"

"I would be delighted to do so," Kittiwake said. Although he actually wanted to talk about the morning's visit from the Children of Knowledge, Kittiwake hoped that a demonstration of his marvelous invention would put Whitedove in a generous, helpful, and protective mood.

Kittiwake swiveled the box so that the outlet pointed at Legislator Whitedove. "Could you take two steps back, please?"

His patron complied.

Kittiwake concentrated on his patron, feeling the man's eagerness and curiosity. His patron's soul also held a touch of fear, but that was normal when facing an unknown magic. Kittiwake could resonate with these feelings easily.

Once he had established resonance with his patron's elemental Emotion, Kittiwake opened the spigot. Emotion poured out. It was Zefi. She was actually in the kitchen across the atrium, but Kittiwake could feel the power of her beautiful brown arms. He guided the outpouring of Emotion into his patron.

Legislator Whitedove's eyes widened and his aura flashed blue-green with surprise, but Kittiwake did not need these cues to tell him how the other man felt. He felt it all through elemental resonance.

Legislator Whitedove rubbed his arm. "What was that?" he asked.

"A hammer blow," Kittiwake said.

"Amazing!" said the legislator. "I could barely restrain myself from swinging my arm."

But he *had* restrained himself. Some part of him had resented the foreign emotion and successfully overcome it. That did not bother Kittiwake. He had not created the emotion box to control people.

Legislator Whitedove suddenly became worried. Kittiwake allowed his resonance with the other man to fade away. It would be dangerous to know something that Legislator Whitedove wished to keep hidden.

The legislator put his concern into words: "I thought the artifact would trap spirits, not create them."

"That was not a created spirit. You felt an emotion I trapped earlier," Kittiwake explained. "I asked my servant to swing a hammer."

"Ah. So that was her spirit trapped and stored."

"Not her entire spirit," said Kittiwake. "Simply an impulse."

"Hmmm. She seems quite fond of you."

"Ah … yes."

"The jewel on the lid—did I see it change color?"

"Yes. That is a sympathetic garnet." Kittiwake was grateful to have the topic of conversation veer away from Zefi. "I aligned it with the holding chamber inside. When the artifact holds Emotion, the garnet is a blood red, but when the artifact is empty, the garnet is this darker color."

"Dark red is also a color of blood," said Legislator Whitedove.

"Yes," said Kittiwake. "The color of dried blood, if you like."

"I am not certain I do like," said Legislator Whitedove. "Blood is ugly."

"Yes," said Kittiwake, fearing he had misspoken. But Whitedove seemed distracted by other thoughts.

"So you can trap spirits," the legislator said. "With the other spigot. Does it require skill to use?"

Kittiwake swallowed. Legislator Whitedove always seemed disappointed that Kittiwake's artifacts required an affinity with elemental Emotion. Usually, only a weak affinity was necessary. Kittiwake's artifacts could be used by people far less talented than he was, but even small talent was rare.

"I have to use magic to guide the Emotion into the box," Kittiwake admitted. "Anyone can let it out again, but you may not have felt it without the connection I established for you."

Legislator Whitedove nodded. "I see."

"However, it should be possible to capture Emotion even without being able to sense it," Kittiwake said. "I would like to work on that aspect of the problem next."

Legislator Whitedove smiled. "That would be useful."

"And then I need to find a way to reverse the process so that people can feel emotions released from the box even if they have no affinity for the element," Kittiwake said. "With light boxes, everything is so much simpler. We have many sources of light and everyone can see it."

"If it can be done," said Legislator Whitedove, "I am certain you will find a way, for you are the most visionary artificer in Dupho."

"Thank you."

"But tell me: With this device, as it now stands, can you hold a soul?"

"A soul?"

"Yes, if a person were to die, could you keep his soul in that box?"

"I— I don't know."

"You told me once that you can sense the souls of the dead."

"I can," said Kittiwake. "I have. They linger sometimes, after death. But it is not pleasant to sense these spirits. I avoid them."

"Yes, of course," said Legislator Whitedove. "But could you catch one?"

"I don't know. If it went into the box it would be trapped. But making a spirit go into the box against its will—why would I want to do such a thing?"

Legislator Whitedove fixed Kittiwake with an intense stare and quietly said, "Because your patron wished you to."

Kittiwake swallowed. "Then I would do my best to comply," he said.

Legislator Whitedove smiled, but his aura did not change. "Good," he said.

"Do you have a spirit here in the villa?" Kittiwake asked. Tales told of ghosts who had made themselves known even to people without elemental sensitivity.

"No," said Legislator Whitedove. "Do you know of a spirit we could test it on?"

"No!"

The legislator frowned. "I would dearly love to display your wondrous artifact at my party tomorrow night, but we must be certain it works."

"We have just demonstrated that," Kittiwake reminded him.

"No, my dear artificer, that is insufficient. We must be certain you can trap a soul."

The legislator's gaze fell on his caged doves. He covered his mouth with a smooth white hand. "I shouldn't," he said. "The doves are so beautiful, and my sister gave them to me."

He approached the cage. One of the birds cocked its head and cooed at him.

"Could you?" he asked. "If I killed it, could you trap its soul?"

"I—" Kittiwake wondered what he was afraid of. It was just a dove. "Perhaps I could," he said.

Spirits were complicated. Trapping one would be a challenge. And when had he ever been afraid to test his skill?

Legislator Whitedove opened the cage. The bird hopped onto his finger.

"This is the male," he said, stroking the feathers. "Isn't he pretty?"

"Yes. Yes, he is."

Was it wrong to let his patron kill the bird just to see if he could trap its soul? Perhaps. But this was the demonstration his patron wanted. It would be unwise to defy the only person who could protect him now.

"What is the matter?" Whitedove asked.

"Nothing, I— Perhaps I am just a bit distracted. You see, I had visitors this morning."

"Yes?"

"Children of Knowledge," Kittiwake said. "And they ... threatened to abduct me."

"What?" Whitedove slipped the bird back inside the cage and closed it.

Words tumbled from Kittiwake's mouth like olives spilling from a bowl. He told how the little couple had seemed friendly at first, but then had become more and more menacing, finally threatening that he would meet the same fate as Otter the Artificer. Kittiwake left out the fact that the little man had accused Whitedove of failing to provide adequate protection for so valuable an artisan. He hoped the legislator would draw that conclusion himself.

"I wanted to keep the emotion box safe," Kittiwake finished. "So I bundled it up and left the shop immediately. I know you told me not to worry, but now I fear for my life. I— I have artifacts to make. I would like to design a new box, with those improvements we talked about. But how can I keep the guardians from confiscating it? Or those Children of Knowledge from stealing it? Only you are powerful enough to protect me."

Legislator Whitedove embraced Kittiwake and kissed his forehead. "Oh, my artificer, please forgive me. I was so concerned with tomorrow evening's entertainment that I failed to consider your troubles. For you see, although I may lack your magical gifts, I did recognize that something troubled you.

"Kittiwake. Dear Kittiwake. I am glad you have brought this problem to me, for you are correct. You need a means to protect yourself and your creations. You need to have some of the power I possess. In fact, you deserve it."

Kittiwake was puzzled. He had hoped the legislator would invite him to live in the villa for a time, or perhaps hire him the services of a guard or two.

"I see you do not understand," said Legislator Whitedove. "You were so kind to demonstrate your gifts; allow me to demonstrate mine."

He removed the emotion box from his desk and handed it to Kittiwake. Then he walked out the doorway to the garden. Kittiwake had not been invited to follow, so he stood there, holding the emotion box until his patron came back.

Legislator Whitedove returned carrying a potted sagebrush. The earthen pot must have been heavy, but he carried it cheerfully, with his youthful face showing no strain. He set the pot on top of his marble desk, then fetched a large glass bell jar from a corner of his office and set it on the desk beside the pot.

"Surely you have wondered what this jar is for," he said.

Kittiwake nodded. It was far too large to be considered an elegant decoration.

"A ritual," the legislator confided. "One in which I hope you will participate."

Kittiwake gave no answer. He had seen rituals at the Temple of Beauty. None of them involved glass jars and potted plants.

Legislator Whitedove seemed to expect no answer. He took out the magnifying lens with the point-work doves and went into the garden to light his lamp.

Kittiwake was intrigued. The Church of Beauty was not the only way to worship the Goddess, despite what the Theocratic Empire wanted its citizens to believe. The Church of the Peaceful Path offered a way to serve the Goddess without swearing obedience to the church hierarchy or, by extension, to the Theocratic Empire. The Church of Three Sisters claimed to serve Beauty, Knowledge, and Sun. Perhaps Legislator Whitedove was secretly a priest of one of these alternate faiths. Kittiwake was willing to accept any blessing his patron had to offer, but he feared that it would not be sufficient to protect him from his troubles. The guardians-of-the-peace were probably blessed a hundred times a day.

When Legislator Whitedove returned, he closed a black curtain over the garden doorway, too, so that now the room's only light came from the lamp in his hand and from their auras. He smiled at Kittiwake.

"Do you know how old I am?" he asked.

Kittiwake shook his head.

"I suppose I look old to you," said Legislator Whitedove, "but when you are thirty-five, you will not think it is so old."

"You really are thirty-five?" Kittiwake asked.

"Is that not how I appear?"

"Yes, but ..."

"Go on."

"It is nothing."

"I insist."

Kittiwake wished he had been able to keep his thoughts to himself. "Everyone says that you have looked thirty-five for the last twenty years."

Kittiwake was relieved to see his patron smile.

"It is not so," Whitedove said. "I have looked this way for *thirty* years. My body has not aged since I dedicated my soul to the Goddess. This is but one of the boons I am offering you."

Kittiwake was puzzled. "I have not heard this about your church," he said.

Legislator Whitedove removed a bottle of lamp oil from its shelf and uncorked it. "You have heard nothing of my church," he said. "My followers and I serve our goddess in secret."

He tipped the bottle so that a thin, steady stream of oil flowed onto the branches of the plant on his desk.

"You have followed me, too, Kittiwake. Faithfully. Now I give you the chance to come further." He lifted the oil lamp. "Stand back, please. We don't want to harm the artifact."

Kittiwake took two steps back. Part of him wanted to keep going back, through the curtain, across the atrium, out of the villa, and down off the Heights. But he was too fascinated to flee.

Whitedove ignited the oil on the sagebrush. At first only the oil burned. But the tiny leaves withered in the heat and then caught fire themselves. The fine tips of the twigs began to curl and glow. Whitedove blew out the flame on his lamp.

"All things die," he explained to Kittiwake. "At every moment. You and I are constantly dying. The only question is:

how fast? The Goddess cannot grant life, but she can slow death."

He lifted the bell jar and set it down over the burning bush. The jar fit snugly against the rim of the terra-cotta pot.

"The fire in the jar consumes the air as it consumes the life of the plant. Now the fire brings light, but soon— See it fading?"

The skeleton of the sagebrush faded until the room was lit only by Kittiwake's and Whitedove's auras. No daylight found its way past the curtained doorways. Kittiwake coughed in the smoke.

"And in the darkness, the Goddess comes, and she grants me her powers!"

Legislator Whitedove's aura winked out. For a moment, Kittiwake thought his patron had disappeared. But no: He could still see the man, by the light of his own aura, which was now a dim green.

"Do not fear," Whitedove said kindly, his aura returning rosy. "Loyal servants need not fear the Goddess. And I am certain you will be as loyal to her as you have been to me."

"I— I've not been very pious since I left my mother's house," Kittiwake said.

"And why should you be?" Legislator Whitedove asked. "Beauty and her Theocratic Empire ask so much of us, but what do they give us in return? What power do the priests of Beauty have other than that which *people* give them? Beauty has the elements at her fingertips, yet has she ever given her subjects the power to do even something as simple as this?"

A gem appeared, spinning in the air, its facets reflecting the darkness of the corners of the room. Kittiwake reached to touch it, then looked at his patron.

"You may," said Legislator Whitedove. "The illusion cannot harm you."

Kittiwake's hand passed through it.

"It is only the appearance of a gem, and yet, is not the appearance the most important part? Would anyone display a garnet that looked like granite?"

"Which goddess lends you these powers?" Kittiwake asked.

"We call her Glamour."

"I've not heard of Glamour."

"You were taught that there are only nine deities," said the patron. "But it is not so. For in the reflection of the mirror, does not everything come in pairs?"

"Glamour is a reflection of Beauty?"

"Forget about Beauty! What has she ever done for you? Has she ever offered you influence? Has she ever offered you the ability to do this?"

Legislator Whitedove reached toward his bird cage and a dove dropped softly from its perch.

The legislator's eyes went wide, and his aura shimmered with horror. "Catch his soul! Catch his soul!" he shouted.

Kittiwake opened the intake spigot on the emotion box. He opened his mind, searching for a bundle of stray Emotion.

"I sense it," he said.

"Do you have it?"

"No," said Kittiwake. "It is still tied to the body, but perhaps I can— Hold out your finger, as though you want it to come to you."

His patron did so.

The tiny spirit did not move, but Kittiwake found the desire in Legislator Whitedove and brought it into resonance with something in the ghost of the bird. Walking toward the cage, Kittiwake gently, gently guided the spirit into his box. The garnet changed color. Kittiwake closed the spigot.

Legislator Whitedove's face filled with wonder. "Is he there? Is he inside?"

Kittiwake nodded.

His patron kissed him. "Marvelous work, Kittiwake. Marvelous! Now, kill his mate and put her in the box so that they can be together."

"Are you certain?"

"She will be forlorn without him. They must be together."

Kittiwake swallowed. "Very well."

The cage door opened smoothly on its hinges. It had been well crafted.

Kittiwake reached inside.

"No!" his patron cried. Kittiwake's hand snapped back as though from a hot forge coal.

"Don't choke her! Don't choke her!"

"I— I'm not!"

His patron regained his composure.

"Use the power, Kittiwake. Use the power Glamour offers you. Kill the dove with this power you deserve to have, so that she can rejoin her mate."

Yes, Kittiwake thought. *The doves are soulmates. He deserves to keep her forever. And I have the power to do this for him.*

Kittiwake extended a hand toward the cage. The life of the dove flowed through his body, disappearing into the abyss that he opened in his soul.

CHAPTER 14
The Servant

I HAD ALMOST GOTTEN HIM TO EAT SOMETHING, Zefi thought as Badger led Kittiwake into the study.

Still, she was glad that the patron had decided to see Kittiwake ahead of the others gathered in the atrium. While walking to the villa, Zefi had prayed for Thafarsi, goddess of knowledge, to help the patron understand that Kittiwake's problem was serious. It looked like her prayer was being answered.

A moment later, Badger emerged and pulled a curtain across the doorway. Zefi realized that the patron's eagerness to see Kittiwake did not imply he was eager to help; the patron was just interested in the artifact. And apparently, he did not want anyone else to see it before the party.

Zefi wished the patron had been more secretive about the earlier artifacts as well. Kittiwake's troubles seemed to be the result of his fame. If his patron had kept quiet about the artifacts, then Commander Fox would never have sent his soldiers. And now word had even reached the Thinker People. Kittiwake loved it when his patron praised his work, but perhaps his patron should not have praised Kittiwake so publicly.

Badger was moving that bench that the patron always made Kittiwake wait on. Zefi crossed the atrium to help him. She picked up one end.

Badger hesitated a moment, then said, "Thank you."

Zefi wondered whether he meant it or not. Possibly he did. His aura did got grow noticeably yellower. They set the bench down by the fountain at the center of the atrium.

Zefi hoped the patron would listen to Kittiwake this time. Somehow that little, dark-eyed man had seemed even more dangerous than Commander Fox's soldiers. The woman had said they were offering protection, but the man had made it clear that if Kittiwake refused to accept the offer, then ... something bad would happen. Was he bluffing? They were too small to overpower Kittiwake. If they threatened him with bodily harm, Zefi would stop them. She would protect Kittiwake from the soldiers, too, if necessary. But the soldiers had spears. She doubted she could prevail against more than one.

Maybe Legislator Whitedove would agree to take Kittiwake in. Zefi would have to live with Whitedove's servants, but she would still be able to see Kittiwake. And she would know he was safe.

A man in a brown gown crossed the atrium and approached Badger. He had an honest smell about him.

"It seems we have many guests today," he said.

Badger nodded in acknowledgment.

"Do you think you could let me slip in ahead of the next supplicant?" the man asked.

Donkey dung, Zefi realized. It was donkey dung that made him smell honest.

"I think the District Lamp Steward and the Mural Inspector would be quite offended if I did," Badger replied. "What news do you have, Tortoise?"

"I found him."

"Ah."

Badger looked at the curtained doorway. "I fear the legislator may be some time. But the information is for his nephew. Snowgull is taking lunch in his mother's room."

"Where is that?"

"I will accompany you there," Badger said. "The legislator's sister will not like having her lunch interrupted, and you may want me to intercede for you."

"Thank you," said Tortoise.

Zefi wondered whom Tortoise had found and why the patron's nephew was interested in him. She wondered why the patron's nephew had not gone to find this mystery man on his own. The patron's sister and nephew never seemed to do anything for themselves. They passed their problems on to the patron's servants. Would Kittiwake become like them if he lived here?

Zefi knew he would not. Kittiwake was always kind, whereas the patron's sister acted as though her servants were not really people. When Kittiwake was working on an artifact, he might forget that Zefi was in the room, but when he asked her to do something, he treated her as an assistant, not a donkey. Actually, Zefi knew several donkeys who got more respect than the patron's servants.

As Tortoise and Badger entered the arched passage from the atrium to the courtyard garden, they were nearly run over by a chambermaid coming the other way. Her aura was dark green with distress. Badger gestured angrily in the direction of the kitchen, and the two men continued through the passage.

The chambermaid, holding an earthenware wine pitcher, scurried across the atrium. Her eye was swelling.

"What happened?" Zefi asked.

The woman stopped to look at her, but instead of answering, she gulped with fear and scurried off toward the kitchen. Zefi followed.

When Zefi reached the kitchen, the chambermaid was surrounded by women offering condolences and wanting to hear her story.

"The legislator's sister asked me for white wine," she said.

"And what did you say?" the cook asked, her aura turning a greenish yellow.

"I— I said I thought she preferred the red wine from the barrel."

"And then he hit you, didn't he?" asked one of the girls.

The chambermaid nodded.

"I know somebody he won't hit," the cook muttered. She grabbed Zefi's hand and pulled her out the doorway, saying, "Come."

The tight-lipped cook led Zefi to the table that was set up in the atrium. She lifted a bottle of white wine and put it in Zefi's hand.

"Upstairs," the cook said, waving vaguely. "Legislator's sister. Upstairs. You take. Understand?"

Zefi nodded.

I understand many things, she thought as she crossed the atrium to the garden passage. *I understand that all of you are too afraid to deliver this wine. I understand that you won't care if I get hit.*

She thought about the patron's white-haired, white-skinned nephew. It was easy to assume he was soft from living his life in his uncle's villa, but Kittiwake said he had once been a captain in the navy, and Zefi had seen the javelin target he had set up in the patron's garden. Even though the patron's nephew just shipped goods for his uncle now, he was still a soldier. If he hit her, it would hurt. Zefi thanked Devlen, god of labor, for giving her a thick skin.

The stairs from the garden courtyard to the second floor were small for Zefi's feet. She walked carefully, for the bottle was uncorked. She could hear their voices drifting down the stairs.

"But I thought the Child of Knowledge had broken the mast," the patron's sister said.

"Mother, we spliced it."

"Oh. I didn't know you could splice wood."

"Yes, Mother. And now—"

"You should have made your crew row all the way," the patron's sister said. "It would have taught them a lesson."

"Yes, Mother. I'm sure it would have. But now that you know the *whole story*, I really would like to hear what these men have come to tell me."

Zefi decided that this would be a bad time to appear with the wine. She waited, immobile, in the stairway.

"I spoke with the harbormaster," said the man known as Tortoise. "He says the glass ship had two bookers as passengers. One man and one woman, probably husband and wife."

"Bookers" was the word Decorator People used for Think-er People when they wanted to be nasty. It was like calling Worker People "leatherskins". Zefi didn't like people who used those words, no matter how honest they smelled.

The nephew asked, "This man—was his hair dark and his skin pale?"

"Yes," said Tortoise. "And his wife was dark-skinned with curly hair."

Them! And apparently they had broken the mast on the patron's nephew's ship. Were they pirates?

"Yes, yes!" said the nephew. "You found the right ship. Did you find the man?"

"I asked around," Tortoise said. "He and his wife are stay-ing at the House of the Flashing Tuna."

"I believe I know the place," the nephew said. "On an avenue near the Fish Plaza, isn't it?"

"That's right."

"Snowgull," the patron's sister asked, "what are you planning?"

The nephew laughed. "I am planning to kill him, Mother."

Zefi's stomach tightened. She had prayed for help defend-ing Kittiwake against the Thinker People. Was this the gods' solution? Then it really was a struggle of life and death.

"Be careful, son," the patron's sister said. "Children of Knowledge are treacherous. The Goddess cannot protect you against them."

"She could have," the nephew replied. "She just chose not to. I serve her faithfully, but she deserts me!"

Such talk made Zefi sad. The patron's nephew should not expect Swalethi, the goddess of beauty, to defend him from pirates. That was a job for Kashram, god of the lith. But Dec-orator People did not understand that different gods handled different affairs. She hated to hear Decorator People deprecate any of the gods, but it was even worse to hear one challenge the love of his own creator. With a quick prayer to Lashrefi, goddess of luck, Zefi stepped up the stairs and into the room.

As she had hoped, the subject of conversation changed immediately.

"What is that?" asked the patron's sister. The many bracelets on her arm clinked together as she raised her hand to her mouth.

"She is an orphan," Badger said. "The servant of Kittiwake the Artificer."

"She was slow enough," the patron's thin-lipped nephew observed.

Yes, Zefi thought. *I'm just slow. I'm bigger than you, so I must be slow, clumsy, and stupid. Please don't think that I might have been standing on the stairs listening.*

Where to put the bottle? She looked around the room without meeting their eyes. A nightstand, a decorative table, shelves—there it was: A table with wine glasses.

"Tell the cook not to send her again," the sister said. "She's too ugly to leave the kitchen."

Zefi set the bottle down very carefully and thanked Devlen for giving her a thick skin.

CHAPTER 15
Strikers

SHIKO WAS IMPRESSED at how Topaz had furnished their room at the House of the Flashing Tuna. The table was the proper height for floor-level dining. The beds were Hicho-made sheepskin cots. The floor was covered with grass mats and seating cushions.

It was incongruous, yet comforting, to have these familiar features in such an exotic atmosphere. The room was as small as rooms in Hicho, but the walls were twice as high. Only two of the corners met at right angles. Because the avenues of Dupho ran in three directions, square rooms were un-common—although perhaps not as rare as rooms without mirrors. For a Child of Beauty, a room without a wall mirror was unimaginable.

Shiko had not expected to use the mirror, but after she and Higomu had snuck back into the inn through the trapdoor in the rooftop garden, she had been glad to have it. She needed to know how bad she looked.

A careful appraisal had told her that she did not look as sore as she felt. Still, she and Higomu were scraped up enough that it would have caused comment had they come in through the front door.

According to Higomu, they were not alone. Oh, they were alone in sneaking in through the hot rooftop garden, but they were not the only guests spending the afternoon resting at the inn. The streets of Dupho grew quiet in the heat, and the only sounds from the avenue below their room's balcony were shuffling footsteps and the occasional rumbles of cart wheels.

Since lunch—which an unseen servant had left discreetly in

the hall on the other side of the curtained doorway—Shiko had been sitting on a cushion near the balcony, looking through Kittiwake's notebook. His work was heavily influenced by optics.

In the early pages, Shiko found notes on the theory of the Emotional mirror, which could reflect Emotion the same way a normal mirror could reflect light. The design for the mirror was preceded and followed by many designs for an Emotional lens, several of which had been crossed out emphatically. It had taken Kittiwake months to find a design that worked.

Kittiwake's genius lay in recognizing that laws of optics might apply to Emotion. Shiko had studied light boxes extensively under Elder Badiki's tutelage, and she could see that the emotion box worked analogously. The most intriguing distinction between the two designs was that, whereas the light box trapped its contents in a mirrored cube, the emotion box used a mirrored octahedron.

Despite Kittiwake's trouble developing a lens, he had discovered the octahedron design without any false starts. Perhaps the shape was implied by the nature of elemental Emotion; unable to perceive Emotion herself, Shiko could not be certain. She wondered whether the other perfect solids could function as vessels for containing other elements. Shiko knew only six perfect solids, but if one were to exclude the material elements—Earth, Water, and Air—then one would be left with only six elements to contain.

However much this idea intrigued her, she did not allow it to distract her from her purpose, which was to identify any ideas that should be classified as forbidden knowledge. She found none.

"I think we should let Kittiwake remain in Dupho," she said.

Higomu, who was relaxing on one of the room's two cots, rolled his head over to stare at her.

Shiko immediately felt contrite at having interrupted Higomu's rest. He had certainly earned it—unlike Shiko, who had slowed him down and then nearly killed herself missing a jump.

"He has built a soul trap," Higomu said. "I don't think we should wait for him to perfect it."

Shiko shook her head. "It is not a soul trap. It's just a box for storing elemental Emotion."

Higomu sat up. Without wincing. Apparently the abrasions on his knees, the bruises developing on his shins, and the cut on his arm—"from an agave," he had said—did not pain him. Shiko could hardly breathe without wincing.

"But you agree that such a box might be able to contain a soul," Higomu said.

"I am telling you: I have read his notes, and that is clearly not his intent."

"His intent does not matter," Higomu said. "What matters is what the artifact can do and how a servant of the demons might use it."

"But every artifact could have a use for a servant of the demons," Shiko countered. "A light box, for example, could be used to read a demonic text, yet light boxes are not forbidden."

"Acquiring forbidden knowledge is not as egregious a sin as preventing a soul from ascending to its proper heaven," Higomu said.

Shiko cast about for a better example. Her eyes fell on the knife sitting on the lunch tray that Topaz's servant had brought.

"Well, then, consider that knife. It could be used for murder, but we do not forbid knives. We use them to slice cheese."

"A knife is not an artifact," Higomu said. "We do confiscate artifacts that could be used as weapons—at least those which would be more powerful than the weapons we could give to the average soldier."

"We don't have soldiers," Shiko reminded him.

"But we will have soldiers when the time comes to fight the demons," Higomu said. "And they will not be at a disadvantage if the opposing army happens to own knives."

"Nor would they be at a disadvantage if the opposing army owned an emotion box," Shiko said.

"Are you certain?" Higomu asked. "Spirits can carry information. Information can win battles. We *might* be at a disadvantage if the enemy has devices for capturing the souls of our dead."

"But that is not its purpose," Shiko said.

Looking up at him when she spoke was aggravating. Shiko stood up from her cushion by the balcony. Her right knee and hip complained. Higomu remained sitting on his cot.

Using the arm that had not slammed into the second-story windowsill, Shiko waved Kittiwake's notebook in the air. "What gives us the authority to enter this man's home and take his belongings?" she asked. "What gives us the authority to threaten him?"

"It is our job," Higomu observed.

"Our job is to protect the world from dangerous artifacts, not to harass innocent people."

"Part of protecting the world from dangerous artifacts is controlling the knowledge of how to make them," Higomu said. "You know this."

His voice, unlike Shiko's, was calm. His deep, dark eyes did not waver from her face.

"Controlling the knowledge, perhaps," Shiko said. "But that does not mean controlling the people with the knowledge."

"Of course it does," Higomu said. "We can't contain Kittiwake's knowledge without containing Kittiwake."

"But we could reason with him."

"And we shall."

"You threatened him."

"We needed him to leave his workshop," Higomu said. "So we convinced him to run straight to his patron, taking most of Fox's spies with him."

Most of them? Ah, yes. The yawning man had not followed Kittiwake. That reminded Shiko of something that had puzzled her: "Why did the yawning man go to fetch soldiers?"

134 JASON A. HOLT

"So that the soldiers could do what we did—search for evidence of wrongdoing."

"Couldn't the yawning man have searched by himself?"

"He could have," said Higomu. "But it seems he was under orders to fetch the soldiers instead."

"But why?"

"Look at it from the yawning man's point of view. Consider the advantages, assets, and allies."

This was a familiar phrase from Elder Badiki's training. Advantages, assets, and allies were the three factors in any tactical decision.

"Entering the House of the Four Wrens would have given him the advantage of expediency," Shiko said.

"He did not know we were coming back," Higomu said. "He believed his opponent was Kittiwake, and he had plenty of time before Kittiwake returned."

"But what does he gain by fetching the soldiers?"

"First consider rather what he risks by entering on his own. Right now, he believes himself to be unknown. If the neighbors see him entering the House of the Four Wrens, they might take note of him. He would risk the advantage of secrecy. Furthermore, the soldiers have the advantage of authority, the advantage of numbers, and the assets of spears, daggers, and armor. So naturally, he called upon his allies."

"One man can fight an empty house as easily as six soldiers can."

Higomu chuckled. "True, but I suspect they were not only there to search. I suspect they planned to arrest Kittiwake upon his return."

"Whatever for?"

"For associating with me. Fox's spies recognized me, remember?"

"Oh. Yes."

"I must stop underestimating Fox," Higomu said. "He seems to have improved his tactics since last we met."

"Should we warn him?" Shiko asked. "Kittiwake, I mean.

Should we warn him that the soldiers might be planning to arrest him?"

"I believe we already did."

"But what if they are waiting to ambush Kittiwake in the workshop right now?"

"Ah," said Higomu. "Then that would quite improve our bargaining position. He will be much more interested in coming with us if he is in prison."

Was that a joke? It did not sound like sarcasm. Shiko decided to take it seriously.

"So we will bargain with him?"

"We will do whatever is necessary to convince him to come with us," Higomu said. "If we cannot convince him, then we may have to do things you are not comfortable with. But a striker does what must be done."

"It just doesn't seem right," Shiko said.

"Then why are you a striker?"

"Maybe I'm not."

This took Higomu by surprise. For a moment he just sat on the edge of his cot, blinking his dark eyes at her. Then he asked, "Why did you enroll for Elder Badiki's training?"

"I started training under Elder Badiki eleven years ago," Shiko said. "When I graduated from the Academy, I didn't want to stop."

"But you were studying locksmithing and metaphysics," Higomu said. "Not ... this:" He gestured at his bruised shins and scabbed knees.

"I was studying artifacts," Shiko said. "And since I have no magical talent whatsoever, Elder Badiki suggested the Order of the Lock as a way I could apply what I had learned."

Higomu's eyebrows rose. "He must have been recruiting you from the moment you set foot in the Academy."

Shiko nodded. "I suspect so," she said.

"And while he was teaching you, he was testing you, trying to find out what you would be suited for."

"Perhaps," Shiko said. "But I am not suited for this."

"No?"

"No," she said. "I won't help you abduct Kittiwake. Either we convince him to come with us of his own free will, or we leave without him. I will not help you coerce him. Not because it makes me 'uncomfortable', but because I know it is wrong. I am sorry that I cannot make a stronger argument. I am sorry that I have not convinced you it is wrong. But I know that if you try to hurt him, then I must defy you, regardless of the consequences."

Higomu smiled. "You are mistaken," he said. "But Elder Badiki was not mistaken about you. You are a striker."

CHAPTER 16

Confession

I HAD NO OTHER CHOICE, Kittiwake told himself as he and Zefi walked down the avenue to the Agave Plaza. *Legislator Whitedove was right: Beauty has done nothing to protect me.*

Kittiwake could feel that his soul had shifted. Existence now felt awkward. It was like reaching for a wooden bossing mallet and picking up a cross-peen hammer by mistake. Even his breathing seemed out of balance.

I will become accustomed to this in time, he told himself. *Like a new pair of sandals.*

Kittiwake could feel the power of Glamour permeating his body. She was watching him—and watching the world through his eyes. His soul had become a window to some place beyond.

Thank you for giving me the power to keep my shop safe, Kittiwake told his new goddess. *I will use it wisely.*

Barefooted Zefi walked beside him with straight back and square shoulders. Where had her confidence come from? Kittiwake had told Zefi nothing except that they would be safe now. How readily she believed him! He was lucky to have her. And now, he could keep her.

He would not tell her what he had done to guarantee their safety. He did not want her to worry. He wanted her to be calm and comfortable, just as she had always been.

On the shady side of the avenue, just beyond a cheese stall tended by a wrinkled, silver-haired woman, two guardians-of-the-peace emerged from a side street and began walking toward Kittiwake and Zefi. Zefi saw them, too. Her straight posture became rigid.

Kittiwake used his control of elemental Emotion to keep fear from coloring his aura. He reminded himself that he had the power to bring death at will. The guardians could no longer harm him.

As the guardians drew nearer, they stared up at Zefi. Kittiwake held his aura at a soft, neutral white glow. When Zefi veered onto the sunny half of the avenue, he followed her lead. One guardian gave them a suspicious stare, but Kittiwake returned the soldier's gaze coolly, and they passed without comment.

"It was just a patrol," Kittiwake said.

"Let's be in the sun," Zefi murmured. "Soldiers like the shade."

"Certainly," Kittiwake said. "If that will calm you. But we no longer have to fear them. I can defend us now."

"How?"

"Zefi, you don't have to worry about it. You are safe with me."

"Your patron will stop Fox?"

My goddess will, Kittiwake thought. But he could not tell Zefi that. She was pious. She would not understand why Kittiwake had chosen to serve a ... different kind of deity.

"Kittiwake?"

"Zefi, do you trust me?"

"Yes," she said. "Always."

Kittiwake reached up and patted her shoulder. "Good," he said. "Thank you."

He felt guilty keeping his secret from her, but she was so simplistic. She could not grasp the political skills artisans required to achieve success in Dupho. Really, Kittiwake's decision had been only about politics. He would never have—

Oh, but he was not displeased! On the contrary, he was honored that a ... goddess would deem him worthy of her attention.

"What is wrong?" Zefi asked.

"Nothing," said Kittiwake.

"You jumped."

"Yes, I—" He had felt the demon pinch his soul. "Perhaps I am a bit unsettled."

"You should tell me," Zefi said.

"Tell you what?"

"The thing that you not tell me that makes you jump."

"Zefi, it's complicated."

"Like your artifact?"

Kittiwake smiled. "It is complicated in a different way."

"You can explain," Zefi said. "Like your artifact. You explain. I not understand your artifact, but I understand enough to help. So explain."

Kittiwake exhaled. "Zefi, I fear that if I explain, you will not like it."

"Why not?"

"You might think I did something bad."

"You did something bad?"

"No," said Kittiwake. "At least, not yet. But to protect us, I might have to do something bad soon."

Zefi frowned.

"See?" said Kittiwake. "I was right. You don't like it."

"What might you do?" Zefi asked.

"Zefi, if someone wants to hurt us, I might have to hurt them."

Zefi still frowned, but she nodded, too. "And you want not to hurt people."

"Not really," Kittiwake said.

"You should let me hurt people," Zefi said. "I think you are too kind to do it."

"Zefi, that's ..."

Unexpected. That was unexpected. Kittiwake had told the truth when he admitted that he didn't want to hurt people, but surely, if the situation called for it ...

Yes. Yes, if they harmed Zefi, he would kill them. But he wished to avoid a scenario in which he could become a killer. He hoped the guardians-of-the-peace and the little couple from

Hicho would simply realize he had become dangerous and leave him alone. But how would they know? He couldn't say, "I serve a demon now, so go away." He did not actually want to kill anyone to demonstrate. Was there a way he could threaten them with this power *before* things got desperate?

"You think I am too kind also," Zefi said. "But I am big. Like a mother. I can spank naughty children if they need it."

"Yes," said Kittiwake, distracted from his thoughts by the image of Zefi spanking a soldier. "Yes, of course you can, Zefi. But I'm talking about killing people."

Zefi stopped and grabbed his arm.

"Kill not," she said.

"Sometimes it needs to be done," Kittiwake said.

"No." Zefi shook her head. "Never kill anyone, Kittiwake. You are not a killer. It would be very bad for your soul."

"I knew you wouldn't understand."

"I understand. Very well. Kill not. It is better to die."

"Zefi, I will do what I must to keep you safe."

"No," said Zefi. "I would be better dead. I can be happy in Heaven. The gods will find work for me. I cannot be happy if my friend hurts his soul."

"Zefi."

"Promise me," Zefi said. "Promise me you will not kill because of me."

"Zefi, I—"

"Promise me."

"Zefi, I have already killed."

She looked at him with a funny expression, as though disbelieving she had heard him correctly. A nearby fruit seller was staring at them. Kittiwake took Zefi by the hand and encouraged her to continue walking home.

"I killed a dove, Zefi. One of my patron's doves."

"By accident?"

Kittiwake shook his head. "My patron asked me to."

"For dinner."

"Not … really," said Kittiwake.

"So you killed a dove, and now you feel bad."

"Yes," Kittiwake admitted. "I mean, no. That is, I feel bad about—"

"You see? Even a dove hurts your soul. It would be much, much worse if you killed a person."

"Zefi, my soul is not going to Heaven. At least, not to Beauty's Heaven."

"Beauty forgives," Zefi said soothingly as they entered the Agave Plaza.

"But I renounced her," Kittiwake said. "I now serve the Goddess of Glamour."

Zefi frowned. She shook her head. "I know your names for all the gods. There is no Goddess of Glamour."

"Perhaps," said Kittiwake. "But that is what Legislator Whitedove calls her. And she has power, Zefi! Real power. I didn't kill the dove with my hands; I killed it with a wish! That's what will protect us: power, not prayers to a goddess who never listens."

"Hush! Say not that!"

"I say it."

"No." Zefi shook her big head. "No, you would not do this. Your patron, he tricked you. You are a kind and gentle man. You cannot serve the demons."

"I will do what is necessary to protect me, my shop, my assistant, and my artifacts! I had no other choice."

They stopped just outside the door to the workshop. Zefi took him by the shoulders and looked down into his eyes.

"You always have a choice," she said. "You cannot tell me you want to be evil."

"Zefi, I just want to be left alone to make artifacts. My patron offered me this power. I had to take it. Now please come inside."

He slipped from her arms and pushed open the door.

The transition from exterior to interior was always abrupt in the afternoon. The thick-walled house was so much cooler and darker than the paving stones outside. The sunbeam's parallelogram of light only caused the room's shadows to deepen. So it took a moment before Kittiwake saw the six soldiers.

"Citizen," said the sergeant, "the guardians-of-the-peace are taking you into custody."

CHAPTER 17

Flight

KITTIWAKE'S SKIN prickled with sweat. Zefi moved to stand beside him, but Kittiwake held out an arm to prevent her. Those spears were his responsibility.

"No, Kittiwake," she said. "Use not those powers."

How much had the guardians overheard? With the sergeant were two other men and three women. On their belts hung daggers, wrist bonds, and identity hoods. Kittiwake was not sure he had the power to kill all six.

Perhaps one would suffice. Just reach out and take one life for his goddess. The survivors would respect him then. He could swear them to secrecy.

"Zefi, go." He did not want her to watch.

The sergeant took one step closer. The others followed. Kittiwake realized that Zefi was right: He did not have the heart to kill any of them.

But he did not need to! His goddess offered him another avenue of escape. With her power over Light, she could make him invisible. He could flee unseen to wherever he wished. All he needed to do was open his skin to Glamour's power. And abandon Zefi, of course. The Goddess's powers were not to be shared with the unworthy.

Kittiwake grabbed his head to force these thoughts from his mind. Abandon Zefi? That idea was not his.

"Bind their wrists," said the sergeant.

Zefi made a sudden movement—not toward the open door, but toward Kittiwake's workbench. Her great, brown hand pulled a shaping wedge from its tool slot.

"You will not harm him," she said, brandishing the wedge at the guardians.

They paused. The sergeant's aura turned a puzzled shade of blue.

Kittiwake, too, was puzzled. What could a shaping wedge do against a spear? Nothing. But that was the wrong question.

"Aha!" he bluffed. "I see you hesitate. I see you wonder: What can she do with that? I warn you, come one step closer and you shall find out; for we are artificers and you are in our domain!"

The sergeant looked at his soldiers, then back at Kittiwake. The sergeant took one deliberate step.

Kittiwake spun on his sandal and pushed Zefi out the door. The guardians' auras brightened into action. Kittiwake seized the brass door handle. As he pulled the door shut, a use for the wedge did occur to him. He snatched the tool from Zefi's hands and pushed it partway through the door handle so that the end held the door shut against the clay wall. Zefi, for good measure, drove the wedge fast with the heel of her hand.

"Good," said Kittiwake. "Now let's run."

He led Zefi around the plaza's rock gardens and past the fountain. Children's voices silenced as they passed by, but the morose woman supervising the children did not even look up. Kittiwake dashed for the passage between the Ladybug House and the House of Autumn Dragonflies. A glance over his shoulder showed him that one soldier had crawled out the window to open the door for the others.

Kittiwake ran through the cool passage with the sound of Zefi's broad feet slapping paving stones behind him. "You were right," he said over his shoulder. "I'm not a killer."

"I know," Zefi said as they sped past the gate and into the courtyard beyond.

The gate was kept open because the courtyard held several shops. Kittiwake and Zefi dodged around the ornamental cedars, ran past the fountain sculpture (believed to be a portrait of the artist's mother), and slipped into the back room of

Shark's woodworking shop.

They stopped behind a stack of lumber, where they could be seen neither from the courtyard nor from the shop's workroom.

"They only want me," Kittiwake said. "You should not be involved in this."

Zefi frowned in confusion.

"Zefi, your term of service ended four days ago. We've passed the middle of Redmonth. Surely you know this."

"Yes," she said.

"So go back to the Orphanage."

Zefi shook her head. "I'm not leaving you."

"Zefi, your work is done. I release you."

"No," Zefi said, the soft lines of her face hardening into determination. "I cannot leave you now. Your soul is in danger."

"You can't stay," said Kittiwake. "If Whitedove realizes you know—"

"I will not leave you! I will fight the soldiers. I will fight your patron. I will fight your demon. I will even fight *you*, if I must. I will not let you go to Hell!"

Footsteps approached from the workroom.

Kittiwake stepped out from behind the lumber pile and greeted the carpenter: "I bid you good day, Shark!"

Shark blinked in puzzlement. "Good day, Kittiwake. I didn't hear you come in."

"Please excuse us," Kittiwake said. "We are just passing through."

He pushed past Shark and led Zefi out through the workroom. They emerged onto a narrow street in the interior of the Insect Jewels district. Kittiwake had lived on the Agave Plaza for several years, but this was as far as he had ever gone into this neighborhood.

"This way," Zefi said, turning moonward.

"Why?"

"The Temple of Beauty is this way."

"Then we go this way," Kittiwake said, turning moonaway.

Zefi followed him down the street toward the busy avenue ahead.

"You are not a killer," she said. "You say yourself you make a mistake."

Kittiwake nodded. "I've made a mistake, Zefi, but the Temple of Beauty would be a bigger mistake. They won't save me. They'll execute me."

He spoke quietly, but a man in a cream-and-rose gown standing in the avenue at the street's end looked at them with interest.

Zefi yanked Kittiwake's arm and took him down a side street.

"That man was standing in the sun," she explained.

"And he was staring at us," Kittiwake observed.

"Should we run?" Zefi asked as they hurried down the street.

"That would draw attention," Kittiwake said.

Then he realized how stupid it was to say that to a woman as huge as Zefi.

"On second thought," he said, "perhaps we *should* run."

"This way," suggested Zefi, pulling Kittiwake down another side street.

"Where are we going?" Kittiwake asked.

"Away."

"Are you certain this direction is away?"

They stopped running.

"Which way *should* we go?" Zefi asked.

"We need to get you to the Orphanage," Kittiwake said.

"We need to get you to a priest," Zefi countered.

"But not one from the Church of Beauty," Kittiwake said.

Zefi nodded. "Yes," she said. "I see."

"Good."

"We go to the Orphanage, then," Zefi said. "Church of Three Sisters. One of those goddesses can help you."

Kittiwake wasn't sure anyone could help him, but at least

the plan would get Zefi to the Orphanage. "Very well," he said. "Let us go."

Zefi nodded and asked, "Where is the Orphanage?"

Kittiwake looked around. None of the city's main avenues could be seen. "Which way is sunward?"

The narrow backstreets were in the shade all the time, but sunlight could reach the tops of the facades. Kittiwake looked up to see which side of the street was lit and saw a man in a brown gown looking down on them from a rooftop bridge. As though being on the roof in the daytime were not suspicious enough, he ran off.

Zefi frowned. "Followed he us?"

"I fear it is so," said Kittiwake. "This way. Quickly."

Kittiwake was just guessing now. If they could find a wider street—one too wide for rooftop bridges—then the man in the brown gown would not be able to keep up. But the man in the cream-and-rose gown was still somewhere on the ground. They trotted halfway down the block before Kittiwake remembered a way to see their pursuers without being seen himself.

He stopped near the end of the deserted street and closed his eyes.

"What you are doing?" Zefi asked.

Kittiwake held up a hand to discourage interruptions.

Relaxing his mind, distancing himself from his pounding heart, Kittiwake tried to make himself open to the emotions of others. Zefi's fear was strong, but Kittiwake forced himself to ignore her and search beyond. He wished he had practiced this. Most of the time, he used his concentration to shut other people out—otherwise his neighbors' emotions would disrupt his work.

With his mind open, he could sense more souls nearby, but he was not certain he could distinguish his pursuers from the other people in the neighborhood.

"Let's go right," he said, because he thought that might be the least crowded direction. "We'll walk."

Zefi nodded.

They strolled casually around the corner. Two guardians-of-the-peace were walking ahead of them.

Behind them, from up above, a voice called, "Fugitives! Fugitives! This way!"

Zefi and Kittiwake stopped. The two guardians looked around, bewildered.

Zefi and Kittiwake ducked back to the deserted street.

"I think they saw us," Zefi said.

Kittiwake just ran.

Three female guardians stepped into an intersection two blocks away. Because one had an identity hood hanging from her belt, Kittiwake recognized them as those he had confronted in his workshop.

"Stop!" she called. "You are under arrest!"

"Keep going!" Kittiwake told Zefi. They ran toward the guardians.

"Stop!" the guardian repeated, her aura glowing uncertainly.

Their unexpected charge froze the women in place. After covering half the intervening distance, Kittiwake and Zefi turned down a side street.

The rooftop voice was still calling, "This way!" but it was growing fainter. Kittiwake and Zefi dashed down another street. Speed was the only way to escape from this tightening net.

The man in the cream-and-rose gown stepped out of a house two doorways ahead. Kittiwake and Zefi skidded to a stop.

He had borrowed a broom, and he held it in such a way that it seemed to be a weapon. Kittiwake could see a blue-green aura glowing in the open doorway, indicating that the person in the door—probably the owner of the broom—was too scared to come out into the street and be seen, but curious enough to watch the man who stood in Kittiwake's way.

"Citizen, you are under arrest," said the man in the cream-and-rose gown.

With the rooftop observer goading them on, the guardians

behind Kittiwake and Zefi would catch up rapidly. From the broom-wielding man's dangerous aura, Kittiwake judged that getting past him would not be simple.

Then Kittiwake saw a perfect way to escape. If he used Glamour's power to kill the man, she would grant him an illusion. He could exchange appearances with his victim, who was obviously allied with the guardians in some way. Kittiwake, supernaturally disguised as the man in the cream-and-rose gown, could tell the guardians that he had killed the artificer, pointing to the evidence at their feet. They would report to Fox that Kittiwake was dead. And then, he could go wherever he wanted and make his artifacts in peace.

Would Zefi corroborate his story? And yet, how could she not? She would not betray him to the guardians, would she?

No. That was madness. Whether she betrayed him or not, she would stop loving him. How could anyone love a demon-worshipping murderer?

Kittiwake spread his hands. "I'll surrender if you let her go."

The man's eyes took in Zefi's height.

Shouts of pursuing guards echoed along the street.

"Commander Fox wants me alive," Kittiwake said, hoping it was true. "Let her go, and I come willingly. Arrest her, and you must kill me."

The man nodded. "Go," he said to Zefi.

"I won't," said Zefi.

"Zefi, I beg you," Kittiwake said as the sandals of the guards struck the paving stones behind him. What could persuade her? "If you are in prison, you can't save my soul."

She enveloped his fingers with her huge, warm, brown hand. "I will find a priest for you," she said.

"Do that," Kittiwake agreed.

The man with the broom held up his hand. The running sandals stopped.

"We don't need the orphan," he told the guardians-of-the-peace. "The artificer will cooperate."

Tears formed in Zefi's blue eyes. Kittiwake would not look away. He knew it would be his last vision of Zefi, and he knew that he loved her.

His hand was snatched from hers. His wrists were swiftly bound behind his back. Someone slipped a black hood over his head, and Kittiwake accepted the darkness.

CHAPTER 18
The House of the Flashing Tuna

FOR ZEFI, it had all begun with the snapping of an oar. Oars snapped. They were only wood, and wood broke down under repeated strain.

This oar had snapped in the hands of Adom, the rower who sat in front of Zefi. She could still hear the crack of splintering wood. Adom, who had been pulling on the oar hard enough to move his share of the fully loaded merchant ship, suddenly found himself applying the same force to a short wooden handle. The power of his stroke had been transformed into a blow to Zefi's knee. She had not rowed since.

That had been the beginning, but at the time, Zefi had thought her life was ended. The foreman had helped her hobble to the Orphanage, where he had chosen Zefi's replacement. She had been cast off like a broken chisel or a leaky kettle.

But Zefi had been repairable. The Church of Three Sisters had skillful healers, and soon they had put her back on her feet. Then they had assigned her to work for Kittiwake.

Every day, Zefi had thanked the gods for sending her to him. Every day, she had asked their forgiveness for succumbing to despair instead of trusting that the snapping of the oar would lead her down a path chosen by the gods. Now, as she wandered the streets of Dupho, she felt lost.

The man she loved had committed his soul to the demons. Had Zefi caused this? Had he done it because he thought it was the only way he could protect her? She tried to make sense of it all.

But perhaps it didn't make sense. Perhaps she had been a fool to think her meeting with Kittiwake was arranged by the gods. She had certainly been a fool to think that she could make a year-and-a-day last forever.

Would things have turned out better if she had left him four days ago? She would not have been home when the soldiers came to deliver their message, she would not have been with him when the Thinker People threatened him this morning, and she would not have been by his side when he was captured. Kittiwake would have faced all those troubles alone. No, not alone. Worse than alone. He would have had only his patron to turn to. This way, at least, he had Zefi on his side. Perhaps this was why the gods had allowed her to stay.

She stopped beside the fountain in the Whale Plaza. Why was she here?

While her mind had been wandering, her feet had taken her toward the harbor. That was only natural. She had promised to find Kittiwake a priest at the Orphanage, which she could reach by walking past that group of sailors, down the steps to the harbor, and then a few dozen paces along the docks. So why had she stopped beside the fountain? Was she still afraid of returning to the Orphanage?

Zefi looked at the sunlight sparkling in the stone whale's plume of water. Mamosi, goddess of the sun, would want her to go down those steps and yield to the authority of the healer-priests. Kashram, god of the lith, would give her the courage if she lacked it. But no. It was not lack of courage that had stopped her. She had stopped because she needed a moment to think things through.

What would happen once she found a priest who would convert Kittiwake's soul? Well, she would take him to Kittiwake. But Kittiwake was in prison. If Zefi appeared with a priest, the soldiers would want to know why. The priest would tell them. And Kittiwake would be executed for demon worship.

Zefi needed to find a better solution. This was a matter for Thafarsi, goddess of knowledge.

Before Zefi could begin her prayer, the group of sailors loitering near the harbor steps was joined by a man with long, black braids. She had seen that sailor before—his thin nose, his spiteful lips. Zefi realized that without the long, black braids, he would be Whitedove's nephew. It was a wig!

The sailors conferred. Zefi was much too far away to hear what they were saying, but she recalled the conversation the gods had allowed her to overhear at the patron's villa. These men were meeting to plot the murder of the Thinker People.

Zefi had interrupted that conversation when the nephew had complained about "the Goddess". At the time, she had assumed he was speaking of Swalethi, the goddess of beauty, but now she realized that he had been referring to this demon that they called "Glamour". Zefi had no way to translate the word into her own language. The closest she could come was "vanity".

The sailors' conference arrived at a conclusion. The patron's nephew, disguised by his wig, led the sailors across the Whale Plaza and down the moonaway avenue. They were going to the House of the Flashing Tuna. Zefi had no doubt that the gods wanted her to follow.

I will do what I am able, she promised Thafarsi. *Please grant me the wisdom to see what I must do.*

The little Thinker People, Thafarsi's people, had offered to take Kittiwake to safety. They had seemed dangerous, but the true danger lurked in the safety of the villa. This was why the gods had wanted Zefi to overhear the nephew's plans. This was why the gods had stopped her in the center of the Whale Plaza.

Zefi tried to keep up with the sailors without being noticed. It was so late in the day that the shadows had crossed the wide avenue to creep up the faces of the buildings on the opposite side. The cooling paving stones swarmed with Decorator People, many of them carrying a freshly decapitated fish in a basket. Zefi could not exactly hide in the shoulder-high crowd, but she looked no different from the rowers who came to explore a bit of the city on shore leave. She was able to follow the patron's nephew and his thugs closely—although she dared not push her way ahead of them.

When the men reached the House of the Flashing Tuna, they stopped to argue in the middle of the avenue. Zefi stopped, too, wary of being recognized if she came closer.

The nephew convinced the sailors to enter the House of the Seven Sawfish, right across the street from where Tortoise had said the Thinker People were staying. This tactical decision was explained several moments later, when a man appeared on the roof of the House of the Seven Sawfish. From his long arms and broad shoulders, Zefi recognized him as one of the nephew's sailors—the biggest one. He stood silhouetted against the late-afternoon sky. Zefi could not see his eyes, but she judged he was watching the door of the inn across the street.

This was Zefi's chance to warn the little people, but what if the man on the roof saw her and realized what she had done? It was a risk she would take if she had to, but she was already in enough trouble. Could she think of a better way?

Just then, she heard the march of approaching feet. Many feet. Turning, she saw a dozen guardians-of-the-peace, auras gleaming off their polished helmets. She stepped off the avenue onto a side street.

"Good evening!"

A short man smiled up at her, standing only two paces away.

"Smells good, doesn't it?" he asked.

He wore white, the traditional color of bakers in Dupho. His loaves were arrayed on a table outside his bakery, and Zefi had to admit that they did indeed smell good.

Behind her, the tramp of feet grew louder.

"Would you like to buy?" the baker asked. "Do you have money?" He jingled a small pouch of coins in case she didn't understand.

"No," Zefi said. "I am sorry. I have no money."

This was true. She got her spending money from Kittiwake, and they had left it all at the workshop.

"That's unfortunate," said the baker, as the soldiers passed by on the avenue behind Zefi's back. "Did you spend it all?"

She realized the soldiers were not coming after her. They would not know she was in this part of town. Nevertheless, she kept her back to the avenue.

"No," she said. "Or maybe yes."

The baker chuckled.

From the avenue came the command, "Squad halt!"

The march of the soldiers stopped. Zefi spun around. They had all marched past, but they must have stopped close by.

Forgetting the baker, Zefi went back to the avenue. The sergeant was talking to a worried man with silver fish painted on his arms. Zefi decided to learn why the soldiers had come. Praying to Kashram for courage, she strolled past.

I'm just big, slow, and stupid. Don't notice me.

"They left after breakfast this morning, and I have not seen them since," the worried man said. "Would you like me to show you to their room?"

"Yes, thank you."

"It is my pleasure to assist Captain Faith in any way I can."

"Of course," the sergeant replied. As Zefi pretended to inspect the wares of a nearby citrus vendor, the sergeant added, "I will also need to send four of my squad to your roof, and I would like to hide four in the kitchen."

The innkeeper hesitated, but he replied, "Very well."

As the soldiers entered the inn, Zefi saw a curly-haired head disappearing from a balcony above.

CHAPTER 19
Reunions

SOLDIERS! Shiko rushed back into the room to tell Higomu, but he already had his ear pressed to the floor.

Shiko did likewise. Footsteps. Getting louder. Coming up the stairs. Now they echoed in the hallway beyond the room's curtained doorway.

Higomu helped her up. "How many?" he asked.

"I saw twelve outside," she said.

At the other end of the hallway, the footsteps halted.

Topaz said, "This is the ladder to the roof."

Had Topaz betrayed their location? Shiko looked a question at Higomu.

He scowled an affirmative.

"Which is Darkheart's room?" a voice asked.

"That one at the—"

Topaz cut himself short and dropped his voice to a whisper, as though he had not known the room was occupied until he had seen the drawn curtain. Apparently, the innkeeper and the soldiers had been planning an ambush.

Higomu picked up his satchel, dropped his sandals into it, and stepped out onto the balcony. Shiko collected her things as well, remembering to also bring Kittiwake's notebook. As sandaled feet began striding down the hallway, she joined Higomu on the balcony.

Shiko looked over the railing. No soldiers remained in the avenue below, but she was not looking forward to another roll on the paving stones of Dupho. Higomu's scowl showed that he concurred.

Higomu took Shiko's hand and nodded at the balcony of

the adjacent room. Shiko agreed.

Higomu wanted her to go first, so she clambered up onto the railing, judged the distance, crouched, and leapt into the air. It would have been an easy leap if she had wanted to grasp the other balcony's railing with her hands, but she could no longer trust her shoulder to hold her weight. Instead, she leapt far enough to grab the railing with her outstretched foot. Unable to plant a landing on the narrow railing, she tucked her legs, extended an arm, and landed with a roll across the wooden balcony. Her satchel cushioned her landing.

A cry of "Who's there?" came from the room. Shiko looked up to see a fellow guest staring at her, his startled face illuminated by his own blue-green glow.

On the other balcony, Higomu tried to distract the guards by shouting, "This way!"

"You are under arrest!" shouted someone in the hallway.

"Innkeeper, what is the meaning of this?" demanded a woman from the other side of the hall.

"Citizens, remain in your rooms!"

"Please be calm," pleaded Topaz.

"He's gone, sergeant!"

"Ranks three and four, check the roof!"

"Topaz!"

The second floor was sparsely occupied at this time of day, but those guests who were present shouted enough to compete with the soldiers. Higomu leapt to land lightly on the railing above Shiko. His eyes sparkled.

Shiko got to her feet and shrugged an apology at the startled man whose balcony they had boarded. Higomu scuttled along the railing and leapt for the next balcony, satchel flying out behind him.

The startled guest turned suddenly at a sound from inside the room. A voice said, "Pardon me, citizen."

Shiko clambered onto the railing to make the jump. Higomu was already two balconies ahead of her.

"Halt!" said the soldier inside the room.

"There's one!" shouted a voice from the balcony behind her.

Shiko leapt, rolled off the next balcony's railing, and crashed into the flower pots on the opposite side. She scrambled to her feet, but could not see where Higomu had gone. Helmeted heads stared at her from the two balconies where she had been. The room she had landed outside of seemed empty, so she ran inside.

Shiko was momentarily disoriented by the size of the room, the massive bed, the huge sea chest, the head-high nightstand with the striped pitcher and matching basin. She was back in the land of the giants. The exit was blocked by Topaz the Innkeeper—two obsidian-black legs inside a blue-and-green gown.

Realizing that Topaz had not seen her, Shiko ducked behind the sea chest. Topaz remained in the doorway, staring down the hall, pleading, "Please be calm!"

A foot, followed by Higomu in his billowing chiton, struck the innkeeper square in the back. Someone else gave a grunt, and a helmet thudded into the floor.

Shiko jumped up from her hiding place and waved.

Higomu turned and gave her a manic grin. "Two with one blow!"

He ran to her side and opened the sea chest.

"Nice work," he said on seeing the contents.

He removed a green cotton gown and took it out to the balcony. Shiko followed.

Higomu shoved the gown through the railing so that it dangled over the avenue below. He tied the sleeves together around a baluster and pulled the knot tight.

A soldier entered the room and shouted, "He's here!"

"You go first," Higomu suggested, and he stepped back inside.

Another soldier entered the room.

"I can't leave you one-against-two," Shiko said, moving to Higomu's side.

Two more soldiers entered the room.

"So where does that leave us now?" Higomu asked.

The soldier with the red triangle painted on his white cheek seemed to be the leader. He said, "Foreigners, you are under arrest."

"Not interested," Higomu replied.

"Do not resist," the soldier advised. "We will kill you if we must."

Higomu shook his head. "Not interested in that, either."

"Albatross, bind his wrists."

The man so named looked apprehensive, but he said, "Yes, Sergeant." He leaned his spear against the wall, and pulled a leather cord from his belt.

Higomu held up a hand and said, "Wait, Albatross."

The soldier looked at his sergeant for direction.

"Shiko," Higomu asked, "do you remember how Vadu won at pegboard?"

"Yes."

Higomu nodded and said, "Thank you, Albatross."

With a shift step and a leg sweep, Higomu toppled the nightstand. Its striped pitcher and basin fell with a crash. Water spread over the clay floor.

"Chaos evens the odds!" Higomu cried.

He ran for the balcony. Shiko followed.

Behind them, she heard the thump of a soldier hitting the suddenly slick floor.

Higomu leapt onto the balcony railing and disappeared over the edge. Tension in the arms of the gown showed that he used the garment to check his fall. Then the cloth went slack and it was Shiko's turn.

She stepped on a flowerpot for extra height, rolled over the railing, and found the cotton gown with her toes. She rapidly descended until she was holding the hem, dangling above the avenue.

The bright yellow head of the sergeant rose over the balcony railing like an angry sun. He bellowed, "Rear guard: To the street!"

Shiko let go. It was a short drop, and her knees absorbed the impact. As she rose from her crouch, she found herself looking up at a familiar face—a face with a scar on its jaw.

The pirate called "Brutal" hardly glanced at her. She was beneath his contempt. Instead his eyes shifted between Higomu and the black-braided pirate captain. The pirates were seven in number and they had Shiko and Higomu surrounded on the avenue in front of the House of the Flashing Tuna.

"You shan't sneak away so easily this time," said the thin-lipped pirate captain. He was speaking to Higomu.

The pirate captain reached over his shoulder and withdrew a knife from a hidden sheath on his back. The thin blade was long enough to pierce all the way through Shiko's tiny body. "I only regret that the guardians are also after you, because I would have liked to savor this."

Something yellow flashed past the pirate captain's ear and bounced off the shoulder of the man opposite him. Higomu bolted out of the circle before anyone could react.

The pirate captain turned and chased after Higomu, ducking a lemon thrown by a huge brown-skinned woman. For a moment, Shiko thought it was the ghost of the rower he had killed. The other pirates turned to follow just as soldiers began running out of the inn.

The resulting chase was like a bizarre parade. The Child of Labor led the way toward the Fish Plaza. Higomu was gaining on her as he passed an angry citrus vendor. The pirate captain was trying to keep up, holding his long knife with one hand and the top of his head with the other. His fellow pirates were overtaking him. Shiko found herself chasing after the pirates, because the alternative was to be captured by the soldiers who brought up the rear.

From the slap of the soldiers' sandals on the paving stones, Shiko could tell that she was maintaining her lead. The pirates ahead of her were unencumbered by spears or armor, and she gained no ground on them until they slowed to match their leader's pace.

"Kill them both!" he screamed at his men.

Brutal glanced over his shoulder at Shiko. She skidded to a halt.

But the pirate captain was not referring to her. "A purse for the booker and a half-purse for the leatherskin!" the captain shouted as he ran. His men, including Brutal, surged ahead of him.

Shiko checked her lead on the guardians-of-the-peace and resumed running. Higomu and the Child of Labor—was she Kittiwake's assistant?—entered the Fish Plaza side by side. Higomu veered away from the giant woman and climbed up onto a fish cart. Four of the pirates and their captain chased after him. The other two drew knives from sheathes hidden near their shoulderblades and ran after … Zefi, wasn't it? Yes. Shiko thought her name was Zefi.

Shiko's feet made a decision at the Fish Plaza, and her mind worked out the logic as she ran. Higomu had, on numerous occasions, proven himself capable of escaping from situations like this one, whereas Shiko had generally made his escape more difficult. It was unwise to try to help Higomu.

Zefi, on the other hand, was not a striker for the Order of the Lock. She was an artificer's assistant who had thrown fruit at killers. She was in mortal danger and might actually need Shiko's help. And Shiko had a moral obligation to this woman who had freed them from the circle of pirates.

Shiko was glad that her feet had decided to do the right thing.

Although the sun was setting, the Fish Plaza still held plenty of vendors and shoppers. These people began screaming hysterically at the two knife-wielding men chasing Zefi. Bystanders recoiled in terror, opening a wake behind the pirates through which Shiko could run unobstructed.

Glancing behind, she could see that the soldiers had stopped on the edge of the plaza. They were only four. Shiko deduced they were waiting for orders or reinforcements. Probably both.

So now Shiko's only immediate problem was that the pirates were fast enough to catch Zefi before Shiko caught them. A distraction might buy Zefi time, but Shiko had nothing to throw, nor did she have any confidence in her aching shoulder's aim. She could shout to draw the pirates' attention, but she doubted she would be heard over the shoppers' screams of fear. It was a wonder they had not drawn the attention of more guards.

Actually, that might be a good idea.

Shiko climbed up onto the nearest stall and looked around the plaza. There they were: a pair of soldiers approaching cautiously from the lithward avenue.

"Zefi!" she shouted. "Run for the soldiers!"

Zefi turned at the sound of her name and saw where Shiko was pointing. She put her head down and changed course.

When the soldiers saw the huge woman running toward them, their auras darkened and their cautious approach slowed to a halt. Zefi slowed, too, as she neared them. Shiko could see her pointing back toward the pirates.

Then the two pirates stopped. They had caught sight of the soldiers. Knives against spears was apparently not worth the potential reward of a "half-purse". Their knives disappeared down their backs and they began walking rapidly through the crowd toward the Grand Market. This prompted the soldiers to find their courage, and they began striding purposefully across the Fish Plaza, although not so purposefully that they would actually catch the two pirates before they made their escape.

"Don't be frightened. They're gone."

From her perch on the awning of the fish stall, Shiko looked down into the friendly face of a copper-eyed man.

"You can come down now," the fish-seller said. "The guardians-of-the-peace will take care of it."

"Yes, of course," Shiko agreed. "It was foolish of me to be so scared."

"Oh, not at all," said the man.

"I hope I did not damage your wares?" she asked.

"Oh, no," he assured her.

"Good." She smiled. "Please excuse me."

She fled.

Shiko hoped to find Zefi before the giant disappeared in the crowd, but she had gone only a few steps when the giant found her. Taking Shiko's hand, Zefi led the way out of the plaza.

"That was well done," Shiko said. "With the lemon."

"I missed," Zefi said.

"But it worked," Shiko said.

The giant nodded. "This way," she said, pulling Shiko into a side street.

"Where are we going?" Shiko asked.

"Away from the soldiers," Zefi said. "Now this way."

The giant led Shiko down a narrow street, between buildings painted with indoor scenes—a mother teaching her daughter to sew, three oranges sitting on a table, a bowl of grapes. Shiko found it unsettling to be outside and see the light and colors of the inside world. And the murals were so big— the bowl of grapes took up an entire wall—that they made her feel like a mouse. The dim, unpainted alley that Zefi led her into was actually more comforting.

Zefi stopped and leaned against the wall. When she had caught her breath, she said, "I was afraid to run to the soldiers, but you gave me courage. That was smart. It worked."

"You played your part beautifully," Shiko said.

"I hope your man escaped," Zefi said.

"Higomu is not my man," Shiko corrected. "But your wishes are appreciated. I don't think you need to worry about him, though. He can take care of himself."

"He can also find a more sensible place for conversation," Higomu said, appearing at the end of the alley. "These walls echo. Let us relocate."

CHAPTER 20
Interrogation and Torture

WITH HIS head inside the identity hood, Kittiwake could see only the stone beneath his feet, but that was enough to tell him he was climbing to the entrance of the Red Palace. His mother had brought him here when he was ten, as part of his education on Dupho's artwork, history, and architecture. Two centuries of sandaled feet had sculpted shallow depressions in the red marble steps. Kittiwake followed in the footsteps of the emperors, soldiers, sight-seers, and criminals who had come to the Red Palace before him.

The Red Palace had been built as the residence of Emperor Zealous, the general who founded the Theocratic Empire. After the completion of the Emperor's Palace on the moonward edge of the city, the Red Palace had continued to serve as the headquarters of the army for a century and a half. In modern times, the recruiting, training, and administration of the Theocratic Army was centered at Camp Shenkerwo, but the Red Palace still played a central role in the city of Dupho as the headquarters of the guardians-of-the-peace. It held administrative offices, a barracks, a mess hall, and—somewhere in the basement—prison cells.

Kittiwake's wrists were still bound, but his captors removed his identity hood when they arrived in the mosaic-tiled foyer. They stopped there to await instructions.

Kittiwake looked up at the balconies and the dome overhead. When he was a child, the sight had inspired awe—the Theocratic Empire was so mighty, and those early masons had been so skilled—but now the domed ceiling reminded him that he might never again see the sky.

Nearby stood a chest-high vase known as "Yezenka's Replica". Unglazed and unpainted, the great vase seemed too mundane to have any value beyond the utilitarian, but in fact, it was a copy of the oldest vase in the world. Yezenka had made the replica with her mind, drawing Earth from the Elemental Realms and forming it into a shape in perfect resonance with the original. Now, eight hundred years later, it was valued as a testament to the skill of Yezenka in addition to being a reminder of the greatness of Moshantyo, the first potter.

I could have done that, Kittiwake thought. *I could have made artifacts that the entire empire would want to see even centuries from now. Instead, I made artifacts for Whitedove, who forced me to twist my emotion box into a soul trap. And instead of resisting, I agreed to serve him and his demon, trapping my own soul more securely than any artifact ever could.*

Glamour caressed his heart and promised him he would still have a chance for fame.

A soldier approached and said, "Captain Faith wishes that the prisoner be taken to the Dark Wing."

The soldier led them to an arched doorway and down a hall with a high-vaulted ceiling. They came to a flight of stone steps and descended to the subterranean cells of the Red Palace.

Although the soldier had referred to this section of the basement as "the Dark Wing", it was lit by ambient daylight from high-set windows in the arch-roofed cells that lined the long corridor. In the cell nearest the steps, a glum-faced boy leaned against the iron bars and watched Kittiwake's arrival. He looked barely twelve years old! What had the boy done? Would his parents come looking for him?

The next cell held a woman who seemed to be wishing herself invisible. She sat curled up with her feet and buttocks on a bench, rocking in rhythm to her own deranged mumbling. Her nose was tucked into her knees, and her long loose hair fell down over her face. Her aura was the deep black of despair.

The next cell was empty, and the next. As the guardians led Kittiwake down the corridor, he saw none of the stereotypical criminals: no colonial sailor who had picked a fight with men from the Theocratic Navy; no egg seller who had been in an argument over whether he were selling week-old eggs; no unregistered fishmonger who had parked his cart too near the Grand Market. All the remaining cells were locked and empty. This was not the main prison. This was a forgotten corner of the building—or perhaps a corner for those whom Commander Fox wanted forgotten.

At the end of the corridor, a flight of stone steps led down to a shadowy wooden door, but the guardians did not take Kittiwake farther. Instead of descending, they unlocked the last cell in the corridor, opening a door made of iron bars. Kittiwake entered. They closed the door and locked it again.

Kittiwake would be kept far away from the other two prisoners. Perhaps that was for the best. He did not want them corrupted by the terrible power he felt writhing inside him. It was a power he had not yet used, and this displeased the being to whom he had aligned his soul. If he refused her again, he would be punished. The idea came to him as a certainty.

The sergeant dismissed most of Kittiwake's escort. One guardian and the sergeant remained outside the cell. Kittiwake wondered if he were so dangerous that he needed to be under constant surveillance.

He was. He could feel the unused power in his bound hands. The sergeant's breastplate was impenetrable to magical resonance and resistant to spear points, but Kittiwake knew it would be no barrier to the power of the being who reached into the world through his self-damned soul.

Kittiwake could kill them both. If the sergeant fell dead where he stood, the key in his hands might land within Kittiwake's reach. Or did Kittiwake think that being forgotten in a cellar like a dusty bottle of wine was a fitting end for Dupho's greatest visionary? Yes, killing was wrong, but wasn't his life worth more than theirs? What would their spears ever do for the world that could match what Kittiwake could do with his hands and his mind?

Kittiwake wondered how many of those thoughts were his.

The two guardians looked down the corridor. They stood up straighter as footsteps approached.

"Captain," said the sergeant, putting his hand to his heart in salute.

"Good afternoon, Sergeant."

The woman who arrived at Kittiwake's cell was one of those people whose hair did not contrast their skin. Her black ringlets were cut to army length, just above the shoulders, and held away from her face by silver combs near the top of her head. In yellow paint on her black forehead, a horizontal line with a dot in the center marked her as a captain in the Theocratic Army. The two downward triangles on her left cheek marked her as an officer of the guardians-of-the-peace. Her eyes held feminine gentleness, but the bearing of her chin, neck, and shoulders left no doubt who was in command.

"Are you Kittiwake the Artificer?" she asked.

"I am," Kittiwake admitted.

"I am Captain Faith. Sergeant, unlock the door, please."

The sergeant did so, and Captain Faith stepped inside, followed by an attendant.

"Please sit down," the captain said.

Kittiwake sat on the edge of the bed attached to the stone wall.

The attendant placed a stool behind her captain.

"Thank you," said Captain Faith, sitting down opposite Kittiwake.

Looking into her eyes, Kittiwake was enamored of her beauty. He realized that if he killed Captain Faith, his new goddess would forgive him for all his failings. This was the opportunity he had been promised. Killing this high-ranking, beautiful woman would make him famous.

She turned to the men outside the cell and asked, "Sergeant, have you explained to the artificer why we have brought him here?"

"No, Captain."

"Very good."

He felt the power in his bound hands. Using it would be as simple as a wish.

"Kittiwake," asked Captain Faith, "do you know a Child of Knowledge who calls himself 'Higomu'?"

Sweat beaded on his brow. He wished to be renowned for his skill, not for his crimes. And yet, if he did not commit the crime, Glamour would take away his skill.

The sergeant barked, "Answer the question, artificer!"

Kittiwake shook his head. *I will not*, he told his demon. *I am not a killer. I am an artificer. I create. I do not destroy.*

Captain Faith looked puzzled. "What is it?" she asked. Her life's blood pulsed through her throat.

No, Kittiwake thought. *I will not kill her.*

Supernatural thorns stabbed into Kittiwake's bound hands. The killing power drained from his fingers, taking with it the vitality that had made his hands so skillful. His skin shriveled. His knuckles bulged into aching knots.

"My— my hands," he gasped.

Captain Faith stood up in alarm. "Sergeant, release his bonds."

The sergeant hesitated a moment, before saying, "Yes, of course." He stepped into the cell and undid Kittiwake's wrist bonds.

Kittiwake squeezed both fists against his chest, trying to make the aching stop. His fingers felt blurry—as though they had passed beyond numb and were on their way out of existence. Captain Faith called for someone to bring water. The sergeant berated his subordinate for binding Kittiwake too tightly. Their voices were muffled by the sound of Kittiwake's own gasps for breath.

"Thorns of Hell," murmured Captain Faith, staring at Kittiwake's hands. "What happened to you?"

Kittiwake spread his fingers. They were still there, but his white skin had lost so much pigment that he could now see his own veins. The fleshy parts of his hand had withered to reveal the outlines of his bones. His aching knuckles were swollen like cysts.

The man who had bound Kittiwake was staring wide eyed. "I didn't—" he said. "I didn't— Sergeant, I didn't know it was that tight."

"He wasn't this way when you captured him?"

"No, Captain," squeaked the frightened guardian.

"What happened?" the captain demanded of Kittiwake. "How did you destroy your hands? Don't pretend it was the bonds. I know what loss of circulation looks like. This was magic!"

Hope for freedom might have inspired Kittiwake to withhold the truth, but even freedom would be hopeless now that his hands were ruined. Why not tell all?

"It was not my magic," he said. "I have been punished by a demon."

CHAPTER 21
Jailbreakers

"A DEMON?" Shiko whispered.

Zefi nodded.

"Now you see why I suggested a change of location," Higomu said.

They were sitting in a hillside vineyard belonging to one of the villas on the Heights above. The sun was setting, and their side of the hill was already in shadow.

"Could he have been mistaken?" Shiko asked. "Or could it be that you misunderstood?"

"He called her 'Glamour'," Zefi said.

"Glamour?" Higomu repeated. "Oh. You mean Vanity."

"Yes!" Zefi said.

Shiko nodded. She recognized that name.

"How much do you know about the demons?" Higomu asked.

"I studied sacred teaching," said Zefi. "But it says small about demons. I know the demons are nine. I not learned their names."

"It can be difficult to fight them without knowledge," said Higomu. "Did you learn about triads? No. I see I have puzzled you."

Higomu took a stick and drew an equilateral triangle in the dirt. "Knowledge, Justice, and Beauty are in the same triad," he said, labeling the corners with those deities' symbols. "Our people usually put Knowledge on top. Then Justice. Then Beauty. But it doesn't matter where you start; you just keep going around the triangle.

"Every deity has a demon that can lead followers astray. Servants of Knowledge are susceptible to the Deceiver." Apparently, Higomu did not think this name was worthy of being written down. He simply made a mark on the side of the triangle between Knowledge and Justice.

"But every demon can be overcome by a deity. The Deceiver is overcome by Justice. Does that make sense so far?"

Zefi looked confused.

"Let me continue and perhaps you will see," Higomu offered. "Servants of Justice sometimes lose control of themselves and become heartless." Higomu made a mark on the side between Justice and Beauty. "But the Demon of Heartlessness can be overcome by Beauty, who helps people realize that rigid laws and cruel punishments harm the souls of those who enforce them."

Higomu marked the third side of the triangle, between Beauty and Knowledge. "Vanity falls here. She is the demon to whom a servant of Beauty would be most susceptible. It does not surprise me that she has clandestine worshippers in Dupho."

Shiko studied the diagram with a sinking heart. "You must think I'm a fool," she said.

"Not at all," said Higomu.

"I have been defending Kittiwake and his artifact, while you were right all along," she said.

Higomu looked at her with his deep, dark eyes. "He was not evil when you met him, Shiko. From what Zefi has told us, it seems most likely that he was coerced into serving Vanity this very afternoon. Your convictions were strong. Your intuition will improve with practice."

Shiko said nothing. It was not about intuition; it was about principle. A man who had done nothing wrong deserved to be free. But a man who had given his soul to a demon …

"The circle completes," Zefi said, nodding. "I see now. Knowledge beats Vanity."

"Yes," said Higomu.

"And that is why, when I pray for help, the gods lead me to you."

"The deities led you to us?" Shiko asked.

"An interesting hypothesis," said Higomu. "Regardless, we are grateful you came."

"Yes," said Shiko. "Thank you for rescuing us from those pirates."

"I wonder how they found us," Higomu said.

"Legislator Whitedove has many friends," said Zefi. "He sent a man to find you. This man found you and told the nephew."

Higomu was as confused as Shiko. "What nephew?" he asked.

"Legislator Whitedove's nephew. The leader of the pirates."

"But that doesn't— Tell me, Zefi, does Whitedove have any interest in glass?"

Zefi nodded. "He is the patron for Chuckwalla the Glass-maker. The new patron. The old patron was Fox, who leads the soldiers. The guardians. Kittiwake says the two men fight over him the way they fighted over Chuckwalla."

"Ah, I see." Higomu rubbed his eyes. "It seems I am the one who has been a fool."

Shiko asked, "So the pirate with the long black braids is Kittiwake's patron's nephew?"

"Yes," said Zefi. "Or, no. Those are not his braids. He really has short white hair."

"A wig," said Shiko.

"Didn't you realize why he holds on to his head?" Higomu asked.

"I should have," said Shiko.

"Thank you, Zefi," said Higomu. "That is certainly good to know. It does not, however, change our plans. We still need to rescue Kittiwake while avoiding the soldiers and pirates."

"Can you do that?" Zefi asked, face full of hope. "Can you rescue Kittiwake?"

"Of course we can," said Higomu.

"Can I help?" Zefi asked.

"Yes," said Higomu. "We will need you to convince him to trust us."

Shiko was not certain the artificer deserved to be rescued, but he was certainly too dangerous to leave in the hands of the Theocratic Army. And speed was important. Zefi claimed that Whitedove intended to use the emotion box at a party the following evening. They did not know what Whitedove planned to do, but they agreed that they should get the artificer and his artifact out of Dupho before that party.

With the rescue agreed to, Higomu left. He came back at dusk with cheese and two loaves of bread, which they apportioned as a loaf-and-a-half for Zefi and a quarter loaf each for Higomu and Shiko.

As soon as they had eaten, Higomu insisted they sleep. The earth of the vineyard was soft, having been recently hoed, but Shiko worried about getting her chiton dirty. Higomu said that dirtier was better, as it would be less visible at night. Shiko was tired enough from the day's exertions, but her aches and scrapes prevented her from lying comfortably enough to fall asleep. She gave up trying, hoping that simple rest would be sufficient. She lay among the rustling grape vines, watching the shadows creep across the ground in the red light of the setting moon.

The moon had set when Higomu woke her. Zefi was already standing, towering up into the starlit sky. Shiko could not see the lith, but she knew that if the moon had recently set, then it must be nearly the eighth lithic.

Higomu said this was the best time for a rescue attempt. Danger would keep the rescuers alert. The soldiers would have no such stimulant. Furthermore, the soldiers were used to dealing only with their fellow Children of Beauty. People who did not glow would seem near-invisible to them in the darkness.

Higomu and Zefi seemed near-invisible to Shiko as they walked the streets of Dupho. They traveled back streets with few lamps. The pale paving stones were white in the starlight, and the forms of Shiko's companions were only hazy shadows on the stone.

However, such dark streets were not always easy to find. The city was surprisingly well-lit at night, considering that every citizen could function as his or her own lamp. Shiko realized the lights were for appearances: Their illumination of the streets was only incidental; they were placed to illuminate the fountains and murals.

"We'll need a pair of pliers," Higomu told them as they passed a house decorated with a twisting school of eels. Before the women could reply, Higomu pulled himself up into the house's window.

Shiko looked at Zefi, but kept her silence. Above their heads, a murmur of low voices told them that the neighbors were making a late night of it on the roof. Shiko hoped the shopkeeper was up above and not sleeping inside, where Higomu thumped gently onto the floor.

She listened. Someone on a rooftop down the street laughed. Zefi breathed with deep-chested huffs, but no sound came from inside the shop. Was Higomu waiting to see if anyone had been alarmed by his entry? Had he been harmed in the fall? What if he had landed wrong? Would Shiko and Zefi wait outside the window all night until the people on the roof came down to find Higomu lying on their floor? But no. Higomu would never land wrong. He must be moving so silently that she could not hear him.

The side street on which they stood had a thirty-degree bend about fifty paces ahead. The house at the bend was painted with jellyfish. Shiko had not noticed the jellyfish when they were walking, but as she and Zefi waited outside the house with eels, the jellyfish were illuminated by a pink glow.

"Someone's coming," she whispered.

Higomu gave no reply. Perhaps she had not whispered loud enough.

Zefi's eyes grew wide with alarm.

Well, Shiko was trained, wasn't she? She didn't need to rely on Higomu to think for her all the time. Taking Zefi by the hand, Shiko drew the giant into a nearby passage.

In the daytime, the passages from streets to courtyards were dark; at night, they were simply black. Shiko could not see whether they were moving toward a gate or an open courtyard, but she could tell from the echoes of their breathing that the tunnel's walls were close around them. Even their footsteps seemed loud, despite Shiko's precaution of leaving her sandals in her satchel, which she had hidden in the vineyard.

The people outside had taken no precautions with their sandals. A gentle scrape of wood on stone accompanied the murmur of voices drawing nearer.

Shiko and Zefi halted. Shiko looked back at the entrance, a barely discernible archway of gray floating in the blackness.

The footsteps approached. The voices seemed to belong to a man and a woman. The outline of the archway began to glow pink.

Shiko hoped Zefi would not move. The footsteps were now too close to risk even a whisper of sound.

Two figures stepped into the archway and stopped. Their bodies seemed vague and shadowy compared to their softly glowing heads.

The man caressed the woman's cheek and his glow became brighter. "We would not be seen in here," he murmured.

The woman looked furtively toward Shiko, then back at the man. "Here?" she asked.

"Yes, my love."

The woman glanced toward Shiko again.

Does she see me? Shiko wondered.

Shiko did not move. Her heart was pounding, but she knew her fear was unfounded. The woman would have been startled if she had seen Shiko. Instead, she simply seemed reluctant to enter the dark passage.

"I do not think I could," the woman said.

The man leaned closer to her and their lips met. Both auras

shone red in the darkness. Shiko held her breath and counted her heartbeats until she lost track.

Finally, the couple's kiss ended, and the man said, "Then let us walk some more, my love, for only in movement can I constrain the passion I feel for you."

Zefi let out a long breath as the red glow faded from the archway. She murmured something with one word Shiko recognized: "Swalethi". Zefi was thanking the Goddess of Beauty for sending the lovers away.

Believing it was now safe to return to the street, Shiko took Zefi by the hand and led her back to the passage entrance. She nearly screamed when she saw a pair of white legs standing there.

"See?" said Higomu's pale face. "A dirty chiton makes it easier to hide."

"Found you the pliers?" Zefi asked.

"I did," said Higomu. "We will need them to get Kittiwake out."

"We give them back after?" Zefi asked.

"You certainly may, if you so choose," said Higomu. "But for now I recommend we continue on our way."

They did continue on their way, but Shiko could not help saying, "She has a point. It's not right to take goods without paying for them."

"Who is saying I didn't pay for them?"

"Did you?" Shiko asked.

"I'm not saying."

"It's not a joke," Shiko said. "We are supposed to be serving the Goddess, not breaking the law."

"Now that is a joke," said Higomu. "Were you expecting to break into the Red Palace legally?"

"That's different," Shiko said, before she could stop herself.

"Is it?" Higomu asked. "Why?"

Shiko winced. He had won again.

"Because the gods know," Zefi said. "They know if you left money. If you didn't, they know why. They know what harm we do to a craftsman when we steal his tool. They know what harm we do to Kittiwake if we do not bring him to a priest. The gods weigh all. Justice will judge."

"I'm impressed," Higomu said.

"So did you pay for the pliers?" Shiko asked.

"Coins jingle," Higomu said. "I left our money in my satchel back at the vineyard."

"So you stole them," Shiko said.

"I do what must be done. Now we must steal some rope."

"Why can't we use your climbing cord?" Shiko asked. She knew he had it coiled about his waist, underneath his chiton.

"Because Zefi would be too heavy for it," Higomu replied.

"Not if you double it," Shiko said. Her time at sea had taught her that a doubled line could support more weight.

Higomu smiled. "Do you know, I had not thought of that? Very well. Enough burglary for the evening, then. On to the jailbreak."

When they were near the Imperial Plaza, Higomu left them at a block of buildings painted to look like a mountain range as seen from the coast. He returned with the news that the Imperial Plaza held "only the usual number of guardians." Unfortunately that number was two at each of the six avenues, as well as others assigned to guard the various buildings of imperial and city government.

"Just stay close to me and act invisible," he said. Then they were off.

Shiko tried to stay as close as a shadow. Higomu led them around the corner and suddenly they were in the middle of an avenue wide enough for a dozen carts to pass. Two halos marked guardians at the edge of the Imperial Plaza. Higomu moved swiftly toward them.

The soldiers stood facing the plaza. Their helmets, armor, and spear points gleamed in the light of their own auras. As Shiko followed Higomu's approach, she wondered if she would be attacking those guards from behind. If so, she hoped that Higomu remembered to moderate his pace when he charged; otherwise, she would not be able to keep up. At least she had her chiton pinned up.

But Higomu did not lead them directly to the guards. He angled across the avenue and stopped at a wall.

"Lift us up," he whispered to Zefi.

Zefi picked Shiko up, and she felt momentarily like a child. Then she was on the wall.

"Can you climb?" Higomu asked, when Zefi had set him beside Shiko.

"I think no," Zefi said.

"Then it is time to put Shiko's idea to the test," Higomu said. He wriggled until his climbing cord was uncoiled from his waist. Apparently, the coils had held the stolen pliers, for he handed them to Shiko. The pliers were too heavy to tuck into her lockpick belt so she kept them in her hand.

Higomu grasped both ends of the climbing cord and tossed the middle down to Zefi. Then he jumped down the other side into the space between the wall and a hedge of ornamental pines. Shiko followed him.

Higomu wrapped the cord three times around a pine and pulled the end tight. A moment later, Zefi's head rose above the wall.

The giant landed among the shrubs with little grace. Shiko was grateful that the garden was deserted. Once Higomu had re-coiled the cord, he handed it to Zefi.

"Judicial Palace gardens," he explained as he led them through the paths. "Two guards in front of the building, but no one patrols back here."

They came to another wall. Higomu followed it to a gate.

"No need to guard a gate that is always latched," he said, lifting the latch.

The three of them slipped outside the walls again. They were in a wide space between the Judicial Palace and a rhomboidal building Shiko recognized from the descriptions in *A Recent History of Dupho* as the Imperial Architect's House.

"That's the garden wall of the Red Palace," Higomu said,

pointing across a wide expanse of paving stones. The size of the building was difficult to judge. Elsewhere around the plaza, murals and statues were well lit, but the Red Palace occluded the plaza's lamps like a black cloud in a starry sky.

"Is that how we get in?" Shiko asked. Zefi could not lift them to the top of a wall that high.

"It is," Higomu said. "But not yet."

Shiko waited for an explanation. Higomu gave none. After a while, the explanation presented itself in the form of a glowing head drifting along the top of the wall.

"A parapet?" Shiko asked. She had learned from Captain Muzer that military fortresses were sometimes designed with walls soldiers could walk on.

"Yes," said Higomu. "Now follow me closely."

Shiko would have liked to wait until the aura above the parapet was out of sight, but Higomu was already moving. He took a line that crossed directly in front of the Imperial Architect's House. That building had no guards, but even so, the three of them were in plain view of the guards at the Judicial Palace. A few strides later, they were also in view of pairs of guards on two avenues.

The haloed head continued bobbing along the parapet, finally disappearing into a wing of the building when they were nearly to the base of the wall.

"She won't be back for a while," Higomu said of the guardian. "And the others know that no one can be climbing this wall because they just saw the patrol pass."

"I understand," said Shiko. "How do we get over the wall?"

"Zefi will throw me."

Shiko heard the frown in Zefi's response: "How?"

"Lace your hands together like this," Higomu said. "Good. Now when I step onto them, lift as fast and as high as you can."

"Very well."

Higomu took the climbing cord off Zefi's shoulder, dropped the coil onto the paving stones, and grasped one end in his hand.

"Ready?"

"Yes."

There was a flapping of linen as Higomu's pale shape flew into the sky. He struck the wall with a thump and a grunt, but Shiko knew he hung on, for the climbing cord remained suspended in air.

A moment later he whispered down, "Tie on the pliers."

Shiko did so, wrapping excess cord around the tool so the metal would not scrape against the stone wall. Higomu pulled the pliers up.

"Now Shiko," he said, letting the end of the climbing cord fall to the paving stones.

Hand over hand, Shiko climbed the cord. It would have been easier if Zefi had been holding the bottom for her. She wished she'd thought to ask. But the wall was not much higher than the climbing wall at Elder Badiki's training grounds. Shiko had enough strength to reach the top.

Higomu wrapped the middle of the cord around a railing and tossed both ends down to Zefi. A moment later, the Child of Labor joined them. Apparently, she was good at climbing rope.

The Red Palace wrapped around three sides of the rectangular garden below, with the parapet closing off the fourth side. Although the building presented a dark exterior, lamplight shone from many of the windows around the enclosed garden. Shiko hoped this would make it easier for them to see without making it easier for them to be seen.

Higomu sent Shiko and Zefi down into the garden first. He dropped the pliers down for Zefi. Then he unwrapped the climbing cord so that it only wrapped around the railing once. When he was most of the way down, he let go of one end of the cord and dropped down to join them. A moment later, the end he had released landed neatly on the ground at his feet.

Higomu re-coiled the rope. Zefi looked up at the parapet. Shiko considered what it would be like to retrace their path while accompanied by a glowing fugitive.

"How do we get back out?" Shiko asked.

"We have many ways out," Higomu said. "First, let's see if I can remember the way in."

He handed the rope to Zefi and set off into the garden, leading them to a wall formed by one wing of the palace. At its base was a line of small, ground-level windows. The glow of lamplight could be seen from the windows at either end of the line.

"Prison cells?" Shiko asked.

"Yes," Higomu whispered.

"How do we get him out?" Shiko asked. "Those windows look too small for him."

"Don't worry," Higomu said. "We just use the window to get in."

"And the pliers are to take the bars off?" Shiko asked.

"Exactly."

They went to the nearest window. Higomu murmured, "Check it."

Zefi knelt down and peered through the bars. "Yes! That is him!"

Higomu knelt beside her and peeked in as well. "Oh," he said, standing up. "That's a problem."

"What?" Shiko asked.

"They left a guard outside his door. I didn't plan for that."

CHAPTER 22
Change of Plans

SHIKO KNELT in the dusty rain gutter and peered through the bars of the basement window. The man sprawled across the bed built into the wall of the prison cell was lying face down. Shiko would not have recognized him. She was glad they had brought Zefi along.

Three walls of the cell were of stone. The fourth was a wall of iron bars, which allowed light to pass into the cell from a ceiling lamp hanging in the hallway outside. The aura of the guard under the lamp was a faint silvery glow, barely discernible in the lamplight. The face-down man's aura was a brown so dark that it actually drained light from his cell.

What made Zefi so certain of the forlorn figure's identity? In the light of the burning olive oil, his gown did not look as red as it had in the House of the Four Wrens. His white skin and long black hair could be seen on half the men in Dupho. Yet Zefi knew he was the artificer, and Shiko believed her.

At first glance, it appeared that Kittiwake was asleep, yet something about his breathing and the attitude of his limbs suggested to Shiko that he was not. He had the air of an exhausted man lying where his body had fallen, too miserable to make himself comfortable enough to sleep.

The guard was standing where he could see every corner of the cell, but he faced down the hallway, as though watching for something that might come from the other end. Possibly, he was simply watching Kittiwake's movements out of the corner of his eye while politely appearing to respect the prisoner's privacy.

The grate over the window was held in place by two bolts.

With the pliers, the grate would be easy to remove; the trick was to remove it without the guard noticing. The bored guard might not see the grate's disappearance from a shadowy corner at the top of the back wall, but the arched stone cell was the kind of place that would propagate echoes.

Higomu pressed Shiko's shoulder and indicated they should move away from the window so they could talk.

He spoke first to the Child of Labor. "Zefi, the window grate has two bolts holding it on. Understand?"

Zefi nodded.

"I think you are strong enough to twist them with your bare hands."

Zefi thought about it, then nodded once.

"When the guard leaves, I want you to twist those bolts and remove the grate. Shiko, you will drop into the cell and unlock the door."

"Will the guard leave?" Shiko asked.

"I predict he will."

Higomu took the pliers and walked away from them along the wall, fading into the darkness. Shiko turned her attention back to the guard, waiting to see how Higomu would make him leave.

She did not have to wait long. Higomu wrenched around one of the bolts on a window grate, and the faint sound echoed through the subterranean hallway. The guard's silver aura shaded toward blue. Shiko guessed he had heard but had not identified the meaning of the sound. Higomu wrenched the other bolt loose.

Zefi knelt down to watch, too, her face close enough that it brushed Shiko's curls.

Higomu removed the grate with a scrape and a clank. Shiko even heard his feet land in the cell. Sound traveled well in that basement.

Color seeped into the guard's aura until it took on the hue of glassy ocean waves in a light breeze on a partly cloudy day. "Who goes there?" he asked. It was a question, not a challenge.

The reply drifted down the hallway: "Darkheart."

"Show yourself!" the guard said, his aura flashing to yellow as he lifted his spear.

"I would gladly show myself," said Higomu, "if you would be so kind as to unlock my cell."

Zefi put her hands on the bolts.

The guard advanced up the hallway.

Zefi twisted, and the bolts were loose. She lifted the grate away from the window.

The narrow opening offered Shiko no dignified way to enter the building. She decided to go in head first.

"Catch me," she whispered to Kittiwake, who, whether he had been asleep or not, was now lying on his side looking up at her.

Voices echoed from the hallway:

"How did you get in there?" the guard demanded.

"Magic," replied Higomu.

The morose artificer made no move to aid Shiko. Zefi, however, gave her a push from behind. As Shiko's bruised hips popped free of the window, she pushed off the wall and flipped to land on her feet in the middle of Kittiwake's cell.

A purple light seeped into Kittiwake's dark aura, but he did not rise from his bed. She hoped he would follow her. She did not think she could drag him.

Shiko turned her attention to the cell door. Reaching inside her chiton, she found her pry levers. These tools were only useful on the largest, crudest locks. Elder Badiki had recommended them as being especially useful in Dupho.

"So will you let me out?" Higomu asked as Shiko approached the cell door.

"No. No, I don't think I should do that," the guard replied.

He was out of sight. Shiko hoped he would not see her arms snaking out through the bars, reaching up to probe inside the locking mechanism with the pry levers. This lever fit in here. That lever found the tooth there. No. There. Lift the tooth out of the catch. Slide the bar like so, and ...

Click.

"Hey, where are you going?" Higomu demanded.

Shiko pushed open the door and stared up at the advancing guard. Advantages: confusion and surprise. Assets: two pry levers. Allies: one woman on the other side of the wall, one man trapped in a prison cell, and one man free but too stupefied to move. Shiko would have preferred to be the armored giant with the spear.

"Curls!" the guard exclaimed.   .

Shiko threw a pry lever at his face. The pain in her shoulder spoiled her aim, but the action had the desired effect: The guard raised an arm to ward off the flying tool and in so doing shifted his spear out of line. Shiko was already charging, deflecting the spear point with her other pry lever. As the guard dropped into his defensive stance, Shiko was flying through the air. She struck his thigh with both feet.

But the guard's stance was firm. Shiko bounced off and landed sitting on the floor in front of him.

The guard leapt back to put Shiko once more beyond his spear point. Shiko rose to a low crouch, hoping to provide only a small target. From the cell behind the guard, a pale hand flicked out and scattered an arc of tiny brass balls on the stone floor.

Ah.

Shiko shifted to the side. The guard pivoted to face her.

Shiko feinted, drawing the spear off line. She shifted in to catch the shaft on her pry lever. The guard stepped back to disengage, and his foot slipped on the tiny brass balls.

Higomu grabbed the foot and yanked it through the bars of his cell. As the guard's body hit the floor, Shiko sprang onto his spear, pinning his hand to the ground.

"Well done," said Higomu. " 'Curls.' "

Shiko could hear the grin in his voice, but she did not dare take her eyes from the man below her. She held the advantage, but it seemed that any move she made would release him. Shiko was mistaken, however.

"You can take his spear," Higomu said. "I do not think he will object."

In truth, the green-faced man's eyes were wide, as though Shiko were holding a knife to his throat. Puzzled, she asked him, "Will you let me have—?"

"Yes!" he squeaked.

Shiko stepped off and swept the spear from his limp fingers.

"You see?" said Higomu. "They can be cooperative. Now, Shiko, would you unlock my door?"

Shiko allowed herself to take her eyes from the suddenly compliant guard and saw that Higomu was holding the foot at an intriguing angle. Possibly, this angle was causing the guard pain, but more importantly—as Shiko knew from her training—it caused the guard to think about the *promise* of pain, which made sudden movement undesirable.

As Shiko moved to collect her thrown pry lever, she heard Kittiwake exclaim, "Zefi!"

"Quiet," the giant said gently. "We are here to save you."

"Oh, Zefi, save yourself! There is no hope for me."

"There is hope," the Child of Labor insisted. "I hope."

"I had hoped he would be a bit quieter," Higomu mumbled as Shiko began working on the lock.

"Zefi, my soul is lost," Kittiwake said. "And my hands are crippled."

Zefi gasped. "What happened?"

Shiko raised the catch and pushed ... just there. *Click.*

"It was my punishment," Kittiwake said. "For refusing to use the powers the demon gave me."

"Good work," murmured Higomu. "Now can you hold him in a wrist lock?"

Shiko nodded. She slipped her tools back into the belt inside her chiton, then picked up the guard's wrist. He looked at her with concern. She gave him an apologetic shrug.

Shiko twisted his hand, bent his wrist, and thus assumed control of the prisoner. Higomu eased the guard's leg out of the bars so that he could open the cell door.

"Kittiwake," Zefi said. "You must believe. You must trust them. Knowledge has sent them to save you."

Shiko wondered if that were true. She considered the lava rock pendant resting against her skin. They were on a mission for the Goddess and they had asked for her blessing, but Shiko didn't pretend she was guided by divine wisdom. Knowledge wanted people to be wise enough to make the right decisions on their own.

Kittiwake's voice echoed down the hallway, "Zefi, I— How can I be saved after what I have done?"

Once out of the cell, Higomu took the guard's dagger and used it to slice the leather hem off the skirt of the guard's gown. He cut the leather into two strips. Then he removed three handkerchiefs from the interior of his chiton.

"Please accept these samples from Long Creek Linen," he said, stuffing the handkerchiefs into the guard's mouth.

After tying one of the strips of leather as a gag, he took the wrist lock from Shiko and persuaded the guard to stand up.

"Higomu will free you," promised Zefi's voice at the end of the hall. "And I will save you. Trust him. Trust me."

"Oh, Zefi."

Higomu indicated that Shiko should use the remaining strip of leather to bind the guard's wrists. She did so, as tightly as she could.

Satisfied, Higomu released the guard and used the guard's spear to encourage him to step inside the cell.

"Can you lock it?" he asked, once the gagged guard was inside.

Shiko nodded.

It took only a moment to slide the locking bar back into place. The Red Palace locks were amazingly simple.

The prison hallway was lit on both ends, with darkness in between. The stairs at the far end presumably led to the upper floors of the Red Palace, but Shiko wondered about the stairs at Kittiwake's end. They led down to a small landing and a closed wooden door.

Shiko followed Higomu into Kittiwake's cell. Even without the grate, the window was too narrow for Kittiwake's body, but Zefi had managed to squeeze her arm through. Kittiwake was holding her giant brown hand.

"I realize we said we would come for you tomorrow," Higomu said, "but under the circumstances, I thought you might have changed your mind already. Would you like to come with us now?"

Kittiwake nodded. Zefi gave his hand a final squeeze and withdrew her arm from the narrow window.

"Shiko," Higomu said, "you will take Kittiwake through the door at the bottom of those stairs." He nodded toward the mysterious stairsteps just outside Kittiwake's cell. "We will meet at the bathhouse on the Temple Plaza."

"And Zefi?" Kittiwake asked.

"Zefi and I will leave the way we came in. Do not worry. We are quite competent."

"How will Shiko and I get—?"

But Kittiwake was interrupted by the march of sandaled feet coming down the stairs at the opposite end of the hallway.

CHAPTER 23

The Sewers of Dupho

SHIKO TUGGED at the artificer's gown, but he insisted on standing in the lamplight to call up to the narrow window, "Zefi, be brave!"

"I will," she promised. "Please go."

With a heavy sigh, the artificer turned and allowed Shiko to lead him to the stairs. Higomu, still holding the guard's spear, stepped into the cell and closed the door. Shiko and Kittiwake reached the bottom of the stairwell just as the marching stopped. Voices echoed from the opposite end of the subterranean hallway:

"Captain? I thought you said he was under guard."

"He was. I thought my orders were clear."

The steps of sandaled feet resumed, but at a quicker pace.

From the landing at the bottom, Kittiwake and Shiko could not see the rapid approach of the soldiers. This was good, Shiko thought, because it meant that the soldiers could not see them … unless they noticed Kittiwake's bright green halo.

The door was locked, but the lock looked simple enough. Shiko pulled out her pry levers and began to feel around inside it. She had eighteen tools in her belt, and every lock in Dupho could be opened with a pair of pry levers! This one was even simpler than the cell doors. Just slide the—

Shiko jumped as something wooden slapped against the floor above.

"Hurry!" Kittiwake said. "Can't you open it?"

Shiko did not take time to reply. Now where was—? Ah. There. *Click.*

Shiko ushered Kittiwake through the door. She followed

him and pulled the door shut behind herself. They stood at the top step of a stairway in an unlit passage only as wide as the door. Although the light of Kittiwake's halo did not reveal much of the stairway, Shiko could at least examine the door's label, which spelled out *Red Palace*. On this side, the door could be locked simply by turning a handle. Shiko did so, and the bolt inside the door clicked back into place.

It seems we are safe for the moment, she thought. *Unless they have a key.*

Voices on the other side began speaking excitedly.

"We should keep moving," Shiko murmured.

Kittiwake nodded.

Where was she? The sign on the door was not helpful. Shiko took the lead down the stairs, wondering what they had been built for. An escape route for the first Theocratic Emperor? A passage to an underground library of secret military texts? The locking mechanism implied that this stairway led someplace that was supposed to be difficult to get to, but easy to get out of.

"It's locked!" exclaimed a voice on the other side of the door. A fist began pounding against the wood. "Open up!"

"It seems they don't have a key," Shiko observed.

"Good," murmured the artificer.

Shiko had no idea why the soldier on the other side of the door thought that pounding on it would persuade her to open it for him. She followed the twist of the stairway to the bottom. It was damper down here and it smelled like water. And a bit like sewage.

"Oh," she said. "We're in the sewer!"

"Yes," said Kittiwake. "How will we get out?"

"That might not be so difficult," Shiko said. "Everything seems to be well marked."

Kittiwake's halo illuminated a sign at the bottom of the stairs that read, *Red Palace Exit.*

"I can see why," Kittiwake said. "If I worked here, I would want to know the way out, too."

They stepped out of the narrow passage into a large space that sounded like it had a river running through it. On one side of the passage exit, the wall was labeled, *Empire's Scope*. On the other side, the wall was labeled, *Army Victorious*. Shiko recognized these as names of two districts near the Imperial Plaza.

"Which district is closer to the Temple Plaza?" she asked.

"Army Victorious," Kittiwake said. "Do you think the sewer will take us to the Temple Plaza bathhouse?"

"It probably leads where we want to go, or else Higomu would not have sent us this way," Shiko said. "And we should not stand here waiting for the soldiers to find a key."

"Very well," Kittiwake said. "Lead the way."

"You should go first," Shiko said. "That way I won't block your light."

In truth, his head was high enough above hers that they both would have been able to see quite easily, but Shiko thought it unwise to turn her back on a demon worshipper.

Their path was a narrow walkway that formed an artificial stone bank for an underground river. Tazhubo's *History of Dupho* said that it was actually the outflow of a large irrigation canal that watered fields upstream. As it approached the city, the canal descended below street level and flowed underground to become the city sewer.

It didn't smell much worse than the Redwood River did in Hicho. Of course, it didn't smell nearly as nice as the Redwood River smelled near the village where Shiko had grown up, but cities were cities. Sewage had to go somewhere.

High water had stained the stone wall beside the walkway, reaching levels that made Shiko glad she had come to Dupho at the start of the dry season. Arches supported the ceiling, above which was, presumably, the avenue that led to the Temple of Beauty.

"I think we are going upstream," Kittiwake said.

"Yes," Shiko said.

"Good," said Kittiwake. "The water should run from the aqueduct to the bay, and the Temple is near the aqueduct."

"Yes," agreed Shiko.

He was calming down and thinking logically. That would have been a good thing, if getting him safely to the Temple Plaza Baths had been Shiko's only concern. She touched her sacred stone pendant and prayed for protection against his demon. The artificer in person seemed as innocuous as the artificer in the notebooks, but Shiko knew that people with affinity for Emotion were good at controlling which aspects of themselves they presented to the world. It would be safest to assume she was being misled—either by Kittiwake or by the demon with whom he had aligned his soul.

But she did not allow this to frighten her. From the way he moved, Shiko could tell he was not trained in combat. Furthermore, he would have difficulty using his size advantage against her on the narrow walkway. As long as she remained vigilant, she could handle whatever threat he posed. And if the situation became desperate, she believed she could escape by out-swimming him.

Shiko decided this was a good time to ask him a few questions. That would keep him off balance, and perhaps she could learn something.

She said, "Zefi says you gave your soul to a demon."

The artificer's back stiffened, but he hesitated for only half a step.

"I did," he admitted.

"Why?" Shiko asked.

"It was a mistake."

And not a small one! she thought. Aloud, she said only, "I see."

"You despise me for what I have done," he said.

Yes, she thought. "I'm sure you had a good reason," she said.

"It seemed good," he said. "I thought I would gain the power to protect Zefi."

"And did you?"

"No. Or yes. I don't know. Glamour gave me power, but I

could not use it."

"Why not?"

Kittiwake shrugged. "It seems I am not a killer."

A demon worshipper with moral scruples? Evil or not, he was certainly a fool.

"Zefi believes a priest can save me," Kittiwake said.

"Yes," said Shiko.

"Do you think she is right?" Kittiwake asked.

"I don't know," Shiko said. "Perhaps it matters more what you believe."

"I am not sure I am worth saving now."

"What do you mean?"

Kittiwake turned on her, his halo flaring yellow. "Look! Look at these withered limbs! Tell me how I am to practice my craft with these!"

Shiko stared warily at his knobby knuckles and wrinkled white fingers.

"What happened?" she asked.

"I have been punished because I would not kill for her." Kittiwake nearly spat the words, but Shiko could not tell at whom he was directing his contempt.

"What if you had a chance to regain her favor?" Shiko asked. "Would she heal you?"

"Why are you tempting me?"

"I'm not," Shiko said. "But I want to know why your hands are more important to you than your soul."

"My hands *are* my soul!" His red eyes stared into hers. "If Glamour offers to heal them, I don't know what I will do. You must find a priest who can save me from that decision. And if you cannot—"

Kittiwake's gaze snapped up in alarm. Shiko turned to see what was in the darkness behind her.

She saw a silver light, unidentifiable without context. It was small enough to be a candle flame on a table, or a single star in an empty sky, or a glowing insect hovering just out of reach. But it had to be a soldier.

Another light appeared and merged with the first. Then another. Shiko deduced they were several soldiers from the Red Palace, stepping onto the perfectly straight walkway and advancing along the canal single file.

Ah, but how would they know which way to advance? That was Shiko's advantage: She knew where she was told to meet Higomu. The soldiers were just as likely to choose the wrong direction … if Kittiwake were not glowing bright green.

"Run," Shiko said.

The artificer ran, but he ran as though his legs were too long for him. Shiko could keep up, and she suspected that was not good. Could they stay ahead of the soldiers long enough to reach the bathhouse? And if they could, was it a good idea to lead the soldiers straight to Higomu?

Kittiwake's aura was glowing brightly enough to illuminate a stone bridge that spanned the sewer canal. Shiko grabbed Kittiwake's flapping gown and directed him to turn there. As they crossed the bridge, Shiko took the opportunity to view their pursuers from an angle: six soldiers, carrying spears. The spears might slow them down. If she and Kittiwake could get out, perhaps they could escape the soldiers in the twisting side streets of the city.

The soldiers had come to a bridge of their own. Three glowing heads bobbed across the darkness over the river. Ah, that was clever. Now the soldiers had pursuit teams on either bank.

At the other end of the bridge, Kittiwake turned upstream. Shiko followed.

Kittiwake's blazing aura illuminated a gap in the wall ahead—a tributary of the sewage canal. The walkway stopped at the point where the influx met the canal, but continued on the other side. A wooden plank spanning the tributary allowed Kittiwake to cross.

"Turn here!" Shiko shouted, when she saw that the tributary had its own walkway.

Kittiwake obediently turned up the dark passageway,

illuminating it as he went. Shiko followed him as soon as she had crossed the plank.

They were forced to slow down then: Kittiwake, because the tributary's walkway was so narrow that he could not sprint; Shiko, because she was behind him. That would give the guards a chance to close the distance, but the narrow walkway would slow them down, too. She just needed to find a way out before the guards caught up.

A side passage labeled *Sandscape Courtyard* offered hope. When Kittiwake ran past it, Shiko called him back. She led the way.

The passage seemed to be neither a tributary nor a walkway. Well, perhaps it was both. Stains on the walls indicated that much water had flowed through it in the past, but Shiko's bare feet were not splashing in water now. Perhaps it was for storm drainage.

She slowed the pace to a swift walk, mostly because she did not want to miss any indication of an exit, but also because Kittiwake was breathing heavily. In a short while, they came to a wall.

"Dead end?" Kittiwake asked.

Shiko looked up at the storm grate. "Yes," she said.

"We're doomed."

"Hold on to that feeling, Kittiwake. Think thoughts as dark as you can."

His face flashed blue—puzzled. Then: "Ah, I see. Very well. I shall do my best."

Actually, with some climbing tools and possibly a crow bar, Shiko might have been able to pop the storm grate loose and escape. But she doubted they had the time to accomplish any such thing. Best to let Kittiwake think that their only hope lay in him holding his aura as dark as possible.

Her assessment of his abilities proved correct: Kittiwake had no trouble making himself melancholy.

Voices echoed in the distance. Perhaps the soldiers were debating. It would be difficult for the soldiers even to find the tributary, and more difficult to guess Shiko and Kittiwake had come down this side passage.

Whether by luck or by skill, they did find the tributary. A glowing head bobbed past the mouth of the passage. Then another. Kittiwake's aura gave the dimmest of green glows, but he regained control, and it winked out again.

A third soldier passed, then came back. The passage was short enough that Shiko could see the triangle painted on his cheek. He turned back and said, "Check this passage." Then he continued on, followed immediately by the fourth soldier.

The fifth stopped and illuminated the arched exit. Her spear point gleamed in her yellow-green aura. She peered at Shiko and Kittiwake's hiding place, then stepped back to read the *Sandscape Courtyard* sign. After a final glance in Shiko's direction, she turned and ran after her comrades.

Shiko waited for the sixth. The sound of footsteps faded away.

"How many did you count?" she whispered.

No reply.

"Kittiwake?"

He was still beside her. She could hear his breathing.

Well, whether five or six, it was unwise to wait for the others to come back. She put a hand on what turned out to be the artificer's knee.

"Kittiwake, we have tricked them. They are gone. Let's go meet up with Zefi."

"Zefi?"

"That's it," Shiko said. "Yes. Zefi."

Kittiwake's aura revealed itself as a silver glow. At its center, the artificer was wiping his eyes. Shiko slipped past him and led the way quietly back to the mouth of the passage.

"Stay here a moment," she warned him.

Shiko stepped out, feeling the edge of the narrow walkway with her toes. The soldiers had continued up the tributary, but she could not count them, as they were all in a line. However, a halo downstream told her that at least one soldier had been left behind to guard against exactly the sort of thing that Shiko had planned to do.

Shiko decided they would have to do it anyway.

"Wait for my signal," she whispered. "Then follow me back the way we came."

The artificer nodded.

Shiko stepped out of the side passage and advanced slowly toward the sentinel, keeping one hand on the wall so that she would not misstep into the flowing tributary. He could not see her—she was confident of this, for she could not even see her hand on the wall—but he was staring at her intently. Shiko glanced over her shoulder and realized that Kittiwake's aura was faintly illuminating the walkway at the mouth of the passage where he hid. Could the soldier see that faint light? Was it backlighting Shiko?

She would not give the soldier time to puzzle out what he saw. She advanced rapidly, trusting her feet to go straight and keep her on the walkway. It was no narrower than Elder Badiki's balance beam.

The sentry's aura flared brightly. He crouched into a defensive stance, yelling, "It's Curls!"

Could she defeat him? Shiko decided to wager on it.

"Now, Kittiwake!" she yelled. "Come!"

The soldier stood on the wooden plank that spanned the tributary. That gave her an opening she could have used to dart past him and run upstream toward the Temple Plaza, but she needed to make an escape for Kittiwake, too.

Why wasn't he right behind her?

She glanced back at Kittiwake's green halo, and the soldier shifted to block her escape.

"Kittiwake, trust me!" she yelled. "This way. Now!"

Shiko feigned a charge at the soldier, pushed her foot off the wall, and leapt onto the plank, landing in a low crouch to keep her balance. The soldier pivoted to keep his spear pointed at her, but he also had to dart glances at the slowly advancing green halo of Kittiwake. If she could only—

Dropping his spear beside him, the soldier knelt and seized the plank. He no longer stood on it, but Shiko did. His move caught Shiko's mind entirely by surprise, but her legs were already moving in to take advantage of the opportunity. As he lifted the board, Shiko's foot snapped up and caught him under the chin. The board slipped from his fingers and landed back in its setting. Since his head was still accessible to her feet, Shiko struck him with a roundhouse to the jaw, which twisted his helmet askew and knocked him off balance. With a slide step, Shiko inserted herself between the soldier and the wall, from which position she was able to give him the push that toppled him into the river.

The soldier's arm flailed out and caught the wooden plank. That was fine with Shiko. She had no wish to drown the man. She looked up triumphantly at Kittiwake and saw that he had chosen to wait until he was certain she had won.

"Hurry up!"

The soldier holding the plank made no move to pull himself out. Instead, he watched Shiko with a wary eye. Shiko picked up his spear to hold him at bay.

Kittiwake did hurry up, but the five soldiers behind him had closed the distance considerably by the time the artificer was at Shiko's side. Not wanting to try her luck against five, Shiko pitched the spear into the water and bolted along the walkway toward the Temple Plaza, trying to stay at the very edge of the light from Kittiwake's halo so that he would be encouraged to run as hard as he could to keep up.

Kittiwake managed a prolonged burst of speed, but too soon his breathing was coming in gasps and his sandals were slapping the stones in a haggard rhythm.

"We're almost there," Shiko called to him.

The soldiers were closing the distance.

They passed a sign reading *Desert Bloom*. It was a district name, but Shiko wasn't sure what that meant.

Up ahead was a side passage with another sign. Shiko stopped underneath it, waiting for her lamp to catch up. Ah!

The sign said *Baths*.

"Zefi," she said, pointing up the narrow passageway.

Kittiwake nodded and followed her.

Higomu will be able to handle this, Shiko thought. *I just have to get us out of here.*

The stone felt cold on Shiko's bare feet as she sprinted along the corridor lit by the green glow of Kittiwake. Ahead, the passage ended in a square chamber, slightly wider than the corridor. Shiko hoped there would be a door somewhere; she hoped she had understood Higomu's plan.

Shiko could see no door in the square chamber, and its walls were higher than she had been expecting. Rungs were set into the far wall, which glistened in the light of Kittiwake's halo.

Shiko looked up. There was a wooden door—or something like a door—high above.

"We have to climb," Shiko told him. "Just one climb, and then you can rest. Higomu will take care of us."

Please let Higomu be there, she prayed. But the prayer was illogical. He was either there or he was not, and not even her goddess could change that now.

CHAPTER 24

Evening Stroll

ZEFI CROUCHED in the Red Palace garden and peered through the tiny window at Kittiwake standing forlorn in the open doorway of his cell. Shiko tugged at his disheveled red gown, urging him to escape, but he insisted on calling out, "Zefi, be brave!"

"I will," she promised. "Please go."

With a wistful sigh, Kittiwake turned and followed the little Thinker Woman out into the hallway.

Higomu, holding a spear twice his height, stepped into the cell and closed the door. A moment later, voices echoed through the basement:

"Captain? I thought you said he was under guard."

"He was. I thought my orders were clear."

As the sound of sandaled feet advanced briskly down the hall, Higomu's black eyes fixed Zefi with an unreadable stare. He held up a hand and cocked his head, judging the sound of the soldiers' approach. After waiting a moment, Higomu nodded in satisfaction and raised the spear.

Zefi had never handled a spear, but she thought the weapon looked unwieldy in the Thinker Man's hands. He was holding it near the end. And why was he pointing the spear at her?

Higomu charged. Zefi jumped back. A moment later, a pale hand slapped the base of the window.

"Zefi!" Higomu hissed.

Zefi peeked in just in time to see the wooden shaft of the spear slap against the cell's stone floor. Somehow, Higomu had used it to bring himself up to the level of the window. Barely.

Zefi grasped Higomu's tiny forearm and helped him climb out.

"Thank you," Higomu said. "Step over here and hold still a moment."

Zefi did so, crouching beside Higomu with her back against the wall of the prison. The Red Palace, so dark from the other side of the parapet, had a dozen lit windows looking out onto the garden in which they hid. She hoped no one could see them. At least they were not within sight of the soldiers who were now shouting in the basement.

"Private Shrimp!"

"What happened to you, soldier?"

"Captain, I thought I saw someone at the sewer access door."

"Check it."

Footsteps continued down the hallway. Coincidentally, a soldier appeared on the parapet above the garden. Zefi understood why Higomu had removed the climbing cord on his way down.

"The artificer is gone," called a voice from Kittiwake's cell. "He used a spear to go out the window."

The reply came from farther down the hall: "Darkheart!"

"Check the access door!" someone shouted.

"I wish they'd be quieter," Higomu said. "They are attracting too much attention."

The soldier on the parapet had stopped her patrol and was now looking down on the garden, glowing blue with curiosity. Did she see Zefi and Higomu hiding? No. She wasn't shouting. Yet. Zefi held herself rigidly still.

"It's locked!"

A fist began pounding on a wooden door.

"Open up!"

"The artificer couldn't have fit through that window," said someone inside Kittiwake's cell.

"No, but Darkheart could," said another voice.

"I saw them go out through the access door."

"Well, now the entire palace will be looking for us," Higomu said as the guard on the parapet ran back inside.

"She saw us?" Zefi asked.

"No," said Higomu. "But she heard them."

"Squad: Form ranks!" a woman commanded.

Feet began shuffling.

"Captain Faith, take your squad and search the garden," a man commanded. "Darkheart will not escape us."

"Yes, Commander. Squad: Double time!"

Zefi said a prayer to Lashrefi, goddess of luck.

"Let's move," Higomu said. "Stay low."

On all fours, he scuttled like a spider down the path and through a hedge. Zefi followed, crawling like a turtle.

Staying low is easy enough for you, little man, she thought.

Trying not to puff too loudly, Zefi struggled around a corner and saw … no one. She was alone in the garden.

A pale hand popped out of a hedge and beckoned her to follow. Zefi squeezed between bushes, tearing her skirt.

Soldiers entered the garden. "Spread out," a woman's voice said, echoing off the palace walls. "If you find Darkheart, call for support."

Soldiers began walking cautiously along the garden paths, poking their spears into bushes.

"We can go over the wall if we run," Zefi said.

"No good," Higomu replied.

Glowing helmets began to array themselves along the parapet.

"We'll stay put," Higomu said.

Zefi crouched in the darkness, peering out through branches of juniper. Here and there, glowing orbs bobbed about the garden. The soldiers seemed to have no system for their search. The greenish tinge of their auras indicated that they had no enthusiasm for it, either. It was as though each was hoping it would be someone else who found "Darkheart".

She wondered about the moniker. Higomu was a dark-eyed man, but was he truly dark-hearted? He would seem cold and impassive to Decorator People, but he was a Thinker Man. He could not let his heart get in the way of doing his job.

His job, of course, was very dark, requiring him to be competent, dangerous, and merciless. Higomu had knowledge of demons. But he used that knowledge to fight them. So perhaps his heart was dark, but Zefi believed it was in the right place.

A voice called, "Shall I fetch some lamps, Captain?"

"No, don't bother," the woman in charge replied with disgust. "He has escaped us. Form ranks!"

The bobbing lights moved swiftly through the garden, returning to the doorway from which they had come.

"Return to your regular duties," the captain said. "Dismissed."

"Fox won't be happy when he finds out his new captain gave up so easily," Higomu said.

"How know you that she is new?" Zefi asked.

Higomu said, "She wasn't here the last time I broke out of prison."

Zefi looked at the glowing heads lining the parapet. They did not seem to be going anywhere.

"How break we the prison this time?" she asked.

"There is a flight of stairs accessible from the corner of the courtyard," Higomu said, waving a ghostly hand to indicate the direction. "We can take those stairs to the roof." He looked at her shoulder. "Good. You still have the climbing cord."

"Yes," Zefi said.

Higomu nodded. "When I double the cord for you, it might be too short. But I'm sure we can figure out some way to get you down."

Zefi hoped so.

Staying low to avoid discovery by the soldiers on the parapet, Zefi and Higomu crept toward the corner of the garden. It was an open area, about ten paces square, with two dark doorways, one in each of the walls that met at the corner. A shaft of light streamed out of a second-floor window and fell across the paving stones. Higomu and Zefi paused in a juniper hedge behind pots of geraniums lining this exposed space.

"That's the doorway to the stairs," Higomu said.

Zefi nodded. "We go now?" she asked.

Higomu shook his head. "No. I don't like this. That captain gave up far too easily. I think she was sent to pin us down in the garden while Commander Fox set an ambush here in the stairwell."

"So what now?"

"You wait here. I'll scout the stairs and see if they are safe."

"And if they are not safe?"

"Then I'll come back."

Zefi didn't understand much about ambushes, but it seemed to her that if there was an ambush on the stairs, it would be best to not go there. What if Higomu didn't come back? She could only stay hidden for so long. Not knowing whether to put herself in the hands of Lashrefi, goddess of luck, or Kashram, god of the lith, Zefi decided to say a prayer to each of them.

Barely discernible by his dark hair and pale limbs, Higomu passed between the potted geraniums, skirted around the rectangle of light on the paving stones, and ducked into one of the dark doorways. He was gone but a few moments when something flashed from the well-lit window above and struck the other wall of the corner. The sound was followed by the familiar tinkle of metal on paving stones. Someone had thrown a coin out the window.

Six guards with hostile golden auras stepped out of the other doorway and formed an arc with their spears pointed at the doorway Higomu was exploring. Zefi heard the sound of sandals running down stairs.

Barefooted Higomu emerged from the stairwell and stopped at the sight of the six spears leveled at his face. Illuminated by the yellow light of the soldiers' auras, he turned to the window on the upper floor and said, "Using a lamp to camouflage your aura was very clever, Fox."

As more soldiers appeared in the doorway behind Higomu, a man with a chevron on his forehead stepped into view at the window above. He said, "Thank you, Darkheart. I knew you would try to escape up those stairs."

Higomu nodded. "Yes, and I knew you had posted guards at the top."

These guards were now at the bottom, arraying themselves to cut off Higomu's possibility of retreat.

"Forgive me," Commander Fox said, "but that seems unlikely. Had you known, you would not have let my guardians-of-the-peace surround you."

"Ah," said Higomu, looking at Zefi, "but it is I who have your guardians surrounded."

Auras flickered. He had confused them. He had confused Zefi, too, but she knew that was a cue to do something.

She picked up a flower pot, lifted it above her head, and shouted, "Rah!"

Startled soldiers turned, and that was enough for Higomu. He dodged between the soldiers and sprinted past Zefi. Her bluff had worked. But it had been only a bluff. Zefi realized she would need to run, too. She turned and raced after Higomu's flashing white legs.

"Throw the pot," Higomu advised when she caught up to him.

Zefi turned and tossed the pot to their closest pursuer. The clang of terra cotta on iron breastplate told her she had hit the mark.

A spear flew past Zefi's ear, soared over Higomu's head, passed through the doorway from which the captain had led the feigned search, and skidded along the tiled floor. Higomu followed the spear into the building. Zefi followed Higomu.

Higomu led Zefi around a corner, up half a flight of stairs, and down a hallway painted with rows and rows of marching soldiers. At the end of the hallway stood a lone guardian, armed with a spear, looking very uncertain as Higomu came rushing toward him.

"Halt!" the soldier tried to shout, but the swift little Thinker Man had already sidestepped the spear and driven his fist up the soldier's skirt. The soldier fell to his knees.

Zefi ran past the unfortunate man and followed Higomu into a domed room ringed with three stories of balconies. Every exit from the room was guarded by a soldier with a spear. Except the biggest exit, leading to the plaza. That one was guarded by six soldiers, including a raven-haired woman with a line-dot-line symbol painted on her black forehead. Higomu ran toward the six soldiers without hesitation. Zefi followed, hoping that was what Higomu expected of her.

Higomu leapt and slashed the air with a white handkerchief, spreading his arms out like wings. The spearmen on either side of his chosen gap recoiled, making space for a suddenly smaller Higomu to slip through.

Zefi skidded to a stop in front of the startled spearmen.

"After him!" the captain shouted to her men. She was already leading the way out the door. Four of the five jumped to obey, leaving one behind to hold Zefi at spear point, while those who had been assigned to guard the internal passageways closed in behind her.

Hoping she could intimidate her foe, Zefi seized a big vase and lifted it off the floor. It was heavy. If she threw it at the guard between her and the doorway, she would have to be very careful, or else it could hurt him.

To her relief, the guard dropped his spear. To her surprise, more spears clattered to the floor behind her.

The guard stepped aside, offering her a clear path to the exit. "We surrender," he said. "We will let you go. Just … please put the vase down."

Puzzled, Zefi gently set the vase on the floor and jogged out of the Red Palace.

A soldier with a dark purple halo was lying on the steps holding his knee and screaming in pain. Another knelt beside him—not to offer aid, but to take the fallen soldier's spear. Apparently he had thrown his own. In the plaza at the bottom of the steps, Higomu was lit by the auras of his three remaining opponents. He had stopped to face them.

Zefi ran down the steps, avoiding the soldier who was trying to extricate the spear from under his fallen comrade. She growled a challenge that she hoped would distract the soldiers enough to give Higomu an advantage. At the sight of Zefi, however, Higomu decided he no longer needed to fight. He turned and sprinted off, but not directly away. Instead, he chose an oblique course that allowed Zefi to run after him without getting closer to the guardians who pursued him. In fact, she and the three soldiers were now on a parallel course in their pursuit of the speedy Thinker Man.

Higomu zigzagged, as though dodging around invisible obstacles. This allowed Zefi to gain ground. The two guardians and their captain, running in slick sandals, carrying awkward spears, were not catching up.

As the captain ran, with her black ringlets bouncing against the nape of her neck, an orange tinge of hatred seeped into her aura. She shouted, "On my signal: Loose spears."

The soldiers' pace slowed. The captain and her men drew their spear arms back.

"Now!" she shouted.

Three spears flew into the air. Higomu planted his foot and changed direction again. Two spears landed in the vicinity of where he had been going. One landed where he was.

Zefi heard him gasp. The spear had only grazed his heel, but Higomu stumbled to the ground.

As Zefi closed the distance, Higomu raised himself, putting no weight on his injured foot. He hopped on one pale leg toward the nearest spear.

"No more work today," Zefi said, scooping him up in her arms.

"I will do what must be done," Higomu said, through clenched teeth. But he made no move to escape her grasp.

Zefi kept running. "I will find a healer," she said.

"Kittiwake first," Higomu said.

"He can come, too," Zefi said. The healers at the Orphanage were priests.

She glanced over her shoulder. The soldiers were loping behind her, but they seemed to be more intent on retrieving their weapons than on catching up.

"Kittiwake is at the Temple Plaza," Higomu said.

Zefi nodded. She was already running down that avenue.

After a few hundred paces, Higomu suggested, "Take this street."

Zefi checked on the soldiers again. Their halos were distant now. She veered out of the avenue.

"Now slow down," Higomu suggested. "Running is loud, and you never know what you might run into."

Zefi obeyed, glad for a chance to catch her breath.

They had entered the Desert Bloom district. It was not a neighborhood Zefi knew well, but Higomu proved to have an intuition for the streets of Dupho. Sitting on her shoulders, he guided her around corners and down alleys until they arrived at the Temple Plaza.

The artwork was so well lit that Zefi could have been walking by moonlight. Life-sized statues of animals with noble intelligence gazed at her as she carried Higomu above the plaza. The statues of people, by contrast, were focused on their own tasks—a painter paused to consider his choice of color, a weaver drew her shuttle through her loom, a singer with closed eyes offered her song up to the heavens, a sculptor poised his hammer to strike a blow behind the ear of a rough-hewn shape which bore a clear resemblance to the finished marble cougar watching with curiosity from a rock nearby. This pair of sculptures had made Zefi laugh by day, but in the light of burning oil, the scene became too fascinating for any sentiment but reverence. This place was truly an homage to Swalethi.

Zefi carried Higomu toward the Temple Plaza Bath, which was adorned with murals of waterfalls cascading from mountain cliffs.

"Think you that they are here now?" she asked.

"I think it unlikely," Higomu said. "Unless they ran as hard as you did."

A glow illuminated the bathhouse's doorway. Higomu seized Zefi's arm and said, "Put me down!"

Zefi did so, quickly. Higomu adopted a casual stance beside her, seemingly on both legs.

A silver-haired couple, elegantly dressed, emerged from the bathhouse, walking hand in hand. It was not until they reached the base of the steps that they noticed Zefi standing in plain view.

The man's aura barely flickered. Waving an arm, he called, "Good evening!"

"Good evening," said Higomu from beside Zefi's knee.

The man murmured something to the woman. She nodded. They turned their steps toward Zefi and Higomu. The pink-haloed elderly couple seemed harmless, but how could Zefi explain what she and Higomu were doing here this late at night?

"Sight seeing?" the man asked.

"Yes," said Higomu. "I had heard that this plaza was even more beautiful at night, but I could not believe it until I saw it with my own eyes."

The silver-haired woman smiled.

"It is worth staying awake for," the man said, patting the woman's hand on his arm.

"Are foreigners allowed to see inside the bathhouse?" Higomu asked.

"Oh, yes," said the man. "You could even bathe there, if you wished. But not tonight. I fear we were tonight's final bathers."

"Oh?"

"Yes. The custodians will be cleaning it. They are letting the water out now."

Higomu hesitated only an instant before replying, "Ah. What a pity."

CHAPTER 25
The Flow

SHIKO CLIMBED THE LADDER set into the damp wall, grasping a metal rung with her injured arm and reaching for the next rung with her good arm. The ladder was offset from the wooden door, high in the wall above. This configuration presented a puzzle: Why was the door so high? Where were its hinges? Why was the wall beneath it damp?

Ah, the dampness explained all, she realized. It was not a door, but a spill gate. Then these rungs must lead to some sort of access hatch. At least, she hoped they did. It was too dark to tell.

Shiko looked down. Kittiwake was not following. The yellow glow in the passage was growing rapidly brighter.

"Surrender or die," a voice shouted.

"Spare us!" Kittiwake yelled. "Spare us! We surrender."

Shiko was certain she did not want to surrender—especially not now, with Higomu so close. She kept climbing.

"Private, bind his—" A creaking noise. "Oh no."

The wooden spill gate moved, and a spray of water arched overhead, flashing green in the light of the auras of the people below. The gate opened wider, and a gush of water caught Shiko by the shoulder, ripped her from the ladder, and slammed her onto the stone floor.

Arms and legs flailed against her body as she was washed down the passage. Realizing the flow was too strong for her to overcome, Shiko curled into a ball, covered her head, and focused on conserving her breath. She bounced and spun like a pinecone in a trout stream, but she knew the rush of bathwater would stop pummeling her once her body reached the underground river. She just needed to keep from being knocked senseless.

An iron helmet punched her in the back. Her body tumbled over it. Then suddenly she was free, ejected from the passage out into the flowing river.

As she extended her arms to pull herself to the surface, something heavy caught her chiton, pulling her down. Shiko loosened her belt, and the linen chiton pulled taut against her shoulders, popping open one of the pins. Shiko slipped her other shoulder free and kicked away. Her head broke the surface of the water.

She had no doubt she was in the main canal. The water was so deep that her feet could not touch the bottom. Her arms found only water on all sides. She could see a few green halos, but their light gave her no idea how far she might be from the sewer's subterranean walls.

The halos she saw were under water. Taking a deep breath, Shiko dove for the nearest one. The pain in her shoulder dulled to a warm ache and became, like the water, simply something she had to push against.

She swam down toward the glow, but the face itself was obscured by something—cloth, Shiko's discarded chiton, clutched in a white hand. The man's limbs flailed frantically. When his face emerged from behind the swirling cloth, she saw that he was wearing a helmet. Not Kittiwake, then.

Not Kittiwake, but she would not let him drown.

Shiko went to the surface to take a breath and to adjust her angle of attack. She knew, as did everyone from her village, that a panicked swimmer would lose all logic and thwart his or her own rescue. Those flailing arms could mean her death if she let the man grab her. Fortunately, desperation made him glow brightly, so she had a clear view of him as she dove.

An arm flashed out at Shiko. She caught it behind the wrist. The soldier used Shiko's grip to jerk her body closer to his. Shiko grabbed his dagger from his belt and kicked away out of reach. She waited until his gyrations put his back to her, then she frog-kicked after him to grab his armor just behind his shoulder. A few quick slices with the dagger were sufficient to cut the cords that laced breastplate to backplate. As the armor slid free, Shiko let go and ran her hand up the back of the soldier's neck to his helmet. It came off in her hand.

Shiko clutched a fistful of black hair and kicked upward. She released the dagger so she could pull with that arm. Their heads broke the surface, and the soldier began coughing.

He was no longer fighting her. His aura had dimmed, but the edge of the canal was just discernible at the outermost reach of his light. Shiko slipped an arm under his to keep his head above water. Wheeling her legs, she dragged him toward the walkway.

A cry that sounded like Kittiwake's drew her attention. Upstream, two helmetless halos were floating together. Neither was recognizable, but the white-faced man had black hair longer than what most soldiers wore. The other man was glowing so brightly that his white curls looked like orange flames consuming his head. He put a black hand in Kittiwake's face and forced him down into the water.

Should she go to Kittiwake's aid? The Academy had taught her how to reason out moral conundrums, but she did not have the time. The Order of the Lock had taught her to make decisions and accept the consequences. Shiko decided to rescue the stranger in her grasp.

She focused her gaze on the walkway, ignoring the struggle upstream. The man she was rescuing did little to help, being preoccupied with the work of clearing his lungs. At least he kept his halo bright enough for her to see the canal's edge.

When her free hand grasped the walkway, Shiko pivoted the soldier's body downstream. His aura brightened when his body brushed the edge, and he reached desperately for the artificial bank. His arm slapped the dry stone and held on. Shiko let go of him and pushed off the wall. His aura seemed to drift away as Shiko floated downstream.

Kittiwake next, she told herself, ignoring her need for rest.

She could see two halos beyond the soldier she had rescued, but the halos were blurry, no longer above water.

Shiko swam toward them, still slipping downstream from the man who clung to the walkway, but slowing her progress enough that the current brought the struggling men closer. One seemed to be a soldier who had lost his helmet. The other was most likely Kittiwake. Their shimmering auras illuminated a tangle of thrashing limbs. Separating the combatants would not be easy. She hoped a means of attack would present itself by the time the men came within reach.

She was startled when her heels struck solid wood. Something heavy slid along her back, forcing her down into the water. As her head passed underneath it, Shiko reached an arm over and grabbed hold.

She was clinging to a log that had been caught against two pillars of a canal bridge. The current was swift between the pillars, causing her legs to stick out behind her as she held the log, but at least it was easier than swimming. Shiko conserved her strength and waited for the two wrestling men.

For a moment, it looked as though their bodies would pass on either side of the pillar on Shiko's left. She hoped to grab Kittiwake as he passed and allow the soldier to be swept downstream. As she reached for Kittiwake's hair, his white hand flailed out of the water and caught the end of the log, just as the soldier's bare head collided with the pillar.

Kittiwake was swept under the log, but his hand did not let go. The end he held dipped into the water and the log popped loose to slip under the bridge. Kittiwake reached out desperately with his other hand and Shiko dove to escape him.

She came up to the sound of Kittiwake's coughs echoing through the canal. He had possession of the log and seemed able to keep himself above water for now. Shiko decided to see what she could do for the soldier who had hit his head.

Where was he? Kittiwake's green aura shimmered off the surface of the water, obscuring what might lie below. Shiko dove.

She saw nothing but a faint silver glow. Could that belong to the man who had been glowing sunset orange when he hit the pillar? How hard had he hit?

Shiko swam toward the light, but it seemed to get farther away. Perhaps the current had caught him, but how could—? No. The light was not diminishing because of distance. It was fading out.

Shiko kicked toward the light and then toward her memory of where the light had been, but her fingers found no trace of the man who had fought the artificer. Her search was brief. She had to go back up for breath. That was one she could not save.

Shiko popped back up. With her wet curls sticking to her temples, she floated in the darkness and tried to rest while treading water.

Kittiwake's voice echoed through the subterranean channel: "Shiko!"

She turned to see Kittiwake with his arms draped over the log, kicking toward her.

"I'm here!" she called.

"I know," he replied. His aura was rosy—affectionate? Perhaps that just meant he was glad to be alive.

"Grab the log," he offered. "Save your strength."

Apparently, he had used his affinity for elemental Emotion to find her in the darkness. He couldn't see her face nearly as well as he could see her exhausted spirit.

Shiko threw her arms over the log. As she rested next to Kittiwake, she realized there was still a chance.

"That soldier," she asked, "can you find him with your senses?"

"He is dead," Kittiwake told her.

"We can't be certain," Shiko said.

"But I *am* certain," Kittiwake said. "I can sense his ghost under the water."

The words brought a chill to Shiko's heart. She had forgotten that those who saw elemental Emotion could also see ghosts.

"He wants to see me drown," Kittiwake said. "He wants to see my soul go to Hell."

"Kittiwake, he cannot harm you," Shiko said. "Ghosts are made only of Emotion and Thought. They cannot affect us physically."

"They can affect us emotionally," Kittiwake said. "If we let them."

"Get control of yourself," Shiko said. "He will go to Heaven soon."

Not all souls could, though. Not on their own. That was why Shiko's people needed ritesmasters, why Kittiwake's people needed priests. What chance did this soldier have with his body drifting in the canal? Would it get stuck on a bridge with other debris? Would it bob to the surface out in the harbor? What if he wasn't found?

"Is his soul still attached to his body?" Shiko asked.

"I— I do not know," said Kittiwake.

"Where is it?"

"Why do you want to know?"

"If his soul is not ascending to Heaven, it means his body needs a funeral."

Kittiwake nodded. "Ahead there. Underwater."

Shiko was sure there were worse fates than being a lost spirit. One such fate awaited Kittiwake if he could not be freed from bondage to his demon. But Shiko felt it was not right to leave the man's body down there where none could find it.

She dove.

When she came up, Kittiwake said, "A bit farther downstream."

Shiko dove again, groping through the black water. She had a feeling she should search more to her left. Now down! Down!

The command was wordless—an impulse, not a thought. Kittiwake was directing her by resonating with her emotions. Shiko reached out, and her fingers found cloth.

The waterlogged body was heavy, but at least it had no armor. She seized the body and struggled to haul it up to the surface, grateful that it was not struggling against her, wishing that she did not have such thoughts. When her head broke the water, Kittiwake was there with the log.

"I sense no gratitude from him," Kittiwake said.

"His goddess will be grateful," Shiko replied.

"Yes," agreed Kittiwake, heaving the body onto the log. "But she will not be grateful to me."

"Do not be so certain," Shiko said. "The deities forgive."

Keeping the dead man on the log was difficult—especially because Shiko also had to watch out for Kittiwake. The artificer was still fully clothed, and he was not a strong swimmer.

They made incremental progress in convincing the log to drift nearer to the edge of the canal, taking care at the bridges to prevent the log and the dead body from being caught on the pillars.

"Is the edge rising?" Kittiwake asked. "Or is the water sinking?"

"The edge is getting farther away," Shiko said.

The ceiling swept over their heads and they found themselves outside underneath the stars.

"We seem to have washed out into the harbor," Kittiwake observed.

"We need to keep kicking across the current," Shiko said. "The tide is still going out. We don't want to be carried into the bay."

Kittiwake and Shiko struggled to move the overloaded log toward the dark piers, but their kicks seemed to have little effect.

"He is too heavy," Kittiwake said. "We should dump him."

"We can't let the body go unless his soul is free," Shiko said. Kittiwake's point had some merit, but Shiko was unwilling to give up so easily.

"Help!" Kittiwake called. "Help us!"

"No one is likely to hear you," Shiko said.

"I thought I saw someone," Kittiwake said. "I hope I did. I don't think I can swim anymore."

"It won't be long until sunrise," Shiko said, stretching the idea of "not long". "The tide should start coming in before the second lithic."

"I can't hang on until the second lithic," said Kittiwake. "Help! Help us!"

"Hellooooo?" called a voice.

Shiko looked up to see a blue halo standing on a pier.

"Help!" Kittiwake called.

The blue halo bobbed along the pier and disappeared.

A while later, they heard the sounds of oars in the water. Two blue lights grew larger in the darkness. Shiko made out the shape of a boat rowed by one man and steered by a man at the stern. As the boat drew near, Shiko recognized the steersman by the thick braid resting on his shoulder. He was the harbormaster.

"Thank you," said Kittiwake. "You've saved our lives."

The boat drew abreast, and the rower shipped his oars.

"Take the body first," Shiko said, looking up at the broad-shouldered rower. "Oh."

From this angle, in the light of the rower's halo, she had an excellent view of the scar on his jaw.

CHAPTER 26
Dawn

ZEFI AWOKE to the sound of women's voices echoing through the stone bathhouse. When had she fallen asleep? She had intended to stay awake to watch over the sleeping Higomu, but apparently, exhaustion had overtaken her.

Higomu still slept, curled up at the bottom of the shadowy stairwell, in front of the locked door. It was a dark, forbidding place hidden in a corner of the bathhouse—a place that Decorator People were unlikely to come—but Zefi worried about discovery now that the morning bathers were arriving.

She and Higomu could not wait beside the locked door forever. Higomu had insisted that Shiko was competent, that Shiko would find a way to make the rendezvous. Zefi knew that Kittiwake was competent, too, but if he had been down there when the custodians had emptied the bath …

Zefi did not want to believe that Kittiwake was dead. She could think of other explanations for why he had not yet come through the locked door. Perhaps he was injured. Perhaps he was captured. Perhaps he and Shiko had gotten lost. Perhaps Shiko had kidnapped him. None of the possibilities made Zefi feel hopeful, but she clung to hope nonetheless. Kittiwake's soul was in danger. Zefi could not believe the gods would allow him to die before she had a chance to save him.

But whatever had happened to Kittiwake, it was plain that he would not arrive at the bathhouse. Zefi would have to go look for him. Yet first, she needed to take care of Higomu.

The spear point had ripped a small hole in passing through Higomu's heel. Zefi had covered his wound with his handkerchief and bound it with a strip of cloth from the sheet that he wore. The wound had not bled badly, although it had bled enough to stain Zefi's clothing while she was carrying him. She should have washed her clothes last night before the stains had set.

Higomu had been in pain. Zefi had seen it in his face. If he felt more pain than he could hide, Zefi doubted he would be able to walk. She could carry him again, but the soldiers would notice a Worker Woman carrying a Thinker Man through the city. Even those who had not heard of last night's escapade would be suspicious. Zefi prayed for guidance from Thafarsi, goddess of knowledge, as she watched Higomu sleep.

More voices arrived at the bathhouse. Liquid sounds suggested that women were immersing themselves in the water. If this neighborhood was anything like the Agave Plaza, most of the bathers at this time of day would be women preparing to go out for a morning's shopping.

Shopping! That was it!

Zefi climbed the stairs and peeked around the corner. No bathers were looking her way. She walked across the tiled floor, knowing the bathers would spot her soon, but hoping they would not worry about where she had come from.

Zefi left the bathhouse with a prayer asking Woshi, goddess of the moon, to keep the sleeping Thinker Man hidden. She strode through the waking city, like a servant on an errand. Everyone seemed to be staring at her, but no one said anything as she passed through the Grand Market on her way to the hillside vineyard where the Thinker People had left their satchels. When she came back to the Grand Market, she had both satchels and Higomu's bag of coins—thank Woshi for keeping them safe. She also had a plan, and she knew exactly what she needed to buy.

The yellow sun was shining warmly by the time Zefi returned to the Temple Plaza. The basket she had purchased disguised her as just another servant going about the morning's business. But it was conspicuous. Designed to hold pumpkins, the basket was so big that only a Worker Person could carry it. What would people think when she brought it into the bathhouse?

Stares followed her up the white marble steps. More stares greeted her as she entered. Worker People were unusual in this neighborhood, with or without a basket. She could think of no way to approach the stairway where she had left Higomu without being watched by the dozen women—and men!—who were taking a mid-morning bath. Why had she thought this was a good idea?

Have faith, she told herself. *Thafarsi will guide you to a solution.*

All eyes followed her across the mosaic-tiled floor to the top of the stairwell. From the shadows below, a pale face looked up at her in surprise.

Zefi set the basket down. The bathers watched her. She was in a corner of the bathhouse where only custodians would go, and their curious halos wanted to know why. Well, what did people usually do when they came to the bathhouse? Thanking Thafarsi for the inspiration, Zefi walked down the stairs until she was out of sight.

Higomu's dark eyes watched her. Zefi realized he had thought she had abandoned him. Now he was trying to figure out why she had come back.

"How did you get here without being noticed?" he asked.

Zefi shook her head and put her hand over her mouth.

Higomu nodded, with a frown.

Zefi put her hand over her eyes.

Higomu looked confused.

Zefi gave up and began undressing. Higomu just looked puzzled.

She folded her clothes and set them neatly on a step. Then she reached into the basket.

Pumpkins would have been the perfect cargo for such a large basket, but they were not in season. Instead, Zefi had purchased a length of yellow cotton cloth from a tailor on the Grand Market. The basket was ridiculously large for such a modest amount of cloth, but Zefi had realized that if she draped the cloth so that a corner flopped out and waved in the air, people would assume that it was on top of many other purchases, all being carried home to whoever had sent Zefi shopping. Now, however, Zefi would use the cloth to tell a different story.

Holding it to cover her nudity, Zefi climbed up the stairs. Curious eyes watched as she approached the bath. Zefi chose an edge as far from the other bathers as she could. Bashfully, she left the cloth on the tiles and descended into the water.

The act worked. Most of the bathers returned to their conversations. Instead of stares, Zefi saw only a few friendly smiles. She was not acting strangely because she had a fugitive hidden in the stairwell; she was just a bashful foreigner.

Some Decorator People were unkind to Worker People, but Zefi's fellow bathers chose to be considerate. They cast only discreet glances her way while she bathed. After an appropriate amount of washing, Zefi walked, draped in yellow, back to the stairwell, feeling confident that although some of the bathers might be watching her, they were pretending that they were not. For some reason, this was a comfort.

Convincing Higomu to be set into the basket between the two satchels was much easier than Zefi had expected. Last night, he had expressed confidence that Shiko would be bringing Kittiwake at any moment, but now it seemed that he, too, had given up on meeting them here. Whether he believed them dead or whether he invented other explanations to console himself, Zefi did not know.

Dressed once again in her skirt and vest, Zefi walked out of the bathhouse with a loaded basket on her head, a corner of bright yellow cloth flapping above her in the morning sunlight.

The shortest route from the Temple Plaza to the Orphanage led through the Imperial Plaza. Zefi believed that the soldiers would be unable to recognize her as the woman who had helped "Darkheart" escape last night, but she chose to take a longer route anyway. Higomu was as still as if he truly were a load of pumpkins. Zefi realized how much trust he had placed in her by getting into that basket—not just trust in her good intentions, but also trust in her competence to carry him safely through the city. She prayed to Lashrefi for luck.

Her path through the side streets eventually spilled out onto the familiar avenue between the Agave Plaza and the Grand Market. She had walked this avenue nearly every day for the past year. She wondered if this were the last time.

Zefi did not know how to get to the Orphanage by back streets. She passed through the Grand Market and took the lithaway avenue. She was nearly to the Whale Plaza when she met the patrol.

The sun was now high enough to give the avenue a sunny side along which she expected to walk unimpeded, but two soldiers—a man and a woman—crossed the avenue to speak with her.

"Good day, foreigner," said the woman. Her aura was a pale, silvery blue. If she suspected Zefi of being a dangerous fugitive, she was doing a good job of hiding it.

"Good day," Zefi replied.

"We are looking for a Child of Labor who keeps company with a Child of Knowledge. Do you know of such a woman?"

Zefi opened her mouth to speak, but couldn't find the words. She feared that her voice would betray her.

"Wo-man," said the male soldier. "Like you. Big wo-man."

Yes, Zefi thought. *That's right: I'm too dumb to understand unless you use two-word sentences.*

Zefi pointed at the female soldier and said, "Wo-man."

"No, no, no," the woman said. "We are looking for a Child of Labor. La-bor. Like you." She pointed at Zefi.

Zefi gave her a dumb grin, pointed to herself, and said, "Wo-man."

The man stared at her, incredulous that anyone could be so stupid. "I don't think she knows anything, Prudence."

The woman smiled at Zefi and said, "You can't understand a word we say, can you?"

Zefi smiled back.

The man observed, "Even if she did know anything, the dumb leatherskin wouldn't be able to tell us."

"I do believe you are correct," said the woman, still giving Zefi her fake smile. "Thank you. Good day."

"Good day!" Zefi said.

The soldiers walked on. Zefi tried not to hurry as she continued toward the docks.

The Whale Plaza was crowded with sailors just arrived in port and the vendors who wanted to sell to them. A group of Worker People clustered around a lemon seller. One of the rowers looked at Zefi, then lowered his eyes after seeing her basket. Zefi knew what he saw—an injured rower doing light work. That was what she had been a year ago, but now—

Well, until yesterday, she had been a valuable assistant to a skilled artisan. She wasn't sure what she was now. Maybe she was just another rower.

Zefi carried Higomu down the steps to the harbor. The Orphanage was tucked in among numerous dockside warehouses. It had once been a warehouse itself, before being donated to the Church of Three Sisters. Zefi had heard the story before she had known the language well, but her understanding was that a successful merchant had donated the building after the healers had helped his daughter recover from a fall out of a second-story window.

The other buildings in the Empire's Scope district were painted with landscapes and cityscapes from the various provinces of the Theocratic Empire, but the Orphanage murals depicted two intimate scenes: To the left of the door, a Worker Man was lying on a bed, watched over by a white-robed healer with a light pink aura; to the right of the door, the same Worker Man was on his feet and smiling as he walked aboard a ship with the healer watching from the background. One year ago, the two murals had seemed an extravagant way to mark the simple building, but now they just seemed practical—and perhaps defiant. The building was in the Empire's Scope district, but the Church of Three Sisters had not chosen scenes glorifying the power of the Theocratic Empire. Rather, they made a promise of help and offered this promise not to citizens, but to foreigners.

They had kept their promise to heal Zefi. She had kept her promise to serve Kittiwake. Now she would keep her promise to return. Zefi took a breath and knocked on the door.

A young man with a white braid opened the door. He smiled up at her and said, "Zefi?"

"Yes," Zefi said. "How—? Have we met?"

The man smiled and shook his head. "I am Healer Lark," he said, "the new keeper. But we have been expecting you. Come in."

Zefi carried the basket into the dim building. The disadvantage to operating the Orphanage out of a former warehouse was that the building had been designed to keep out animal pests, not to provide good lighting. The ceiling trapdoors could provide sunlight when needed, but the windowless chambers were lit primarily by oil lamps—and by Healer Lark's friendly pink glow.

"I wish you had come in a few days earlier," he said. "A foreman had to leave port with a crew of thirty-five. I don't know when I'll be able to find you another crew, but you are welcome to stay here until I do. Your service has paid for that. Shall I show you to the well-patient room?"

Zefi shook her head. "My patient is not well," she said, as she set the basket down on the packed clay floor. She removed the cloth and Higomu sat up.

"Good day," Higomu said.

Healer Lark jumped.

Higomu twisted to work the stiffness out of his back, but he gave no word of complaint. He just fixed his dark eyes on Zefi and said, "Nice work."

"His leg— His heel is hurt," Zefi explained.

"What happened?" asked Healer Lark, recovering from his surprise.

"Many things happened," Higomu replied. "Cloth is a dangerous business. But I don't want to bore you with my stories."

"Oh, no, you are certainly not boring me! In fact, I am quite intrigued! How did you injure yourself dealing in cloth?"

Higomu sighed and shook his head. "Don't you also want to ask why I was hiding in the basket?"

"Certainly I am curious as to why you— Oh."

"It is a terribly boring story and I am certain you do not want to be interested," Higomu said.

"Ah," said Healer Lark. "Of course. Forgive me. I did not mean to pry."

"Thus spoke the crowbar," Higomu mumbled. In his normal voice, he asked, "Would you like to look at my leg here in the dark? Or should we move to a room with sunlight?"

"Of course," said Healer Lark. To Zefi, he said, "If you could follow me?"

Zefi picked up the Thinker Man and followed Healer Lark to a room with three empty beds. They were Decorator People beds—a lattice of wicker supporting a rag-stuffed mattress—but big enough for Worker People. The healers refused to believe that Worker People could heal while sleeping on the floor. Zefi laid Higomu down on one of the beds while Healer Lark climbed ladders to open up the ceiling hatches.

After appraising the shafts of sunlight streaming into the room, Healer Lark put a stand mirror in one of them and adjusted it until it reflected the light onto Higomu's bed. He dragged a stool over and sat down at Higomu's feet.

"Under the bandage, I presume?"

Zefi nodded.

Healer Lark gently lifted Higomu's leg. "Can you hold this here?" he asked.

Zefi did so, while Healer Lark unwrapped the bandage. Higomu wore a sour expression as though he thought they were wasting his time, but he kept silent.

226 JASON A. HOLT

Healer Lark frowned at the wound. "Let me get my tools," he said.

Higomu rolled his eyes. Not knowing what to do, Zefi remained standing at the bed, holding Higomu's leg in the air.

"If Kittiwake escaped, where would he go?" Higomu asked as soon as Healer Lark was out of the room.

Just Kittiwake? Had he given up on Shiko?

"He has a sister in a near village," Zefi said. "He would perhaps run to her."

"Would you be able to take me to her?" Higomu asked.

Zefi nodded, thinking it more likely that Kittiwake would kill himself if he escaped. Even if he could free his soul from the demon, he would still be a crippled artificer trapped between Legislator Whitedove and Commander Fox. It was depressing to realize that the most hopeful possibility was that the soldiers had recaptured him.

Healer Lark entered carrying a tray of tools, accompanied by a thin-faced woman who introduced herself as Student Yucca. She carried water and bandages. She looked old for a student, but youthful Healer Lark was clearly instructing her. Zefi held Higomu's leg while they washed the wound.

After an inspection that involved various repositionings of a small hand mirror, Healer Lark asked, "Can you stand on it?"

"I can't put weight on it, if that's what you mean," Higomu replied.

"Can you point your toe?"

"... Yes."

"Will you please do so?"

"No."

"Ah," said Healer Lark. "Very well."

"The tendon is snapped, isn't it?" Higomu asked.

"Not completely," said Healer Lark. "That means it could heal on its own, given time."

"How much time?" Higomu asked.

"You could be walking on it within half a year," the healer replied.

"Or you could heal it with elemental resonance," Higomu said.

"I couldn't," said Healer Lark. "But there are those at the temple who can."

"But it will cost money," Higomu said.

"Not necessarily money," said Healer Lark. "But some form of exchange is expected so that we can continue to train students. As a Child of Knowledge—"

"I appreciate that, of course," said Higomu. "Please send your student to fetch someone immediately. And as for payment—" he turned to Student Yucca, "—tell the bursar that I identified myself as a theologian and that I asked you to tell him I touched the two fingers of my right hand to my left temple."

"But you didn't touch your fingers to your temple," the thin-faced woman replied.

"No," said Higomu. "I didn't. But tell him I asked you to tell him I did."

"I fear I do not understand," she said.

"Of course you don't," Higomu said. "But he will."

When the Decorator People had left the room, Higomu looked to Zefi and said, "They won't be able to heal this in time."

"Have faith," Zefi told him. "They are very good. I know. They healed my knee."

Higomu shook his head. "Even magical healing takes time, Zefi. And it won't give me my body back. If I were a young man, I might be able to regain my skills with six or twelve months of training, but ..."

His dark eyes seemed sad. "It doesn't matter. If they can just heal it enough so that I can put weight on it this evening, perhaps walk a few steps, then that will be enough. It will have to be enough."

"Perhaps we can stay all the night," Zefi said. "I think we could hide here many days." *While I look for Kittiwake,* she thought.

"But Zefi, we must leave this evening. Have you forgotten that Legislator Whitedove is giving a party? You and I must attend."

CHAPTER 27

Brutal

SANDALS SCRAPING AGAINST STONE. A voice asking, "Is she still asleep?" An answering grunt.

Shiko became aware of the cold floor pressing against her cheek. Yes, she was still asleep. And she was still lying naked on the stone floor with her hands and feet tightly bound.

She had no reason to wake up. Every time she opened her eyes, she saw the scar-faced man sitting on a stool by the red-curtained doorway. If she was watched, she could not escape, and if she could not escape, then she should save her strength until Higomu came.

"Wake her up," the voice said. It was the harbormaster. "And help her put this on."

"Where did you get that?" asked a second voice. That was the scar-faced guard.

"It was your sister's," said the harbormaster. "Or, rather, your half sister's. My wife kept all the children's clothes in a trunk."

A grunt.

Shiko opened her eyes to see the scar-faced pirate coming toward her. As he stepped over her prone body, his head with its mop of short braids obscured the light of the windowless room's ceiling lamp. Then he was behind her, and Shiko could see the harbormaster standing in front of the curtained doorway, his hand smoothing his braid of silver-streaked hair against his shoulder.

Green cloth fell from above and landed in a pile in front of her face. Her bonds loosened from her wrists. She pushed herself to a kneeling position and looked up over her shoulder at the pirate with the scar on his jaw. Brutal.

He folded his arms and looked down at her. One hand held the rope that had bound her wrists.

Her feet were still bound. She could not punch him very hard without a firm fighting stance. And even if she could, she would be unlikely to free herself before the harbormaster caught her.

Shiko glanced at Kittiwake lying nearby in his flood-stained red gown, his hair fallen across his face in black strings. He was also bound hand and foot. Their time to escape had not yet come.

Brutal nudged the heap of green cloth with his sandal and said, "Put it on."

It was a gown, she saw as she unfolded it. She slipped it on over her head. It was only slightly too big.

As soon as she had it on, Brutal grabbed her arms and wove the rope around her wrists again. She hoped that had not been her only chance to escape.

Shiko had only a rough idea of how long she and Kittiwake had been held in the windowless room. She did not know whether it was day or night. It had been dark morning when the harbormaster had brought them here, to a place he identified as his "store room", built against the shore cliff at the rear of his dockside office. Bolts of cloth, jugs of grains, and barrels of wine rose in stacks along the room's walls. Shiko did not know whether these goods were bribes, taxes, or confiscated contraband.

As soon as Brutal had pulled the knots tight, he went back to sit on his stool. The harbormaster approached and crouched down in front of her.

"Good afternoon," he said. "I trust you are feeling refreshed after your nap?"

"Yes, thank you," Shiko said, without trying to reconcile the incongruity between his pleasant tone and her unpleasant situation.

"That is good to hear," he said. "I made some inquiries

about your departure. None of the ships in port are expecting you."

Kittiwake was stirring now. The artificer wiggled on the floor and tossed his head to flip the hair out of his eyes.

"I will tell you nothing," Shiko said. "I know you work for Legislator Whitedove."

In truth, the evidence was only circumstantial: The harbormaster associated with Brutal, who was a subordinate of the man Zefi had identified as Whitedove's nephew. But stating it as a fact was a good way to get a reaction that would tell her if she had guessed right. It was also a good way to warn Kittiwake of her suspicions.

"I do what I can for the legislator, it is true," the harbormaster acknowledged. "But this is true of many well-known people in the city of Dupho. So many of us are in his debt. Is that not so, Kittiwake?"

So he had recognized Whitedove's artificer. He believed Shiko had made plans to leave Dupho, and he had tied both of them up. It seemed that he had come to the conclusion that Shiko was helping Kittiwake escape from Whitedove.

How closely was the harbormaster tied to the legislator? Had he been converted to serve the demon Vanity?

"What happened to the drowned man?" Shiko asked, watching for a reaction from either of their captors.

"Yes, do let us talk about your third companion," the harbormaster said. "When I reported that the body of an unarmored guardian had washed out of the sewers, the guardians-of-the-peace showed no surprise at all. Will you tell me why that was so? No? How about you, Kittiwake?"

Shiko doubted a demon worshipper would have given the soldier a chance for a proper funeral. It seemed that the harbormaster served Whitedove for the usual political reasons. She could make no guesses about Brutal. He showed no reaction to her question or to the harbormaster's words.

"Come, Kittiwake," the harbormaster cajoled. "Tell me something. Anything. At least try out your story so I can help you make it more convincing."

From the adjacent room came a demanding shout: "Harbormaster!"

Brutal cringed.

"In here," the harbormaster called, rising.

Before the harbormaster reached the doorway, the curtain was thrust aside by the thin-lipped, white-skinned pirate captain—although, since he was not wearing a wig over his close-cropped white hair, he was probably there in his capacity as Whitedove's nephew. He stepped into the storage chamber. A knobby-kneed sailor—probably another pirate—followed him in.

The pirate captain wrinkled his nose in disgust. "You thought I needed to see this? What are they?"

"I caught two in one net!" the harbormaster said quickly. "She is the wife of that booker you have been seeking. And he is your uncle's artificer."

Whitedove's nephew peered down. "Kittiwake?"

Kittiwake nodded miserably.

The nephew turned on the harbormaster. "My uncle's artificer, and you have him tied up?"

The harbormaster's halo became greener. "I didn't want him to get away."

A white fist flashed out. The harbormaster, holding his throat, sank to his knees on the storage room's stone floor.

The nephew crouched down and jerked on the harbormaster's long braid, forcing the man to meet his eyes. "The greatest artificer in the city of Dupho," he said in a deathly quiet voice, "and you bind his hands."

The harbormaster opened his mouth to speak, but he could only gasp.

"Cut him loose!" the nephew roared.

So the nephew, at least, had not jumped to the conclusion that Kittiwake had defected. If Shiko could encourage him to think that she had taken the artificer against his will, then perhaps he would let Kittiwake go free. Of course, that also relied on Kittiwake being clever enough to follow her lead.

"You have him now, but you shan't have him for long," Shiko said as the knobby-kneed pirate hastened across the floor to free Kittiwake from his bonds.

"Are you addressing me?" asked the nephew.

"My partner slipped past your men to sabotage your ship," Shiko replied. "He will have no trouble stealing your artificer."

The nephew looked to Kittiwake. "Is this true? Have these bookers tried to kidnap you?"

"Ha!" said Shiko. "We succeeded. We abducted him from the depths of the Red Palace. I doubt your uncle's home will present half the challenge."

"I do not fear you," Kittiwake said to Shiko, glowing yellow. "My patron has powers beyond your comprehension. His protection is far stronger than stone walls and iron bars."

The speech was well delivered. Not only had he deduced what Shiko was trying to accomplish, he had found the focus to control his emotions and shape them into what was needed to make the deception work.

The patron's nephew nodded.

The knobby-kneed pirate withdrew his knife and sliced the ropes that bound Kittiwake's hands and feet. The artificer sighed and began massaging his wrists.

"Thorns of Hell," gasped the nephew. "What happened to your hands?"

Kittiwake froze.

With a snarl, the nephew drove his knife into the harbormaster's eye.

"Contemptible fool!" he shouted at the spasming body. He knelt on the harbormaster's chest and gave the knife a twist. "What have you done to him?"

But the harbormaster could no longer answer. Shiko hated herself for the thought, but she instantly realized how much safer Kittiwake was, now that the harbormaster could not offer his theory as to why she and Kittiwake had been found together.

She looked at Brutal. The scar-faced pirate regarded the gruesome scene with an expressionless face. Only his peach-tinged aura revealed any hint of emotion.

Kittiwake looked sick, but he managed to force a smile onto his face as he said, "Ah, I see that his soul is going to the Goddess. She is pleased."

The murderer was too enraptured to notice he was being deceived. He popped his knife out of the harbormaster's eye socket and licked his thin lips.

"Do you think so?" he asked eagerly.

"I know so," said Kittiwake, regaining his control. "My power allows me to see souls beyond death."

The nephew looked greedily at his victim and asked, "Do you think she will reward me?"

"The faithful always receive their reward in the end," said Kittiwake.

His performance was more convincing than Shiko had expected. It was ... disturbing.

The murderer wiped his knife on his victim's yellow gown. "We should go to my uncle's villa at once," he said. "Can you walk?"

"I shall be able to," Kittiwake said, wincing as he rubbed his legs. "But please give me a moment."

"Certainly," said Whitedove's nephew. "What should we do with that, do you think?" He gestured at Shiko.

Kittiwake shrugged.

"We could toss it in the harbor," the knobby-kneed pirate suggested.

That didn't sound good. Shiko doubted she would be able to slip free of the ropes before she ran out of breath.

"You will have to," Shiko said. "For if you leave me alive, my partner will find me."

"Ah," said the nephew. "Yes, that is a good point." He smiled to himself, as though using her as bait for Higomu were his own idea.

He spoke to the knobby-kneed pirate: "Eely, untie her legs.

She will be walking with us." To the scar-faced pirate, he said, "Brutal, keep your knife handy in case she thinks she would like to run away."

He grinned down at the corpse of the harbormaster. "Always keep your knife handy."

CHAPTER 28
Higomu

THE SURGEON removed her hands from Higomu's calf and opened her eyes. "That should help," she told him. "But the rest will be up to you."

Higomu knew that. Everything was always up to him.

From the way the surgeon brushed a strand of mint-scented hair from her face, he could tell she was worried about him. He had rushed her, and she feared that the mended tendon would not hold. Her aura revealed nothing, but Higomu had learned not to be distracted by the auras of Children of Beauty. He had trained himself to look beyond their halos and see the words written by the lines of their faces.

The surgeon sighed. "Do you still insist on walking on it today?"

"I do."

"Very well. Then I will insist that you wear a splint."

"Understood."

And Higomu did understand. He just wouldn't wear the splint.

The student, a thin-faced, older woman named Yucca, took over for the surgeon, binding wood to Higomu's foot to prevent him from putting strain on the tendon. While she did so, the surgeon gave instructions to Healer Lark, the keeper of the Orphanage: "Encourage him to take as much rest as he will. Don't let him use stairs unassisted. And elevate the leg as often as he will let you."

"I shall do my best," Healer Lark said.

"I am sorry to leave you with such a difficult patient," the surgeon said. "Or rather, I am not sorry to leave, but you do have my sympathy."

Healer Lark smiled a grim smile.

Children of Beauty had to make a drama out of everything. Higomu wasn't being difficult, just disobedient. He was glad the surgeon had explained the limitations of her healing, but that did not mean he would promise to stay within the limitations. He would do what must be done.

It seemed likely that the artificer had drowned when the custodians had cleaned the bath. Higomu had not said this to Zefi, however. He needed her to remain calm and hopeful, so he encouraged any hope she expressed, no matter how improbable. He had also encouraged Healer Lark to accept her offer to help with the Orphanage's laundry. She wasn't needed during the surgery, and a little outdoor work might keep her mind off Kittiwake for a time.

Higomu also nurtured his own irrational hope. Shiko, being a skilled swimmer, could have survived. Her failure to arrive at the bathhouse last night indicated otherwise, but clinging to hope was necessary right now. The alternative was grief, and that would just distract him from his mission.

For he still had a mission. The artifact had to be destroyed.

Zefi's description of the "emotion box" matched the diagrams in the notebook. Zefi remembered many construction details, but Higomu concluded that she did not have the ability to replicate the thing. She would be free to go once she had helped him steal the artifact from Whitedove's villa.

As at the Red Palace, Higomu felt guilty for involving the girl—she was barely seventeen!—but he saw no way to complete the mission without help. He was crippled. His choice of combat stances would be limited. He would not be able to run or even climb stairs swiftly.

He needed at least a week's attention from elemental healers. He could pay for it, thanks to the Order's account with the Church of Three Sisters, but he could not afford the time. Zefi said the artifact had been constructed for a party tonight.

Higomu doubted that a demon worshipper would be planning to put soul-trapping magic to a benign use.

Higomu would do what must be done. And if he was physically incapable of doing it himself, he would get help from the able-bodied Zefi.

As soon as Lark and Yucca left the room, Higomu got out of bed. How much freedom of motion would the splint give him? How could he move quietly on a foot that couldn't bend? Higomu crossed and recrossed the floor, trying side steps, glide steps, walking steps—anything that might let him move without making noise. He had about a lithic before they would have to leave for Whitedove's party.

No one could learn silent movement in a lithic. Higomu's skills had been honed by years of experience and maintained by daily practice. What would be left of him once he finally healed? How many years would it take to regain his skills? He was only six years from retirement. Was this his last mission?

Then I'll end my career with success, he answered himself. *Don't give up, Higomu. Failure is not allowed.*

Higomu was still walking across the floor, trying to discover what his crippled body could do, when Zefi came back from her laundry chores. He recognized the tread as Zefi's because it was too heavy for a Child of Beauty and too rapid for the Children of Labor recovering elsewhere in the Orphanage. She was moving so fast that Higomu expected to hear sounds of pursuit, but she entered his room alone.

"I saw him. Kittiwake. At the docks." The girl was out of breath.

Higomu knew how it was. While Zefi had carried him through the city, he had kept an eye at a hole in the basket, watching for Shiko. Every curly-haired woman had looked like her, no matter that they were twice her height.

"Are you certain?" he asked.

"I know him anywhere!"

"Of course you do," said Higomu. "Absolutely. Now tell me how you knew it was Kittiwake."

"It was him!" Zefi insisted. "I saw his face!"

"Certainly," said Higomu, wondering if anything short of a blow to the skull would make the giant calm down. "And did he see you?"

"No," said Zefi. "I hid. He was with the patron's nephew. And Shiko."

"Shiko?" Could it be?

Zefi nodded. "But her hands were behind her back." She demonstrated.

Captured! Shiko lived!

"Two sailors guarded her," Zefi added.

"Sailors? You mean pirates?"

"Yes. Two pirates from the inn."

Higomu thought about it. Why would anyone parade fugitives from justice through the streets of Dupho? Whitedove's nephew was either very stupid or very certain of his uncle's power. Of course, given Higomu's history with the man, there was also the possibility that he was issuing a personal challenge. If that were the case, he would be disappointed. Higomu never fought a battle on his opponent's terms. And now that he was incapable of fighting, this was doubly true.

"Zefi, I think the nephew will take them to Whitedove's villa. If Kittiwake is going to the villa, that gives us the perfect excuse to get inside as well."

"How?" she asked.

"I need you to tell a story," Higomu explained. "The story is that Kittiwake told you, 'If anything happens to me, go to my patron's villa.'"

"'If anything happens to me, go to my patron's villa,'" Zefi repeated.

"Correct," said Higomu.

"I do not lie well," Zefi said. "But perhaps Moon will help me."

"I am certain she will," said Higomu. Well, at least he was certain that the Moon Goddess could help if she chose to.

Higomu wondered if Fox's spies had seen Kittiwake and Shiko in the custody of the patron's nephew. It seemed likely.

Fox would certainly order the docks watched to prevent Kittiwake or his abductors from escaping by sea. If Zefi had noticed Kittiwake while she did the Orphanage's laundry, no doubt the dock spies had also seen him—and perhaps even followed him.

The guardians-of-the-peace could turn Whitedove's party into a memorable evening indeed. It would be a social event that Higomu just could not miss.

CHAPTER 29

Withering

FRESH SPRIGS OF JUNIPER hung below every window around the atrium, and a bouquet of mint hung above every doorway. Two of the statues had been moved away from the central fountain to accommodate the tables over which the flustered servants were now spreading linen tablecloths embroidered in the longstitch style. An occasional breeze carried the aroma of roasting turkeys, reminding Kittiwake that it had been some time since his lunch in the harbormaster's storage room.

That meal he had eaten with bound hands. Now his limbs were free, but his soul was still imprisoned by the demon he had agreed to serve.

The patron's nephew led them across the atrium, calling, "Uncle Whitedove?" as though the patron were a kindly old uncle instead of a powerful legislator and an earthly intermediary for a malevolent, life-draining demon.

Kittiwake had no doubt that the nephew knew the source of his uncle's power. When Kittiwake had told him that "the Goddess" was pleased by the harbormaster's death, the nephew had assumed she was pleased by the gruesome murder. Clearly, he had not been thinking of the Goddess of Beauty.

Why had Beauty chosen to take the harbormaster's soul immediately up to Heaven? Why had she bestowed mercy on the man who had ordered that Kittiwake and Shiko be tied up? Perhaps it was because the harbormaster had himself been merciful—feeding his prisoners a meal, giving his daughter's dress to Shiko, taking the time to hand over the drowned soldier's body. Or perhaps it was as Zefi said: The deities have their own reasons, and people were not given authority to judge. Regardless, Kittiwake was grateful that the harbormaster had not remained to haunt him. Kittiwake prayed that he, too, might receive Beauty's mercy someday.

The black hand inside his chest gave his heart a squeeze, reminding him that he was beyond Beauty's mercy now. How many others had Whitedove converted to this "Goddess of Glamour"? Kittiwake had seen Whitedove's villa visited by people high and low from all across the city. If Whitedove managed to convert even a twelfth of the people who depended on him, that would amount to far too many demon worshippers in Dupho.

Legislator Whitedove's manservant, Badger, emerged from Whitedove's study, followed by Whitedove himself, who frowned at his nephew's approach. Looking from uncle's face to nephew's, Kittiwake was struck by how alike they seemed in age. Many citizens of Dupho would consider that a fair exchange—to forsake their goddess in return for an ever-youthful face.

Ignoring his uncle's frown, the nephew strode ahead of their little group, proclaiming, "I have found your artificer, Uncle."

Whitedove slowly nodded and his aura shaded toward pink. "So you have," he admitted. "But what has happened to him?"

Under his patron's scrutiny, Kittiwake reached within himself for something to mask his fear. He found tedium. Many times he had sat in this atrium, staring at the four statues and the fountain, waiting for his turn to speak with Legislator Whitedove. He focused on this sense of tedium and amplified it, allowing it to mask his desire to be free of the demon and his fear that this desire would be discovered.

"He says he was captured by the guardians-of-the-peace," the nephew replied.

"He was," said Legislator Whitedove. "But how did he get free?"

"I do not know exactly—"

"You do not need to stand there," Whitedove called to Kittiwake, who was still a respectful distance away, along with Shiko and the nephew's thugs. "Come inside and we shall discuss this privately."

Turning to his manservant, Whitedove added, "Badger, please find a clean gown for Kittiwake."

Kittiwake reminded himself that he was the most brilliant artificer in Dupho. Of course he should be part of a private conversation between Legislator Whitedove and his nephew. Summoning his arrogance was easier than amplifying his boredom. As he strode across the remaining distance, he wondered how long he could hide his true feelings before he began believing his own lies.

Whitedove disappeared into his study. His nephew did likewise, but not before calling over his shoulder, "Put her in the wine cellar for now."

Kittiwake restrained himself from glancing at Shiko. He should not show concern for her. He planned to claim she had been abducting him. It was a good lie because it was true.

Inside the study, Legislator Whitedove stood behind his marble desk, as he always did, with his back to the garden doorway. Inside the doorway's rectangular frame, red sunset combined with red moonlight to give the garden trees an eerie glow.

"Perhaps you should start at the beginning," Whitedove suggested.

"I will do so gladly," said the patron's nephew as Kittiwake opened his mouth to speak. "Last night, I instructed the harbormaster to watch for that booker I have been trying to catch."

He paused.

"Or perhaps I should say, I asked him to 'keep an eye out.'"

He grinned.

Kittiwake pushed down the memory of the nephew's bloody knife emerging from the harbormaster's eye socket.

"My prudence paid off," continued the nephew. "The harbormaster couldn't find the booker, but he did find the booker's wife!"

"Ah," said the legislator. "That would be the young lady that you decided to put in my wine cellar."

"Precisely so. When the booker goes to look for her, everyone between here and the docks will be able to tell him that we have her."

Legislator Whitedove shook his head. "Snowgull, your intellect never ceases to amaze me."

"Ah, but that is not even the best part of my plan!" the nephew replied, oblivious to his uncle's tone. "When he comes to offer his life in exchange for hers, I will accept his offer, and then kill them both!"

Whitedove sighed. "Yes, I am certain you will."

His nephew finally caught his mood. "Are you thinking I should kill only one?"

"I am thinking, dear Snowgull, that your mother and I have been planning for our brother's birthday party to be an intimate gathering, and that now I must adjust the plan to account for several unexpected guests. But before you leave to be certain your men have the prisoner well guarded, do explain how you found my artificer."

"The harbormaster sent a message that he had something I needed to see," said the nephew. "When I arrived at his house, I found Kittiwake, along with the booker's wife. She helped him escape from the guardians-of-the-peace."

"Yes," Kittiwake said. "She broke me from the Red Palace only to take me prisoner herself. I am very grateful for your nephew's intervention."

At these words, Kittiwake felt the otherworldly hand of Glamour seize his left arm. He could feel the elbow joint swelling, the muscles withering, the skin wrinkling, but he struggled to maintain his composure. He hoped the room's lamp would not reveal Glamour's punishment, but Whitedove must have had senses beyond the ordinary, for he started in alarm.

"Ah, you have noticed his hands," said the nephew with a smile, misinterpreting his uncle's reaction. "Yes, I have yet to mention our harbormaster's oversight. He was overzealous in apprehending the booker's wife. Not only did he tie her up, but he tied up your artificer as well—and much too tightly. Whether Kittiwake will ever again be able to practice his art, I cannot say, but our harbormaster will not make that mistake again. Nor any other."

The patron looked up sharply. "You killed the harbormaster?"

His nephew nodded.

The patron put a hand to his forehead. "In front of how many witnesses?"

"Just your artificer," the nephew replied. "And two men from my crew."

The patron frowned and nodded. His aura showed that he was containing his anger by working out a puzzle.

"Perhaps you should stand guard over your prisoner personally," the patron suggested.

"Ah, my men can be trusted with the task."

"No," said Whitedove. "I insist that you stand guard with them. Run along now. If you want to eat, stop for something in the kitchen on your way. I will explain to your mother why you are absent this evening."

"Oh," said the nephew, frowning. "Well if you insist ..."

"I assure you, I do."

"Very well, then."

Shaking his head, Whitedove drew the black curtain over the atrium doorway as soon as his nephew had left.

"You must forgive Snowgull," he said. Kittiwake, as the only person remaining in the room, assumed he was being addressed, although Whitedove seemed to be speaking more to himself as he stepped softly toward his bird cage. "He was in the Theocratic Navy, you know. I fear that his military training awakened within him every barbarity of the soul, leaving him ill-suited for more refined pursuits."

Whitedove reached out a finger and stroked the nearer dove's wing. Kittiwake blinked. Both doves were sitting on the perch. Legislator Whitedove cooed at them and smiled as though they cooed in answer. But they did not. They were immobile.

"Do you think I approve of casual murder?" Legislator Whitedove asked.

Kittiwake shook his head. Whitedove was not looking at him, but Kittiwake found himself unable to speak.

"I do not," Whitedove said. "I want you to understand that I never order a death without a purpose. Life is precious to the Goddess. It is among the things she craves most. Death should never come suddenly, violently. It should be slow, deliberate, and meaningful, so that the Goddess has a chance to savor it. Do you understand?"

This time Kittiwake could not even move his head in answer, but his patron seemed to require no more response from Kittiwake than he did from the stuffed birds.

"Service to the Goddess is truly service," Legislator Whitedove said. "You must consider *her* needs. My nephew is too selfish to understand this, so she will never grant him the powers she has given me." Whitedove turned and stared directly into Kittiwake's eyes. "But I have hope for you, Kittiwake."

Kittiwake blinked. "Thank you, Legislator Whitedove."

Whitedove smiled.

"Now tell me what happened," Whitedove said. "Why did you choose to reject the Goddess's gift?"

Kittiwake's emotions were slipping from his grip. Fear was always so difficult to control. What was worse, he knew he *should* show fear in the face of such an accusation, but only the proper amount.

Kittiwake was too frightened to muster such fine control. Whitedove knew. Kittiwake had given Glamour a window into his soul, and through her, Whitedove saw all.

The truth then. But only as much as he had to reveal.

"I could not kill the soldiers," Kittiwake said. "Glamour

granted me the power, but I could not bring myself to use it."

"And why not?" Whitedove asked mildly.

Because killing is wrong. That was how Kittiwake felt, but he would not say it. Whitedove didn't think killing was wrong. He thought it was sacred.

"It seemed like a waste of life," Kittiwake said.

Whitedove nodded sadly. "Yes. You see? We understand each other. We are not like the imperial soldiers. Life means something to us. But tell me truthfully this time: How did you escape?"

"Those Children of Knowledge—the ones who threatened me yesterday morning—they helped me escape."

Zefi had been there, too, but Kittiwake hoped she would be safe if he did not mention her name.

"I see," said Whitedove. "And before you 'escaped', did you have a conversation with my old friend Commander Fox?"

"No," said Kittiwake.

"No?"

"No. He did not arrive at the Red Palace until late last night, and I escaped just as he was coming to talk with me."

Legislator Whitedove studied Kittiwake's healthy arm, waiting to see Glamour's reaction to these words. There was none. Kittiwake had not lied.

"Most interesting," Whitedove said. "And so how did you end up at the docks?"

"We, ah, escaped through the sewer."

"Ah! That explains much … but not everything. Tell me: Why did the harbormaster tie you up?"

"I do not know," Kittiwake said, spreading his hands. Then he wished he had not made the gesture. It was unwise to flaunt the evidence of his disloyalty.

"The harbormaster feared you would escape," Whitedove said.

"Possibly," Kittiwake said. "That seems likely."

"Because you were planning on boarding a ship with that Child of Knowledge."

"The idea never occurred—" Kittiwake could feel the grip of Glamour on his right arm.

Whitedove shook his head sadly. "Admit it, Kittiwake. You wanted to run away from me."

Away from you, away from the soldiers, but mostly away from this demon to whom you have bound my soul. "I did," he said.

Glamour let go.

Whitedove gave him a gentle smile and put a hand on his shoulder. "You see? The Goddess can be merciful." He lifted one of Kittiwake's shriveled hands. "This must pain you," he said.

"It does," Kittiwake admitted.

"You must want your hands back," Whitedove said.

Kittiwake's throat tightened. "I do," he said.

"The Goddess does not heal," Whitedove said.

Ah. Then she cannot tempt me.

"But," added Whitedove, "your body can heal itself."

"It will?"

"No. It *can*. The Goddess decides whether it will. Do you see?"

Kittiwake nodded. The demon could not tempt him, but she could punish him for disloyalty.

"And so you will have the opportunity to make your artifacts again, my dear artificer, if you but serve us tonight."

"What do you require of me?" Kittiwake asked, wishing that his curiosity were only an act.

"It does not matter," said Whitedove with a fatherly smile. "What matters is that you comply."

He went then to a high shelf and retrieved the emotion box, placing it on his marble-topped desk. "Is this the spigot that releases the souls?" he asked.

Kittiwake nodded.

Legislator Whitedove turned the spigot and two confused spirits fluttered out. They flitted about the room for a moment before disappearing through the wall. Legislator Whitedove could not see them. He simply watched the red garnet in the lid as it darkened. The color change was obvious, even in a lamp-lit study. Kittiwake had chosen a good stone.

"It is almost like watching them die again," Whitedove said with sorrow.

He looked up at Kittiwake. "And remember why they died, my artificer. They died to forge the agreement between you and Glamour. If you continue to fight against your obligation to serve her, then you will waste their deaths. Think on that. Very carefully."

With darkened aura, the legislator stepped past Kittiwake and opened the black curtain. Badger was standing just outside in the atrium, holding a red gown with gold trim.

"The guests have begun arriving," Badger said.

In truth, this was obvious, for their voices echoed around the atrium above the splashing of the fountain. Kittiwake realized that he had been hearing their voices for quite some time, in the same way that he sometimes awoke from a dream and realized he had been immersed in the morning sounds of his neighborhood without being conscious of them.

"Excellent, Badger," said Legislator Whitedove. "Please inform my sister and our guest of honor."

"As you seemed to wish for privacy, I took the liberty of informing them first," Badger replied.

"Well done."

"And I am also pleased to inform the artificer that his servant has arrived."

"Zefi? Here?" She had made it out alive!

"Yes," said Badger. "She said that you had given her instructions to come here in the event that the two of you became separated."

Kittiwake had given her no such instructions. Moreover, Zefi now knew that Kittiwake's patron was a demon worshipper. She would certainly not come to the villa unless she—or that dark-eyed Child of Knowledge—had seen him being escorted to the Heights. Yes, that would explain it. Kittiwake had to find a chance to talk to her. Then he noticed that Legislator

Whitedove was giving him a considering look.

"I see you are eager to be reunited," he said.

"Zefi is a very good assistant," Kittiwake said. "She helped me make your box."

Legislator Whitedove smiled. "Yes, I am sure she did. Well, you should go greet her, then, as soon as you are dressed. Badger, would you help Kittiwake dress in the garden?"

The manservant nodded.

"And ask his servant to stay and help with the celebration this evening," Whitedove added with a smile. "I am very glad she came, Kittiwake, for I know how much she means to you."

CHAPTER 30
Advantages, Assets, and Allies

SHIKO stood in the dark wine cellar with her arms bound tightly behind her back. She examined the rope's loops with a free fingertip while considering her tactical situation.

Darkness was an advantage. It would allow her to hide or to strike unseen, while the Children of Beauty would be illuminated by their own halos. Her bonds, too, would be an advantage—once she was free of them. She would take the pirates by surprise if they believed she was bound and powerless. And perhaps the rope could be an asset.

What she really needed, however, were allies. She now had three guards outside the cellar door—the two pirates who had brought her down here and their captain, who had joined them later. She hoped the captain would leave soon—partly because escaping three captors seemed impossible, but mostly because the captain was a capriciously violent murderer.

Shiko considered ways to secure the cellar door. Most of Dupho's interior doorways closed with a curtain, but protecting wine from heat required a thick wooden door—not unlike the door to Elder Badiki's quiet room, where her mission had begun. Shiko had seen neither lock nor latch when they had brought her in. The door opened inward. That was an advantage, for that meant she was on the side from which the door could be wedged shut. And perhaps the wooden door itself could be an asset.

Aha. Her fingertip had found the end of the rope. She wiggled her thumb until she could grasp the loose end; then she walked her thumb and forefinger along, taking up the slack.

From the way Brutal had wrapped her arms, Shiko suspected he had bound her in a seizing—a technique normally used to fasten two ropes together. Shiko had been taught to secure a seizing with a clove hitch, which could be undone by pushing the end back through its loop.

But it wasn't working. She could not push on the end because the rope was not stiff enough. Another way to undo the hitch was to pull on a loop, but the right loop seemed to be out of reach. She probably could have reached it with a lockpick, if the harbormaster had not taken her tool belt. At least he had allowed her to keep her cord-and-stone. The sacred stone was not a rope-untying tool, but it was a comfort.

Where should she look for a tool? Near the entrance was a stand holding a wine barrel. An untapped barrel stood on the floor beside it. She had seen them just before the pirate named Eely had closed the door. She did not recall seeing any tools for tapping the barrels, though. Perhaps they were deeper in the cellar.

With her bare feet, Shiko felt her way to a wooden rack. She turned her back to it and ran her fingers over glass bottles. These could be assets, she decided. An overhand throw, aim for the halo, duck out between their legs while they were still looking for her. Yes, that could work.

Could she use the rack itself as a weapon? She gave it an experimental push with her shoulder. It would not tip over easily. But perhaps it was still an asset. Put a board against the rack to make an inclined plane. Put a wine barrel at the top. Tie it in place with a knot that could be slipped to release the barrel when the pirates opened the door ...

The door. It must have hinges—hinges on her side. Her toes guided her toward the door. The smell of musty wood told her when she was close.

Shiko's fingertips found the lowest hinge. As with everything in Dupho, it was pointlessly ornate—or rather, pointedly ornate, for the hinge took the form of a stylized grapevine with an artistic curl to the leaf tip that would allow Shiko to catch her rope on its point.

Shiko brushed the rope against the ornate hinge, searching for the right loop to tug. Not that one. Try again. No, the loop should run the other way. Ah, there was one of the loops of the clove hitch. But not the right one. Try again. Did that pull against the rope's end? Try pulling this way. Slipped off the hook. Just a little patience. There. Is it? Yes!

Shiko worked her arms until the rope loosened and fell away. That had not taken long, but it was certainly trickier than the locks in the Red Palace had been. She had been so proud of her locksmith training, but it turned out that her mission's most challenging puzzle could be solved only by using what she had learned on the Academy's fishing boat!

As she began coiling the rope for future use, voices spoke outside the door. Shiko put her ear against the wood and heard the pirate captain say:

"No one goes into the wine cellar tonight."

A pause.

"I have wine."

It was Zefi's voice! … Except she sounded stupid.

"Set it down here. No one goes into the wine cellar tonight. Set wine down."

"I go kitchen," Zefi said. Then she gasped.

"You'll do what I say or I'll fillet you and serve you as the dessert course. I dare say my uncle's followers would like that. Now set the barrel down."

There was a clunk.

The pirate captain muttered something inaudible.

Shiko considered whether to burst from the cellar at that moment. She would have the advantage of surprise. Her combat training was an asset. But was Zefi her ally?

The Child of Labor had been willing enough to be their ally last night, but now the situation had changed. Kittiwake was no longer in prison. He was free to wander about the villa.

Zefi was loyal to a man Shiko could not trust. True, Kittiwake had seemed remorseful about giving his soul to Vanity, but he had also led the pirate captain to believe that he was eager to return to Legislator Whitedove. He was certainly using his Emotional affinity to lie to someone, and Shiko had to acknowledge the possibility that he was lying to her—and possibly to Zefi as well.

Zefi was devoted to Kittiwake. She would not aid the demon worshippers, but nor would she aid Shiko if Kittiwake told her not to.

It didn't matter now. Shiko had hesitated long enough that Zefi was probably gone.

Shiko had just decided to explore more of the cellar when the knobby-kneed pirate, Eely, said something in his high voice.

She put her ear back against the door.

"You drink booker wine?" the pirate captain asked.

"Sometimes," Eely said.

"So does my mother," said the captain. "It tastes like wood."

After a few moments more, the pirate captain said, "Well, I won't have you staring at it all night. Brutal, put it in the cellar."

Shiko leapt away from the door and put her hands—and the coiled rope—behind her back.

The door opened to reveal the halos of the scar-faced man and the knobby-kneed pirate. Behind them, the pirate captain slouched against the wall of the stairwell, playing with his knife.

Shiko backed away as Brutal rolled a wine barrel toward her. She feared him, and she hoped her action would seem logical. She also hoped it would keep her in darkness so that he would not see that her hands were free.

Brutal tipped the barrel up next to the other one. He barely glanced at Shiko before turning his broad back to her and stalking out.

The thing to do, Shiko thought as Brutal closed the door, leaving her alone in the darkness once more, would be to hide somewhere near the door the next time someone came in. If they didn't see her, it was possible that all three would come in to investigate, giving her a chance to reverse positions.

Had she seen a good place to hide? The wine barrels were near the door, but behind them was the first place a searcher would look. She could stand on the hinged side of the doorway so that the door would hide her when they opened it. But wouldn't they think to look behind the door? And if they opened the door wide enough to hit her, not only would she be immediately found, she would also be trapped.

Shiko thought of the horizontal ceiling poles that had been illuminated by Brutal's halo on his way out. If she could wrap her rope around one of those, perhaps she could suspend herself above the door. That would be an incredibly clever place to hide. But could she even get up there?

Perhaps. With the help of the wine barrels. They were nearly as tall as she was. How quietly could she move them?

Shiko felt her way to the wine barrels and gave one of them a gentle nudge to get an idea of how difficult it would be to move. It wobbled.

It wobbled, but it did not slosh. The wine barrel did not hold wine.

Shiko pushed it again. It was heavy. It held something solid. Perhaps salted fish?

She felt around the top and found the cork. So it had been tapped, like a barrel of liquid, but it contained something solid. This wasn't making sense. She pulled out the cork and sniffed. The barrel smelled of wine.

"Zefi?" whispered a voice from within.

"Higomu!" Shiko gasped.

"Shiko," he said. "Are we alone?"

"Yes, but three of the pirates are just outside the door," Shiko whispered into the hole.

"Step back."

Shiko did so.

The barrel's wooden lid popped off and slapped against the stone floor.

"Ah," said Higomu. "That's better."

The barrel wobbled a moment, and then the cellar was silent again.

"This is the wine cellar?" Higomu asked.

"Yes."

"And Legislator Whitedove's nephew is holding you prisoner here?"

"Yes. He's just outside the door."

"With only two others?"

"Yes."

"Is the door locked?"

"No."

Higomu thumped the lid of his wine barrel back into place. "Three guards could be a problem," he observed.

"I was thinking that myself."

"I doubt we can depend on Zefi's help," Higomu said. "She's more of a runner than a fighter. She's a good runner, though. I'll tell you all about it on the trip home."

"You are always so confident," Shiko said.

"Not really. I just never plan for failure."

"I'm worried about Kittiwake," Shiko said.

"Is he being held prisoner, too?"

"No. That's what worries me. He has convinced them that he is still a demon worshipper. And I'm wondering if he didn't also convince himself."

"If he's a good enough actor," Higomu said, "only the deities will know his true intentions. Oh, and the demons, of course."

"So what do we do about him?"

"Let's assume that he wants to escape with us and convert back. If he doesn't, we have to kill him."

A striker does what must be done, Shiko thought.

"But I doubt it will come to that," Higomu said. "If he were suited for evil, I doubt Zefi would be so fond of him."

"Young girls don't always make good decisions," Shiko observed.

"She looks even younger to me than she does to you," said

Higomu. "But she's old enough to tell good from evil. The deities may be the only ones who can know Kittiwake's true intentions, but Zefi talks to the deities frequently."

"It sounds like you two had an interesting night."

"Yes. Although we didn't get washed down the sewer canal and out into the harbor."

"How did you find out about that?"

"Deduction: The custodians were cleaning an empty bath when we arrived, and you smell funny."

"You smell like wine."

"I imagine I do."

"So you must have looked for us at the docks," Shiko said. "If you waited long enough, you would have seen the pirates escorting us away. You could deduce we were coming here and get Zefi to smuggle you inside. But how did you know I would be in the wine cellar?"

"Shiko, if I had known they would hold you prisoner in here, I would have thought up a different way to sneak in. The plan was for Zefi to leave me where no one would be watching. As it is, I do not think we are in the best tactical position."

"We have the advantages of darkness and surprise," Shiko said. "And perhaps the wine bottles could be thrown as weapons."

"Actually," said Higomu, "if you break the neck off a glass bottle, it can be as deadly as a knife."

That was logical. Shiko realized she should have thought of that. On the other hand, she had not practiced much with knives.

"So we have advantages and assets," Shiko said. "And now that we have each other for allies, perhaps we can solve the problem of the three guards. We just need a good plan."

"Ah, and now which of us is sounding confident?"

"I am learning from my mentor. He said, 'Never plan for failure.'"

"Excellent," said Higomu. "You are missing only one more piece of information that you will need to make your plan."

"And what is that?" asked Shiko, glad to have help.

"I was injured last night," Higomu said. "I cannot run, jump, or fight."

CHAPTER 31

The Birthday Party

ZEFI CARRIED A ROASTED TURKEY out to the atrium. Two tables were set up near the fountain. One table held the staples of bread, wine, cheese, citrus slices, and olives, as well as rarities like dried apples from the lands of the Thinker People and fresh pineapple from the lands of the Leader People. The other table held platters of pickled yellowtail, smoked sardines, and spiced oysters. Zefi set the turkey platter down inside a circle of boiled quail eggs.

She walked back to see if they needed help with the other two turkeys, but the cook intercepted her.

"Stay here," she said. "Help serve." She waved at the tables. "Help."

Zefi nodded. "Help," she said.

But she didn't want to stay in the atrium. The demon-worshipping patron frightened her, and his sister was stomping about like a fly-bitten donkey. The woman's aura was a nervous, angry, yellow-green. She glowed far too brightly for someone who was expected to do nothing more than make pleasant conversation all evening.

Yesterday, the patron's sister had told Badger to keep Zefi out of her sight, but tonight both Badger and the cook had made it clear that Zefi was expected to help serve. Serve what, though? Brightly colored earthenware plates had been provided, and the convivial guests were already helping themselves, even though the other two roasted turkeys had yet to arrive. A slender middle-aged woman with a pretty face—the floor sweeper, Zefi thought—had already taken the job of pouring the wine. The cook's assistant was carrying the hand-washing bowl. Zefi was not certain what else needed to be done.

The patron's brother—like his sister—was not enjoying the party nearly as much as the guests. He stood aloof chewing on a chunk of bread, his wrinkled face as dour as if he were chewing wood.

A long-legged boy came running across the atrium to speak to Badger. The broad-shouldered manservant nodded somberly and sent the boy off toward the kitchen.

Legislator Whitedove had kept Kittiwake close by his side for most of the evening, but he separated from him now as his manservant approached. Zefi put a slice of cheese and a chunk of bread on a plate and walked toward Kittiwake, who stood near the fountain.

"Do not allow the guardians to enter until the artificer has completed his task," Whitedove told Badger as Zefi passed them.

So Higomu was right: The soldiers were coming.

Zefi handed Kittiwake the bread and cheese and said, "I am so glad to see you alive."

"And I, you, Zefi," Kittiwake said, laying a withered, knobby-knuckled hand on her shoulder.

"It spreads to your arm," she said.

"It is part of my punishment," Kittiwake replied. "But that is not our concern right now."

"What is wrong?" Zefi asked.

"I suspect that Whitedove does not intend for us to live past the evening," Kittiwake said. "I fear for your life in particular, Zefi. Be careful."

Zefi glanced at Whitedove. Badger was now striding away from the party toward the entrance. Whitedove was whispering with a group of guests.

"He will not hurt me," Zefi said. "Because people are here. And the servants say I must stay in the atrium. We are safe here."

"I am not so certain," said Kittiwake. "Did you see the look the admiral's wife gave us when the legislator spoke to her?"

Zefi watched the patron move to a new group of guests, like a foreman mingling with the other workers during the midday break—except that instead of causing the guests to laugh and relax, his words caused them to quiet down and look at each other with intense eagerness, as though expecting something important to begin. Zefi did not know what was about to happen, but she realized she did not have much time.

She murmured, "Higomu is here."

"Where?"

"In a barrel. He told me to hide him in the wine cellar," Zefi said. "But your patron's nephew guards it."

Kittiwake nodded. "They are keeping Shiko in there."

"Why?" Zefi asked.

"The patron's nephew is using her as bait to lure in Higomu."

"Oh," said Zefi. "I understand."

"Do you? I don't."

"Higomu breaked his ship," Zefi explained. "So he wants to kill Higomu."

Kittiwake shivered. "Zefi, you must get out of here. If you see any chance to leave, you must go to the Orphanage. Get out of Dupho. I can't keep you safe from any of this."

Zefi shook her head. "I can't leave you. And I can't leave Higomu. The nephew said I must put the wine barrel outside the cellar. He and his men guard there. If they open the barrel, they will find Higomu. Then he will die. Perhaps Shiko, too."

"I am not so certain," Kittiwake said. "I think they can take care of themselves."

"Higomu cannot," said Zefi. "No more. His leg—his heel is hurt. He limps now. He cannot run. I believe he cannot fight."

"Oh."

Thafarsi, goddess of knowledge, granted Zefi an idea. "Can you make the patron call for his nephew? Then I could pretend I fetch wine and open Higomu's barrel."

"But what about the other two guards?"

"I open the cellar, too. Shiko, Higomu, and I are three."

"Shiko is tied up," Kittiwake said. "And the guards have knives."

"We can have knives, too," Zefi said, pointing to the array of cutlery on the table.

"You can't fight with knives, Zefi."

He was right of course. She should have learned to fight, but she had not known she would ever need to. She asked Kashram, god of the lith, to forgive her.

"Here he comes," said Kittiwake.

The baby-faced patron approached them with his lips stretched across his face in imitation of a smile. Zefi prayed that Thafarsi would inspire Kittiwake to think of a good excuse to ask for the patron's nephew. But would Thafarsi help Kittiwake? Zefi believed she would, because by helping Kittiwake, she would really be helping her faithful servants, Shiko and Higomu.

"Kittiwake," said the patron. "Would you be so kind as to fetch our little box from my office? I would like to show it to my brother."

"I shall be glad to do so," said Kittiwake so smoothly that only Zefi noticed the tension in his voice. "Has your nephew seen it?"

"My nephew?"

"Yes," said Kittiwake. "Please forgive an artist's weakness for self-aggrandizement, but I thought perhaps your nephew would also be interested."

"My dear artificer, do you know my nephew well?"

"No."

"Ah. Then believe me when I tell you that crafts such as yours fail to hold Snowgull's interest. I beg you to understand that this is not an insult to your craft, but rather an explanation as to why I do not wish to have my nephew present at this, your moment of greatest achievement. I assure you, your glory shall be much greater without the presence of the less enlightened."

"Ah," said Kittiwake. "I see."

"Yes," said Legislator Whitedove. "And now, do fetch the box. It is my brother's birthday, and it would be rude of us to keep him waiting."

"Certainly," said Kittiwake. He gave Zefi an apologetic look before he turned away.

Several guests had joined Whitedove's sister in talking to the sour-faced guest of honor. Others were milling around the cheeses, where Zefi and the patron stood. They seemed more interested in Zefi than in the cheeses.

Shouts arose outside the villa. The patron glanced across the atrium to the villa's main entrance. Silver-haloed Badger nodded to him. Something bad was about to happen. Zefi decided, nephew or no, she needed to get Higomu out of the wine barrel. She took a step toward the kitchen.

"Please remain here for the moment, Zefi."

Zefi stopped as though her feet had turned to stone. The patron knew her name?

"In fact," Whitedove said, "would you like to rest on this bench?"

"I believe I should get more wine," Zefi said, so frightened she forgot to speak in two-word sentences.

"Nonsense," said Whitedove. "I have plenty of servants who would be willing to fetch wine. See? There they go now."

Indeed Badger had gathered the servants and was driving them like a flock of ducks into the kitchen. The patron's brother and sister were in an argument over whether the brother should sit down. It looked like the sister would win, for half the guests were insisting that he listen to her. The other half were moving to surround Zefi. Two men held short lengths of stout rope. Others held knives they had acquired from the table. Kittiwake was nowhere in sight.

"Do sit down," Whitedove insisted.

Zefi sat down.

CHAPTER 32
Unexpected Allies

HIGOMU stood on his good leg in the back of the dark cellar, holding the end of the rope that Shiko had tied to the top of the rack of wine bottles. The rope had been used to bind his partner's hands, and it pleased him to think that he would now be using it to confound her captors.

"Ready?" he asked.

"Ready," said Shiko from across the room in the vicinity of the door.

Using his injured leg for balance only, Higomu pulled on the rope. The tension increased, but in the darkness, he could not see if the wine rack was tipping. Perhaps he was only stretching the rope. Then the tension relaxed, and Higomu knew the wine rack had passed its balance point.

Higomu shifted onto his injured leg and pulled his good leg clear of the rack's path. Pain shot through his tendon, but he had practiced the maneuver beforehand, until he could perform without hesitation. An instant later, four dozen glass bottles crashed onto the stone floor. The noise was Shiko's cue to break the bottle in her hand, in the hopes that it would fragment into a weapon. It was also their opponents' cue to rush into the room.

But no one did. If there was any conversation outside the door, it was in voices too low for Higomu to hear.

Perhaps he and Shiko had been left unguarded. Anyone outside the door would certainly have heard the crash. Were they indifferent to the destruction of the wine cellar? Perhaps, but even so, how could they not be curious?

If the guards were gone, the wise action would be to sneak

out now. On the other hand, if the guards were present, opening the door would be inviting death. Higomu decided he would have to call them in—loudly enough that someone outside the door would hear, but quietly enough that, if the guards had left, they would not come rushing back.

He took a deep breath, but before he could shout, the door opened.

The dark cellar was illuminated not only by a bright blue halo, but also by the light of an oil lamp. That explained the delay. It also indicated that these three pirates would not be as easy to fool as Higomu had hoped.

The pirate captain's eyes flicked around the room, taking in the thick spiderwebs woven across the corners, the stand with the tapped wine barrel near the door, the bottles stored in racks along the wall, and of course the mess Higomu had made in the back corner.

The wine racks divided the cellar into two aisles. The fallen rack blocked Higomu's aisle. Higomu, in the back corner, stood in shadow.

"You are too slow," Higomu said. "I have already freed her."

The pirate captain's aura flashed with surprise, illuminating the long, thin knife he held in his right hand. Instantly, the scar-faced pirate was by the captain's side, also with knife at the ready.

The pirate captain's eyes narrowed, and he moved the lamp to give himself a better view of Higomu's face. "You could not have freed her. There is no way out."

The knobby-kneed man remained in the doorway. *Don't be such a coward,* Higomu thought. *Take three steps inside so Shiko can get behind you.*

"If there is no way out, how did I get in?" Higomu asked.

A worried frown crossed the pirate captain's white face. The scar-faced man glanced at his captain.

"The wine barrel," the captain said. He turned to his associate. "Brutal, why didn't you notice the wine barrel held no wine?"

The scar-faced man shrugged. "Lots of strange things happen in this villa. People who notice them end up dead."

"You will be dead right now if this booker gets away."

The pirate captain spoke over his shoulder to the man in the doorway: "And you, too, Eely. Stay there and don't let him past you."

Eely appeared quite willing to stay back while the other two did the work.

The pirate captain indicated that Brutal should advance up the other aisle to cut off Higomu's escape in that direction. Behind the men, hidden by the open door, Shiko waited for her chance.

The pirate captain held up his lamp and squinted into the darkness. "Where's the woman?" he asked.

Higomu glanced at his empty wine barrel by the pirate captain's leg, then hastily returned his gaze to the pirate captain's face. "I told you: I have already freed her."

"Ah," said the pirate captain. "I see."

With contempt, he pushed the barrel over with his foot. It struck the floor perfectly, with the lid popping off and wobbling through a half-circumference before falling over. The pirate captain did not need to look inside to realize that Higomu had tricked him.

Higomu smirked.

With an incoherent cry of rage, the pirate captain bounded up the aisle and leapt over the fallen wine rack. Higomu dove away from him and rolled into a single-footed crouch just in time to see the faint form of Shiko slamming the door on the timid pirate who had remained in the doorway.

The scar-faced pirate had stepped to block Higomu's escape down the otherwise-unobstructed aisle, but the sound of the door thumping into his companion's skull caused him to turn around. Had Higomu possessed a sound body, he could have chosen to kick the scar-faced man from behind or dash past his legs, but Higomu's quickness was limited to single-footed leaps. He dove under one of the racks that divided the wine cellar and slid through wine and glass shards to the other side. By the time he was back on his good foot, the knobby-kneed pirate was slumped in the doorway like a heap of rags, moaning and holding his head.

Shiko had not fled, however. Instead, she had turned to confront the scar-faced man. Higomu bounded for the door with the loosely knitted parts of his tendon threatening to separate again.

The pirate captain chose not to leap over the wine rack a second time. Instead, he continued his lap around the wine cellar, running down the scar-faced man's aisle

The scar-faced man stood puzzled, as though he were deciding whether a woman half his size armed with only a sharp piece of glass posed a threat that he should take seriously.

Grunting through the pain in his tendon, Higomu reached the fallen pirate at the door. He took the knife from the man's limp hand.

Pushing past the scar-faced man, the pirate captain snarled, "He's mine! You can kill the woman!"

Focused on Higomu, the pirate captain drew back his knife to strike. Shiko's broken bottle flashed out at his leg.

The pirate captain flinched—only slightly, but it was enough to disrupt the thrust he aimed at Higomu's throat.

Higomu had a knife of his own. His blade caught the captain's thrust and directed it to the side. The pirate captain gasped and his aura suddenly dimmed.

Shiko stood behind him, a drop of dark blood falling from the piece of broken wine bottle in her hand. She was staring up in shock, her face lit by the golden glow of the scar-faced man.

As the pirate captain fell to his knees, the scar-faced man pulled his knife free from his captain's back. "I don't want to kill the woman," he said. "I want to kill you."

Higomu caught the lamp as the pirate captain's aura snuffed out. The body fell face down on the cellar's stone floor.

"Take his knife," Higomu said to Shiko. "You might need it."

Shiko nodded and did as she was told.

Higomu and the scar-faced man locked eyes.

"I will guess that you are not actually a demon worshipper," Higomu said.

"My soul belongs to me," said the scar-faced man. "The demons don't keep their promises any better than the deities."

If I had two good legs, I could run you through and improve your understanding of theology, Higomu thought.

Instead he asked, "Can you keep your friend with the headache from causing us trouble tonight?"

The scar-faced man glanced at the moaning man. He nodded.

"Then, since you helped me, I'll help you," Higomu said. "Stay here. Stay quiet. And listen. In a short while, you should hear a disturbance within the villa, and that will be your chance to escape unseen."

It wouldn't be a very good chance, not with the villa swarming with guardians-of-the-peace, but it would be a chance. And that promise might be enough to keep the pirates in the wine cellar until Higomu and Shiko had accomplished what they needed to do.

Higomu left the lamp on the floor, took Shiko by the hand, turned his back on the two pirates as though they were trusted allies, and limped up the stairs.

"Did that make any sense to you?" he murmured.

Shiko swallowed and nodded. "The captain killed the harbormaster today. I think the harbormaster might have been Brutal's estranged father."

"So you were expecting this?"

She shook her curly head. "For an instant, I thought I had killed him with my bottle." She seemed somewhat dazed.

"Don't worry," Higomu said. "It was not your last chance to kill someone."

He had to keep her looking ahead. They had escaped the

makeshift prison, but their duty to the Goddess required more of them than that.

Higomu had to climb the stairs one step at a time. Shiko kept pace with him. At the top, it was too dark to see the steps. Shiko moved quietly. Her breath and the touch of her hand were Higomu's only clues to her position.

Higomu was not stepping as softly as he would have liked. He had worked out a technique for moving swiftly and quietly without putting strain on his tendon, but his legs were not accustomed to it. He had to be careful not to tire his muscles. Fatigue would make him sloppy.

Zefi said the stairway opened into a storeroom, so Higomu assumed that was where he was, although nothing in the room was visible except as a silhouette against the doorway to the lamp-lit kitchen. Figures in the kitchen shuffled nervously. Their green halos provided no illumination. On the contrary, the halos shrouded the servants' faces. From Zefi's description, Higomu had counted on the noise and bustle of the kitchen to mask his movements, but the kitchen's occupants spoke only in low murmurs.

He risked a whisper to Shiko: "I fear the soul trap may be in use."

"What now?" she asked.

"The plan is the same," said Higomu. "We still need chaos to even the odds."

"Understood."

"But Shiko, if you can't steal it, you must destroy it."

"Very well," she said. "And Kittiwake?"

"The same."

"... Very well."

We do what must be done, Higomu thought as Shiko dashed up the next flight of stairs. Yet he regretted he had been forced to involve Zefi. As he followed Shiko to the second floor, he prayed for a way to get the Child of Labor out of the villa alive.

The mission was mostly out of his hands now. Success would be up to Shiko—a situation he would have to get used to, because all the missions would be hers from now on. She was able-bodied, intelligent, and capable. As he hobbled toward the ladder in the corner of this upper storeroom, Shiko was already running across the roof. Higomu envied her, yes, but he was also proud of her.

Rungs. Only a day ago, he had climbed the ladder in Kittiwake's workshop as though running up the wall. Now he hoisted himself one rung at a time through a shaft of red moonlight to the hole in the ceiling.

Higomu paused on the roof to close the hatch so that no one exploring the upper storeroom would know where he had gone. The dark auras of the servants in the kitchen suggested that they were unlikely to venture out to investigate anything, but Higomu saw no need to become sloppy in his old age.

Higomu limped toward the corner of the villa above the entrance. As he had expected, three dozen glowing heads illuminated shining iron helmets below. Most of the guardians-of-the-peace wore patient silver auras, tinged pink by the red glow of the moon. The exception was the man in front, golden as sunset, shouting at the barred door:

"Tell Whitedove we demand entrance immediately!"

It was Fox, of course.

The response was in tones too quiet to hear, but the tones did nothing to calm the commander. "Not 'as soon as he becomes available.' Now! Tell him now. Or if he is not within, then say so plainly and unbar the door."

But of course they had not brought a ram. They were thirty-six soldiers armed with shield and spear, but they would let a wooden door keep them standing outside if that door had pretty carvings.

Higomu checked himself. He was being unfair. Fox had no military reason to remain outside the villa, but politically a siege was wiser than an assault. The longer Whitedove waited to let the guardians in, the more guilty he would appear.

But Higomu did not have time to wait out a siege. He dropped a handkerchief from the roof.

Fox was too busy arguing with the door to notice a piece of falling linen some distance away, but the captain with the black ringlets turned her head in Higomu's direction and ordered a guardian to investigate. With his newly acquired knife, Higomu dug a small chunk of clay from the roof. When the soldier bent over to pick up the handkerchief, Higomu dropped the clay on his helmet.

The soldier looked up.

"Ask your captain to come here," Higomu said, keeping his voice lower than Fox's bellows.

The puzzled guardian brought the handkerchief to his captain and pointed at Higomu. She looked up at him, her brightening aura illuminating her symbols of captaincy—the line-dot-line painted on her forehead and the two triangles on her cheek. Taking the guardian and two others with her, she broke ranks and approached Higomu's section of the villa's front wall.

"We should speak softly," Higomu suggested.

"Very well," she said, matching his tone. "Of what do you wish to speak?"

"I wish to speak of a ladder that is used to prune trees or harvest fruit in the garden of this house," Higomu said. "And of how it has been left outside, propped against the back wall."

At the corner of the building, Fox stopped yelling and turned to look at the captain. She made hand motions encouraging him to continue. He grasped her meaning and began shouting once more, this time berating the individual at the door for his or her lack of civic spirit.

"I must confess," she said, "that I would be more inclined to discuss this ladder if I knew who had put it there and what would await me on the other side."

"On the other side, I believe you will find another ladder, leading down into the garden. And as for the person who is putting them there, I believe you name her 'Curls'."

"Darkheart!" gasped the only one of her three subordinates who had not guessed Higomu's identity immediately.

"I fear I must refuse her generosity," the captain said. "I am here to get someone she has taken from me."

"I am offering you something better," Higomu said.

The captain inclined her head.

Higomu said, "I know who is responsible for the pirate attacks on my people's glass shipments."

"That is not our jurisdiction," she said.

"It is if the pirates use your port," Higomu said. "Tell Fox he will find two pirates in the wine cellar beyond the kitchen. Offer the scar-faced man amnesty, and he will affirm that Legislator Whitedove funded the pirates to protect his newly acquired school of glassmakers."

"Perhaps the courts work differently in Hicho," she replied. "But in Dupho no one will believe the word of a scar-faced pirate against the word of a dashing legislator."

"And why do you think he looks so dashing?" Higomu countered. "What if you could find proof that he has given his soul to the demon Vanity?"

"I had proof," the captain said. "But your partner stole my witness."

"Inside you will *see* proof," Higomu promised. "You can be your own witness. Please ask your commander if he would like you to sneak over the wall and discover the nature of this party that the legislator will not let you attend."

And hurry, Higomu added to himself as the captain considered his words.

"Return to ranks," she told the three soldiers.

As they hastened back into formation, she turned and strode along the wall. Fox stopped shouting as she approached him. Commander and captain retreated from the entrance and held a brief exchange during which Fox scowled up at Higomu.

The commander nodded, and the captain returned to her position in the middle of the formation.

Fox addressed his troops. "Company: Close ranks of nine!"

The soldiers arrayed themselves shoulder to shoulder in

four ranks. The captain rapidly passed along the two lines in the rear, turning auras blue.

"Front squad: Advance!" commanded Fox. "One, two, three, halt!"

He strode to the building and put his entire face in the tiny window beside the barred door. "Here we stand!" he shouted. "We are the guardians-of-the-peace, and our vigilance is tireless. Tell Legislator Whitedove that we will stand here all night. I do not intend to move until this door is open!"

Behind him, screened by his shouting face and two ranks of guards, the captain was leading eighteen barefoot soldiers around to the back side of the villa.

CHAPTER 33
Choices

KITTIWAKE found his emotion box on Legislator Whitedove's desk. How beautiful it had seemed while he had worked on it. How much love he and Zefi had built into it. It was not meant to be a cage for animals' souls.

Now Whitedove wished to demonstrate the box to his brother. What perverse sacrifice would the legislator perform this time? Did he have a goat to slaughter?

But refusing Whitedove was out of the question. The legislator held them all like goats on a rope: Shiko tied up in the wine cellar, Higomu trapped in the barrel, Zefi under orders to remain in the atrium, and Kittiwake bound to do whatever the legislator asked as long as there was hope that he and Zefi might go free afterward.

Kittiwake took the box from the desk, hoping it was only concern for Zefi that made him willing to comply with Whitedove's request. He wished he did not know that an appeased Glamour might allow his hands to heal.

When he stepped back into the atrium, the scene had changed. Someone was shouting outside the villa, but the guests were paying no attention. The patron's brother was now sitting on a bench, with his hands unnaturally behind his back, almost as though they were bound. The old man was surrounded by party guests—the Feathered Flowers Mural Inspector, the Inspector's daughter and son-in-law, the Chief Inspector of Aqueducts. What were they doing? Why were their auras filled with triumph and hatred? And was that a gag tied over the old man's mouth?

Whitedove's brother felt a stomach-chilling fear that resonated with Kittiwake's own Emotion. And Kittiwake sensed another who was afraid ... Zefi! Like the patron's brother, she was sitting on a bench surrounded by Whitedove's followers, with her hands tied behind her back. Her legs appeared to be bound as well.

Legislator Whitedove's aura flushed with affection as Kittiwake approached. Kittiwake held his own aura to a neutral silver. What could he do? He would do whatever it took to get Zefi untied. The Admiral's wife sneered at Zefi with contempt. Temerity the Glassmaker wiggled her knife in Zefi's face.

Knives! They all held knives! Kittiwake forced himself to be calm.

What did Legislator Whitedove intend to do to Zefi? Kittiwake looked into the man's eyes. Whitedove smiled pleasantly.

"My friends," said Legislator Whitedove, in an easy, gentle voice, "my loyal followers, I thank you all for coming to my home this evening to honor the life of my brother. I wish that I had time to tell you all that he has meant to me, and yet I fear that such a chronology could last all night. Permit me, then, to give you but the briefest of sketches."

Walking leisurely toward his brother, Whitedove said, "I surely would run out of voice before I could fully describe the details of my brother's heroic service in the Theocratic Army, even as the Theocratic Seat was confiscating our father's gold mines in the inland provinces. I should stutter searching for words sufficient to describe how inspired I was when my brother won a seat on the Provincial Assembly. As a lowly cotton importer, working to help my father rebuild his lost fortune, I had no idea that the people of Dupho still held our family in such high regard. When my brother, grief-stricken by our sister's untimely death, vacated his seat and endorsed my candidacy in his stead, the honor that this defender of the Empire transferred to my humble head is a gift I have long sought means to repay. Content he was, he said, to leave the politics to me. All he asked in return was the privilege of managing our father's most productive vineyard."

Shouts arose again outside the villa. This time several heads turned. "Ah, pay them no mind," Whitedove murmured. "We will let them in once the celebration has ended. They are merely here to clean up the trash.

"My dear brother." Legislator Whitedove's young and gentle face looked down on the old man with kindness. "After all you have done for our family, after seventy-two years of life, do you not feel that it is time to retire? If not, please tell me."

The old man's biceps strained, and harsh sounds stuck in his throat, but he uttered not a single intelligible word. He was gagged so tightly that the rope made bloody abrasions in the corners of his mouth. Black and white hands seized his shoulders to constrain his struggles.

"You see?" asked Whitedove, raising his voice to drown out his brother's muffled ravings and the barking challenges coming from outside the villa. "Although my brother has not accepted the Goddess into his heart, he is willing to do his part to serve her. And you, friends—are you willing to do your part?"

Whitedove's guests made sounds of assent.

"Then let me hear you say, 'Glory to the Goddess!'"

"Glory to the Goddess!"

"Glory to the Goddess!" Whitedove repeated.

"Glory to the Goddess!" they cried.

"She is with us," Whitedove murmured. "Feel her power."

It was not mere pageantry. The guests' faces were awe-struck. Glamour caressed Kittiwake's heart, promising that his hands would be rejuvenated or he would be dragged immediately to Hell, whichever he desired more. Kittiwake looked to Zefi then. She was bound, but ungagged. Her eyes now held neither awe nor fear. She was praying.

"See her power," Whitedove said, and darkness engulfed

him and his terrified brother.

"Taste her power," Whitedove called from the darkness.

The air took on the flavor of sweet wine from the vineyards that bore Whitedove's name.

"Witness her power," Whitedove said, and the darkness surrounding him disappeared. The gag that had been in his brother's mouth was now in his left hand. His right hand held a dagger.

Kittiwake expected the old man to be slumped over dead, but he was sitting bolt upright with his eyes full of terror, his aura glowing bright green. His bloody mouth was working like that of a dying fish, but he made no sound. A breeze blew lightly past Kittiwake's cheek.

Whitedove dropped the gag on the atrium's stone tiles and put his hand on Kittiwake's shoulder. "My dear artificer, I regret making you work in haste, but please prepare your artifact. I have asked the Goddess to remove my brother's air, and I fear he will not live long."

"Wh— What do you want of me?" Kittiwake asked, watching the silently gasping man.

"Catch him for me, please," the patron said gently. "Do not let his soul drift wastefully to Heaven, but rather use your craft to help me hold on to my beloved brother forever."

"No!" said Zefi.

A dozen hands grabbed her and held her down on the bench.

"Kittiwake, save your own soul!" she cried. "Pray to Knowledge for help!"

"Kittiwake's soul has been saved," Legislator Whitedove told Zefi as his brother's aura darkened from panic to despair. "Glamour will preserve him forever. See how well I have weathered the years compared with that old man over there?"

Whitedove moved to stand beside Zefi. He gently pushed the point of his dagger against her breast, until it seemed that it must pierce even Zefi's thick skin.

"Don't," Kittiwake pleaded. "Let her go and I'll do whatever you wish."

"My dear artificer," Whitedove said. "I have no desire to harm your pet. You must know this. When have I ever shown you anything but kindness? I merely stand here so that you feel properly motivated to perform the delicate task which I now require of you. I hope my intentions are clear?"

Whitedove's fist moved fractionally and Zefi gasped. Blood seeped into her vest. She closed her eyes and her lips began moving, forming whispered words in her own language.

"I will drive the blade no deeper," Whitedove promised. "She will be spared. Because you will join me in service to the Goddess."

Kittiwake looked down at the artifact he held in his withered hands. He could fill the box with any emotion. The garnet would turn blood red, and no one who lacked Kittiwake's senses would know what he had done. But Glamour would know. She would kill him, and then Whitedove would kill Zefi.

Knowledge help us, Kittiwake prayed. *If I have a way to get Zefi out of this, please show it to me.*

But Knowledge was not Kittiwake's goddess, and he received no reply.

"It is time," Whitedove said as his brother's aura faded away to nothing. "Catch my brother's soul."

Kittiwake turned the spigot on the emotion box and focused on his resonance with the deceased man's ghost. The soul's fear was gone, for he did not understand that Kittiwake had the power to put him through even more torment. Whitedove's brother felt suddenly free.

Kittiwake envied him, for although Kittiwake had the power to take the soul's freedom, he could not make that freedom his own. He had no choices. He had to stop Zefi's murder.

But Zefi would rather die than be used as a tool of evil. She would rather die than force Kittiwake to trap a man's soul. She wanted him to defy his patron. Whitedove would kill her, but her kind soul would go to Heaven, where she would be happy. She would accept that. She would love Kittiwake for it. But Kittiwake could not live with that pain.

And that was why he had failed her before. He had not been looking for a way to protect Zefi. He had been looking for a way to keep her. It was selfishness, not love, that had driven him into the service of a demon. If he truly loved Zefi, he would answer her prayers.

I reject you, he said to Glamour. *You must destroy my soul, for it will serve you no longer.*

Death seeped into Kittiwake's chest and spread through his body. Glamour demanded that he do her bidding. She would kill him if he wished, but death would be no escape. Was Kittiwake so eager for Hell that he would refuse his goddess this simple request?

Kittiwake looked at his own soul and saw that his desire to be Zefi's hero was not strong enough to overcome his fear of Hell. He would give in. Glamour would win, because deep in Kittiwake's heart, he was a coward.

Hating himself, Kittiwake reached for the dead man's soul.

You are a coward, the Goddess of Knowledge told him. *But you are a coward with control over your emotions.*

Kittiwake nodded. That was true.

If fear was the only thing keeping him from being Zefi's hero, then he should eliminate that fear. He did not have to overcome it. He could simply release it, trap it in the box. The intake spigot was open.

Kittiwake opened his heart, allowing his fear to drain away into the artifact. The indicator garnet turned blood red. Kittiwake closed the spigot.

Death breathed through Kittiwake's body, down to his toes and out to his fingertips. Whitedove would not be fooled. Kittiwake's death would reveal the truth. But Kittiwake had made his stand. The dead man's soul was floating up to Heaven now, beyond the reach of mortals and demons.

The thought filled Kittiwake's bones with a warmth that flowed gently outward, brushing aside Vanity's grip as though the demon's power were nothing but a few cobwebs.

Kittiwake looked to Zefi in awe. Her eyes were bright with triumph. She knew that Knowledge had saved his soul.

CHAPTER 34
Leap of Faith

THE SOLDIERS were already coming around the corner as Shiko heaved the ladder over the wall. Their silver halos glowed brightly, but their tread was quiet. It seemed they ran without sandals.

She wiggled the ladder to make sure it was on stable ground, then hurried back down the ladder on which she stood. Higomu might be amused by the idea of working with the police, but she was not.

She waited in the middle of the garden to see if they would come over on their own or if they would wait until she gave them assurances. When the first helmeted head appeared above the wall, she thanked the Goddess for giving them wisdom and hurried toward the wing of the house that divided the garden from the atrium.

According to what Zefi had told Higomu, that doorway there should lead to the study. That was where Zefi had last seen Kittiwake with the emotion box. Shiko stood outside the doorway and listened. She heard voices in the atrium but no sound from inside the chamber. If it had been as dark as the cellar, she would have had no fear of finding a Child of Beauty inside, but the red moonlight streaming in from the atrium-side doorway could hide someone's aura.

Soldiers began creeping into the garden. Shiko stepped into the study and took a defensive combat stance. Her eyes scanned the shadows beyond the beam of moonlight. The room was unoccupied.

She was looking for an ornate wooden box with an indicator garnet set into the top. The desk was empty. Perhaps the artifact rested on one of the shadowy shelves high above her head.

"Don't! Let her go and I'll do whatever you wish."

Kittiwake's voice.

A pleasant-voiced man responded in a kindly tone. Shiko stepped across the room and crouched by the atrium doorway. She peered out.

Kittiwake held the emotion box, his hand on the intake spigot. He regarded a middle-aged man who held a dagger embedded in Zefi's breast. Zefi bled, but it seemed that the wound was not yet deep enough to harm her. She was praying.

"I will drive the blade no deeper," the middle-aged man said. He was the one with the pleasant voice. "She will be spared. Because you will join me in service to the Goddess."

Shiko knew the man served no goddess. He must be Whitedove.

"It is time," Whitedove said. "Catch my brother's soul."

Kittiwake turned toward a group of Children of Beauty clustered around a man sitting on a bench. He opened the intake spigot and closed his eyes in concentration.

Don't do it, Shiko thought, fingering the handle of the pirate captain's knife.

Kittiwake opened his eyes, watching what no one else could see. He considered it a while, then turned to look back at Zefi. Making his decision, he nodded and closed the spigot.

Kittiwake faced his patron, priest of Vanity. Raising the artifact into the light of his bright white halo, Kittiwake shouted, "For the Goddess, I keep this soul! Glory to the Goddess!"

"Glory to the Goddess!" the crowd replied.

Whitedove glowed with triumph.

Kittiwake had failed. His will to escape the demon had been broken by the threat of his friend's death. Shiko did not presume to judge him, but she would kill him. She would do what must be done.

Reverently, Whitedove reached out his hands, leaving his dagger dangling from Zefi's flesh. He took the artifact from Kittiwake and peered at the garnet set into the top. Shiko could tell from Whitedove's smile of satisfaction that it had turned bright red.

The group of people nearest to Shiko stepped away from the man on the bench. A short, middle-aged woman with golden bracelets cut ropes binding the man's hands and feet. He slumped sideways into her arms and she gently eased him off the bench onto the stone tiles.

"Inform Commander Fox that his presence is required at once," Whitedove commanded loudly as his guests encircled Kittiwake.

Two men, one in a sky blue gown and another in a purple robe embroidered with bird wings, seized Kittiwake by the arms and held him as others threatened him with their knives.

Kittiwake's aura flared green as he looked to Whitedove for an explanation.

Whitedove looked up from the artifact. "My dear artificer, forgive me. You have served me well, and your artifact shall have a place of honor in my home, not only because it holds my brother's soul, but also as a reminder of your loyal service—to me and to our goddess. If I had known your conversion would be sincere, I would not have planned things this way. But my nephew has brought the guardians-of-the-peace to my door, and I must give them a criminal."

"And why should we be satisfied with only one criminal, Legislator?"

All heads turned toward Shiko—or rather toward the garden passageway adjacent to the doorway through which Shiko was watching. A black-skinned, black-haired woman stepped into the red moonlight, followed by a file of barefoot, spear-wielding soldiers.

Shiko wiped her palm on her chiton so she could take a firmer grip on her knife. The guardians-of-the-peace had arrived to even the odds.

It seemed unlikely that Whitedove would have spoken those words to Kittiwake if he had known the soldiers were entering through his garden, yet so great was his political skill that his face showed no flicker of surprise.

"Dear Captain Faith," he said. "How glad I am to see you. And yet, I fear you are too late. Foolishly, I agreed to provide this wretched artificer with one night's lodging, and he has repaid me by murdering my brother."

The captain considered the body lying on the tiles. During Whitedove's brief speech, her soldiers had formed a line beside her. She returned her gaze to Whitedove. "Legislator White-dove, the guardians-of-the-peace will be escorting you to the Red Palace."

"Ah, not at this late lithic," Whitedove said. "At the artificer's trial, I shall be happy to provide witnesses—" he gestured to indicate the knife-wielding guests, "—but Kittiwake is the only one who will be going with you tonight."

Heads turned at the sound of sandaled feet entering through the opposite corner of the atrium. A soldier with a chevron painted on his forehead took up a stance between the party-goers and the villa's exit, proclaiming, "Legislator Whitedove, you are under arrest!" Golden-haloed soldiers emerged from the doorway and arrayed themselves behind him.

"Dear Commander Fox," said Whitedove, "thank you for your prompt assistance. Your escaped prisoner has murdered my brother. I will be ever so grateful if you would take this man back into custody."

"The escaped prisoner will testify that you are a demon worshipper," Commander Fox replied.

None of the guests expressed shock at this accusation.

"Commander, they are all accomplices," the captain said to her superior across the atrium. "I recommend we question them separately and offer amnesty to the one who gives the most truthful and complete account."

Commander Fox nodded. "Very good, Captain. Legislator,

instruct your guests to drop their weapons."

Whitedove laid the artifact on the nearby table. He regarded the people holding Kittiwake.

"Release him," he said.

They did so. Uncertain, they stepped away from the artificer.

This gave a better opening. Now only Captain Faith's line of barefoot soldiers stood between Shiko and Kittiwake. If she could kill him with a single strike, she might be able to snatch the artifact and run past Whitedove before anyone could react.

"My faithful followers," said Whitedove, moving to put an arm around Kittiwake's shoulders. "Let no one say the Goddess is not merciful. Because of Kittiwake's loyal service, she has decided that he will not be taken tonight. Rather, she gives us permission to demonstrate her powers to our enemies!"

Whitedove raised a hand and Fox's corner of the atrium turned from shadows to black darkness. The blinded soldiers began shouting with confusion.

Captain Faith leveled her spear at the party-goers and called, "Squad: Advance!"

"Face them!" Whitedove cried to his followers. "The Goddess shall protect you."

He took a step away from the advancing soldiers and frowned at them with concentration. A mist condensed out of the air.

"Charge!" the captain shouted, but the soldiers at the center of the mist cloud were already collapsing.

On the right, the soldiers advanced two steps before they, too, fell choking to the ground. The mob of guests rushed in, unaffected by the mist. The woman with the many bracelets stabbed a fallen soldier in the face, and the other party-goers joined her in a frenzy of bloody knives.

On the left, a few soldiers staggered onward, led by Captain Faith. Kittiwake's eyes widened with terror, but he was unable to move.

For an instant, it seemed that Captain Faith would do

Shiko's job for her, but the raven-haired soldier was not attacking the artificer. She stepped around him and planted her feet to thrust her spear into Legislator Whitedove.

But Whitedove did not even flinch. He raised a contemptuous hand and made a gesture like squeezing the juice from a lemon.

Captain Faith's legs collapsed underneath her and her lifeless body fell to the ground.

Knowledge, protect us, Shiko thought, placing a hand on her sacred stone.

As the knife-wielding demon worshippers completed their massacre of Captain Faith's helpless soldiers, the other half of the troops emerged from the supernatural darkness in the opposite corner of the atrium. Whitedove turned to confront them. Spreading his arms, he became seven ethereal Whitedoves, each of them laughing.

He asked, "Do you need more targets, Fox?"

"Do not fear his magic!" the commander shouted to his soldiers. "Your armor will protect you. Advance!"

The soldiers advanced at his command, but the bodies bleeding in the moonlight were proof that he was wrong. Whitedove's displays of power were beyond normal magical skill. He was acting as a conduit for the demon Vanity, and Shiko doubted a little iron would confuse a demon.

The best protection from demonic power was divine power, but Beauty, the goddess of the soldiers, was vulnerable to Vanity. Against the powers Whitedove had revealed, the advancing line of armored, spear-wielding warriors was actually defenseless.

But perhaps Shiko was not. Vanity's powers could be overcome by Knowledge. Perhaps Shiko need not fear the incapacitating mist. As Whitedove's followers moved to intercept Fox's squad, Shiko decided it was time to find out.

She sprinted from the chamber, hurdling the bodies bleeding on the tiles as she passed through the astringent cloud of mist. Unnoticed behind the backs of Whitedove's followers, she leapt onto the bench on which Whitedove's brother had been murdered and jumped from there onto the table.

Now she was at Kittiwake's eye level. He turned to look at her as she raced toward him. She hoped his damned soul would forgive her.

Running along the table, Shiko closed the distance on the confused artificer. As she sprang at him, his eyes widened in horror. Shiko soared through the air and poised her knife to strike.

From this vantage point, Shiko had a good view of Zefi's face. Despite the dagger dangling from her breast, Zefi was calm. Despite Kittiwake's decision to serve the demon, Zefi's chin was high. She was triumphant.

Which meant that Kittiwake had not done what Shiko thought she had seen.

Any Emotion could change the color of the artifact's garnet. Kittiwake could have chosen to trick Whitedove. Perhaps he could even trick Vanity, if his soul had been converted. That was what Shiko saw in Zefi's face: the certainty that Knowledge watched over all three of them.

The chain of thoughts flashed through Shiko's mind with supernatural speed. She pulled her knife-arm back and reached for Kittiwake's shoulder with one outstretched foot. Seven surprised Whitedoves turned to stare at her. Which one was real?

The one who met her eyes.

Shiko pushed off Kittiwake's back. Whitedove raised his hand, and for an instant, a phantom fist gripped Shiko's heart. But her heart slipped free, and Shiko sliced through Legislator Whitedove's throat.

Blood sprayed into the air and fell to earth as dry, brown flakes. Whitedove's cheeks collapsed with wrinkles. His black hair turned silver, then fell away from his scalp as his wrinkling head hit the ground. His four limbs jerked inward, and dry fingernails scraped the sole of Shiko's right foot as she stepped off the evil priest's husk.

Shouts of combat from across the atrium told Shiko where Whitedove's followers were currently occupied. She pulled the artifact down from the table. The garnet was bright red.

What had Kittiwake put in there? Shiko would have to ask him later. He was busy cutting Zefi's bonds with the dagger he had pulled from her wound.

"The kitchen," Shiko told them. "Then upstairs. Higomu will get us out."

Zefi led the way. The frightened servants stood aside to make room for the bleeding Child of Labor. In her wake, Kittiwake and Shiko ran unobstructed.

Zefi knew the stairs. Kittiwake's bright aura gave them plenty of light. As they entered the upstairs storage room, the hatch in the ceiling opened, guiding them toward the roof with a beam of red moonlight.

Higomu greeted them as they popped onto the roof. "That was well played, Kittiwake. You convinced even me."

Zefi grinned at Higomu and said, "You need more faith."

Higomu gave her an appraising look. "Perhaps," he said.

An order floated up from the atrium: "On your knees." Peeking over the edge of the roof, Shiko saw Whitedove's surviving guests surrendering to the surviving soldiers. Shiko looked away. Too many had not survived.

Higomu pointed to his climbing cord hanging off the outside edge of the villa. "That way down," he said.

"So we run?" Shiko asked.

Higomu nodded. "Run for the docks."

"But you can't run," Shiko said. "I don't want to leave you behind."

Zefi put a hand on Shiko's shoulder and said, "He is not stupid. He knows I will carry him."

CHAPTER 35
Paths

IN THE ORPHANAGE'S well-patient room, Kittiwake lay asleep in a bed big enough for Zefi. His dim aura—the room's only light—was affectionately pink. Zefi wondered if he was dreaming of her. She hated to wake him; he had slept so little.

She laid a gentle hand on his shoulder and his aura flickered into consciousness.

"You must go now," she said to his blinking eyes. "Shiko has found a ship. It leaves soon."

Kittiwake sat up in bed. "Will you not come with me?"

Zefi shook her head.

"Ah, Zefi. You have saved me, but what have you saved me for?"

"Knowledge has saved you," Zefi told him. "And she has saved you for yourself."

The room grew dark.

"We love each other," Zefi said. "But we do not fit together anymore."

"It's my fault, isn't it?" Kittiwake asked. "If I hadn't ..."

"If you had not served a demon, then I would not have tried to save you," Zefi said. "And then I would not know that the gods want me for their priest. Do you see?"

"I see nothing," said Kittiwake. "I am lost without you."

"You are not lost," Zefi told him. "Your foot is on the right path now."

Lamplight flickered outside the room. Zefi could hear footsteps limping up the stairs. It was Higomu—intentionally noisy. He could move silently up those stairs. Before their rescue mission, he had spent half a lithic practicing.

Zefi embraced Kittiwake and helped him out of bed. Together, they walked to the top of the stairs where they met Higomu, who held a lamp in one hand. With his other, he offered Kittiwake a handkerchief.

"Thank you," Kittiwake said, dabbing at his eyes.

"Shiko will take you to the ship," Higomu said. "I will be along in a moment."

Kittiwake hesitated, looked at Zefi, then nodded.

"I will miss you, Zefi," he said.

"I will miss you, too," she said.

Kittiwake walked down the stairs, more slowly than Higomu had come up.

Zefi knelt down to look into the tiny man's dark eyes. "Take care of him for me," she said.

"I will see that he is in good hands."

Zefi shook her head. "No. *You* take care of him. I trust you."

Higomu chuckled. "Not many people do."

"Promise me," Zefi said.

"You are serious."

Zefi nodded.

"Zefi, I can't— Oh, very well. I'll keep an eye on him. At least until he gets his feet under him again."

"Thank you," Zefi said.

"And you'll do something for me?" Higomu asked.

"What?"

"Ask Thafarsi to bless our voyage?"

Zefi smiled and laid a hand on his shoulder. "I already asked."

CHAPTER 36
What Must Be Done

A WAVE STRUCK THE BOW, spraying a salty mist onto Shiko's face. They were out of Dupho Bay, heading home, bearing the fruits of their successful mission. Shiko felt empty.

"I see you look forward," Higomu observed, appearing beside her as though emerging from a fog. "Our artificer friend is still looking back."

"He'll get sick," Shiko said.

"I believe he already is," Higomu said. "I hope it makes him feel better."

Shiko looked into his dark eyes. "Was that a joke?" she asked.

Higomu shrugged. "Perhaps it was. It made me feel better."

Shiko went back to staring at the waves, wondering if anything would ever make her feel better.

Higomu sat down beside her. "Tell me about it," he said.

"Why?"

Higomu regarded her. "You aren't looking forward at all, are you?"

No. She wasn't. Or maybe ... "Perhaps I am," she said. "I've been considering what I should do when I get back to Hicho."

"We will escort Kittiwake out to Elder Badiki's estate, where we will give a full report," Higomu said. "But I suppose that is not what you meant."

"No," said Shiko.

"You want to quit, don't you?"

Shiko nodded.

"Tell me about it."

"I'm not sure it is any of your business," Shiko said.

"Between you and Elder Badiki, then?"

"I suppose so," Shiko said. Yes, that was true. She could not leave the Order of the Lock without telling Elder Badiki. But it was her decision to make. She did not need consultation.

"Shiko, if you don't do the job, who will?"

"You will, of course."

"I can't even walk anymore."

"But you will heal."

"Shiko, I don't have time."

She looked into his face. For an instant, she glimpsed the pain behind his mask.

"What are you talking about?" she asked.

"I'm forty-eight."

She waited for him to explain, but he acted as though this revelation explained everything. It meant that he had entered the Seminary before she was born. It meant that she would never catch up to him in knowledge, skill, or experience. But why did it mean he had no time?

"I'm afraid I don't understand," she said.

"In six years I will be fifty-four."

"And I will have to call you 'Elder'," she said. "And perhaps Elder Badiki will ask you to stop running around on rooftops and become a teacher. But that is still six years away."

"Shiko, even with the full-time care of a healer, it could be a year before my leg is back to full strength. And then I will need two, perhaps three years of training to relearn the skills I had when we started this mission—if I can relearn them at all. My body grows older every year. I found a hair on my chin last month. I don't have much active life left, Shiko. This was, in all likelihood, my last mission. The Order of the Lock needs you to take my place."

"You sound as ridiculous as Kittiwake," she said.

"Look at it logically and tell me it is not so," he said.

"Higomu … I can't do it. I killed a man. I almost killed the wrong man. I can't spend my life doing this."

"But you're good at this life," he said.

"I don't want to be good at it! I don't want to become like you. Like some stone-faced … Darkheart."

That made him smile. "It is a good name, isn't it?"

He was proud of the name—of what he had done to earn it. Shiko could not feel proud of what she had done.

"Killing doesn't make you a killer, Shiko."

"Doesn't it?"

"No," he said. "It makes you a judge."

"I am a poor judge," Shiko said. "I nearly killed Kittiwake."

"But you realized your mistake in time," Higomu said.

"I made too many mistakes," Shiko said. "First, I believed Kittiwake and his artifact were harmless. Then, I believed he had to die. Only with the grace of the Goddess did I ever see the truth. No, Higomu. I have proven to be an incompetent judge."

"But when we look at the outcome," Higomu said, "it appears you are more capable than you believed."

Shiko watched a gull glide low above the waves.

Higomu asked, "Will you leave it up to Po, then?"

Shiko shrugged. "Po's a good man. And a better fighter than I am."

"But does he have the courage to face what you faced? Will he do what must be done?"

Shiko thought of her sparring partner … and friend, more or less. Po would push her off the balance beam into the sand pit, but would he be able to take a knife and strike for the throat?

"Only Po can answer that," Shiko said. "And he won't know until he is forced to make the decision."

"And will he make the right decision?" Higomu asked. "Do you really want to trust decisions like that to Po?"

"Why do you think they should be trusted to me?" Shiko asked.

"Because you listen to the Goddess."

"I should have listened more carefully."

"That can be said of all of us. I should not have pushed him so hard." Higomu looked aft at the artificer. "A few of my missions have involved demon worshippers, but this was the first time I created one myself."

"His grasp of theology is a bit muddled," Shiko said.

"He is weak-willed," Higomu said. "And yet, after all he went through, he still found the strength to do what was needed when it mattered most."

Shiko nodded.

"The deities know that we will fail sometimes," Higomu said. "They know we will make mistakes. But when they needed beings that could protect the world, we were the most capable things they could create."

"Is that the sort of thing they teach at the Seminary?"

"I reasoned it out myself."

Shiko sighed. "And now you will tell me that, regardless of how many mistakes I made, I am still the person most capable of doing the job. And therefore it would be wrong for me to quit."

"Ah. I see the Academy, too, teaches students how to reason."

He had beaten her, but she would not let him win.

"If I stay with the Order of the Lock," she said, "I will make you stay, too."

"How?" he asked.

"I will point out to Elder Badiki that you are the most experienced striker in the Order's history, and that it would be irresponsible to allow people like me and Po to go on missions without you to advise us."

"He won't send me on missions, Shiko. He knows that old people slow down."

"Once you have full use of your leg again, I will remind him that even an old Higomu is faster than a young Shiko."

Higomu shook his head. "I'll never be as fast as young Higomu."

"No one will be," Shiko said. "But you will not quit serving the Goddess just because you can remember a time when you were quicker. You will not sit in Hicho feeling sorry for yourself. You are Higomu. You will do what must be done."

Higomu stared at her with his dark eyes. "If I let you win this argument," he said, "you will think you can win another someday."

"Perhaps," she said.

"Ah well," said Higomu. "I do like working with a partner."

"You do?"

"Of course," said Higomu. "It's nice to have at least one person with whom I can share my true thoughts."

Shiko laughed.

"That wasn't a joke," Higomu said.

"As you say, Higomu. But thank you for trying to make me feel better."

"And I thank you. Will you come aft with me, Shiko? Our artificer is also melancholy, and I promised a friend I would take care of him."

Acknowledgments

I'D LIKE TO THANK MY WIFE, SIERRA, for reading an earlier draft and suggesting improvements.

Justin Barba and CthulhuBob Lovely organized the MisCon writing programming from which I have learned so much. From the MisCon Writers' Workshops, I would like to thank M.J. Engh, Di Francis, Deby Fredericks, and Sharon Roest for critiques of an earlier draft of Chapter 1.

Bob Dischert read the nautical scenes and suggested ways I could improve them. Andrea Howe of Blue Falcon Editing suggested ways I could improve my English. All the mistakes that remain are my own.

The Northwestern University Karate Club let me hang out with them long enough to learn a few things. Other stuff, I learned at cabins in Moravia. Thanks, Tygr and Hadži.

Finally, I'd like to thank my father, Bill Holt, for all those basketball games and for consultation on achilles tendon injuries.

About the Author

JASON A. HOLT has a Ph.D. in mathematics. He is fluent in Czech, and he lives on a remote Montana cattle ranch. In other words, he is well qualified to write fantasy novels.

To learn more about Jason, visit `JasonAHolt.com`.

To learn more about the world of Edgewhen®, visit `edgewhen.com`. Or look for *The Klindrel Invasion* at your favorite retailer.

CHRONOLOGY OF EDGEWHEN® ADVENTURES

1002: The Dragonslayer of Edgewhen
1311: The Artificer of Dupho
1500: The Klindrel Invasion

and coming soon:

1577: The Bladesman of Darcliff
1670: The Burglar of Sliceharbor

www.ingramcontent.com/pod-product-compliance
Lightning Source LLC
Chambersburg PA
CBHW021504240626
47154CB00002B/502